HURTLING TOWARD A SHOCKING COLLISION

- A Space-Messiah on a doomsday mission . . .
- A world devoted to pleasure and seething with death . . .
- A ruthless financier hungry for new galaxies to conquer . . .
- A proud woman seduced by an alien consciousness . . .
- A mind-stunning masterpiece to liberate a planet . . .

MONUMENT
by
Lloyd Biggle, Jr.

THE EXPLOSIVE NEW NOVEL
OF AN ULTRADEADLY EXPERIMENT

MONUMENT

Lloyd Biggle, Jr.

This low-priced Bantam Book
has been completely reset in a type face
designed for easy reading, and was printed
from new plates. It contains the complete
text of the original hard-cover edition.
NOT ONE WORD HAS BEEN OMITTED.

RLI: $\dfrac{\text{VLM 7 (VLR 5–9)}}{\text{IL 9+}}$

MONUMENT

A Bantam Book / published by arrangement with
Doubleday & Company, Inc.

PRINTING HISTORY

Doubleday edition published February 1974
Science Fiction Book Club edition published April 1974

The short story "Monument" was first published in Analog
Magazine, June 1961. Included in Analog 1, edited by John W.
Campbell, Jr. (Doubleday, 1963). Copyright © 1961 by Street
& Smith Publications, Inc.

Bantam edition / May 1978

Bantam Books are published by Bantam Books, Inc. Its trade-
mark, consisting of the words "Bantam Books" and the por-
trayal of a bantam, is registered in the United States Patent
Office and in other countries. Marca Registrada. Bantam
Books, Inc., 666 Fifth Avenue, New York, New York 10019.

PRINTED IN THE UNITED STATES OF AMERICA

To John, Bee, and Jack Flory,
who had a vision

1

It came to Obrien quite suddenly that he was dying.

He was lying in a gently swaying gourd hammock, almost within reach of the flying spray where the waves broke in on the point. The caressing warmth of the sun filtered through ragged, scarlet-leaved sao trees. Shouts of the children spearing marnl off the point reached him on fitful gusts of fragrant wind. A full drinking gourd hung at his elbow. The sweet, clear tones of a girl's voice uplifted in an old, old song, and the tremulous twanging of the nabuls stroked in accompaniment, had embroidered his reverie with bittersweet nostalgia. His first wife had sung that song at a moment in time that now seemed remote almost beyond the reach of memory.

Then the realization snapped coldly across his thoughts and roused him from half-dozing, drowsy contentment to icy wakefulness.

He was dying.

The sudden surge of panic he experienced brought pain in its wake, and while the spasm lasted he lay quietly, hands clutching his abdomen, eyes closed, perspiration oozing from his forehead and soaking the hammock's brightly patterned robes. It passed, and he jerked erect and shook his fist at the mocking emptiness of the cloudless blue-green sky. "What are you waiting for, damn it! What are you waiting for?"

The song stopped abruptly. A nabul struck the ground with a soft thud and a dissonant rattle of strings as Dalla, the singer, leaped to her feet and hurried to his side. He sat on the edge of the hammock wearily looking about him. The multicolored vegetation encircled him with a curtain of riotous beauty, and its glistening, drooping blossoms wafted a soporific invitation to rest, to meditate.

Obrien leaned back, Then he felt the first stabbing thrust of the pain's return, and he slid determinedly to his feet and brushed the blossoms aside.

Dalla fluttered about him concernedly, her face tense with unspoken questions. Obrien's great-great-grandson, Fornri, hurried toward him. Fornri and Dalla: Obrien regarded the two of them benignly, suddenly comprehending why Dalla had sung that old love song. In a year or two they would be partners at a betrothal dance. He wondered whether he would be alive to offer his blessing.

The other young people were on their feet and looking on with grave concern. They came frequently to ease the burden of an old man's boredom with music, and they would not understand if he told them he no longer needed to be entertained because he was dying. The pain's thrust continued, but Obrien resisted the impulse to futilely clutch his stomach.

"To the Elder," he said curtly.

Consternation touched their faces. Fornri said slowly, "It is a long and tiring journey. Perhaps in the morning—"

"To the Elder," Obrien said again and turned his back on them.

Their words drifted after him; they spoke unaware that an old man's hearing could be as sharp as their own. Dalla said tremulously, "If you go only a short distance and then return, he may fall asleep and forget."

There was a pause, and then Fornri answered, his voice deeply troubled. "No. He is the Langri. If he wishes to visit the Elder we must take him."

Obrien left them to their dilemma and stumbled down the slope to the beach. The moment he appeared, the children came splashing toward him. "Langri!" they shouted. "Langri!"

They crowded about him excitedly, holding up marnl for his approval, waving their spears, laughing and shouting. The marnl was a flat, broad, reptilian-looking creature with a multitude of legs and a small head on a ridiculously long neck. It was unlovely and inedible, but as a bait it was priceless. On this world children learned to swim before they could walk, for there was nothing in the sea that could harm them, and as soon as they could wield a spear they took to this game of catching marnl and made their play an indispensable economic asset.

Obrien paused to admire the more choice specimens before he gestured toward a dugout hunting boat drawn up on the beach. "To the Elder," he said.

"Ai! To the Elder! Ai! To the Elder!"

They dashed to the boat, hauled it into the water, and began a furious struggled for places. Then Fornri arrived, and he waded into the melee, restored order, and told off seven boys for paddlers. They brought the boat back to the beach for Obrien to board. His pain had diminished, so he shrugged off Fornri's proffered assistance, waded to the other end of the boat, and hopped aboard native fashion. As the boat moved away, the crowd of children splashed after it, swimming around and under it until the paddlers got up speed. Behind them, Dallas stood on a rise of ground with her arm uplifted in farewell.

The boys shouted a song as they dipped their paddles—a serious song, for this was a serious undertaking. The Langri wished to see the Elder, and it was their solemn duty to make haste.

And Obrien leaned back and wearily watched the foam dance under the outrigger, for he was dying.

It was not the imminence of death that disturbed him, but the realization that he should have thought of it sooner. Death was inevitable from the instant of birth, and Cerne Obrien was a long lifetime from babyhood. He wondered, sometimes, just how old he might be, for in this dreamy land, where the nights were moist and the days warm and sunny, where there were no seasons, where men measured age by wisdom, it was difficult to keep an alert finger on the pulse of time.

But Obrien did not need a calendar to tell him he was an old man. The solitary hut he had built on the lovely rise of ground above the point had become the center of a community as his sons, and grandsons, and great-grandsons brought home their wives. It was the village of Langru, the village of fire-topped men, already celebrated in legend and song; and though few of his descendants inherited his red hair, all were considered people of fire. Maidens were eager to mate with them, and the sturdiest youths came to court the daughters of fire. Many of them defied tradition and settled in the village of their wives.

A man who lived to watch his family thrive into the fifth generation had to expect a time of reckoning. Obrien's limbs were stiff and swollen each morning from the night's dampness. He moved slowly and tired easily, and the flaming red hair of his youth had faded to rusty gray. He had been ill for several years as a twitch of discomfort in his stomach became a throbbing irritation and then a sharp, prolonged pain and finally a searing agony. It was the corrosive touch of death, and so slowly did it come upon him that he had not recognized it.

He had received more happiness than he'd expected from life and far more than he deserved, and he should have been able to face death without fear or regret; but the dream that had grown until it shaped his life among these people was unfulfilled, and he knew, with an absolute and terrifying certitude, that if he died now this lovely world was doomed to utter ruin and this beautiful, generous, loving people to extinction. He *knew*.

He had known it almost from the moment of his crash landing. In his younger days the knowledge had made him frantic with worry, and he had pondered and debated with himself on long nocturnal walks along the beaches, and paced his hut through innumerable hours of misty darkness while he devised stratagems, and with inspiration and luck and stubbornness he finally fashioned the answers he had to have. He was the one man in the far-flung cosmos who could save this world that he loved and these people that he loved, and he would do it. He painstakingly rehearsed in his mind every step that had to be taken, and every opposing move that would have to be countered, and he was ready to act the moment the world was officially discovered.

The discovery did not happen, and he, Cerne Obrien, had played the fool. He had been content to wait. It was pleasant lounging in his hammock with a gourd of fermented juice at his elbow, acting the part of a veritable oracle, respected, even worshiped. When he was younger he had roamed the length and breadth of this world's lone continent. He had taken long sea voyages. He was first in every adventure and courted danger with a grin on his face, scorning the world's hazards and revering its beauties wherever and whenever he found them; but his zest for hazards diminished with age, and he became aware that the view from his own village encompassed as much breath-taking beauty as a man could comprehend in a lifetime.

He was a simple man, an uneducated man. The natives' awe of his supposed wisdom alarmed and embarrassed him. He found himself called upon to settle complex sociological and economic problems, and because he had seen many civilizations and remembered much of what he had seen, he achieved a spectacular success and enjoyed it not at all.

And now the long pageant of unumbered, wonderful years had come to this bitter ending: he was the one man in the cosmos who knew how to save this world and this people, and he could not do it because he was dying.

Kilometers of coast drifted past, and scores of villages, where people recognized the Langri and crowded the shore to wave. The afternoon waned and evening came on. Fatigue touched the boys' faces and their singing became strained and breathless, but they worked tirelessly and kept their rhythm.

Dusk was hazing the sea about them and purpling

the land when they entered a shallow bay and rode the surf up onto a wide, sloping beach studded with boats. The boys leaped out and heaved their own boat far up onto the sand. Then they slumped to the beach in exhaustion and bounced up a moment later, beaming with pride. There would be feasting tonight, and they would be honored guests. Had they not brought the Langri?

All native villages lay on hillsides overlooking the sea, with their dwellings arranged in concentric circles about a central oval where, at dusk, cooking fires sent fragrant plumes of smoke skyward. Obrien's march up the village's central avenue was a triumphal procession. Respectful adults and awed children solemnly trailed after him. He skirted the enormous signal gourd that stood in the center of the oval and continued on to the top of the slope where the Elder's dwelling stood. The Elder stood waiting for him, a smile on his wrinkled face, his arms forming the native salute: one arm uplifted; the other held across his breast with hand resting lightly on his shoulder. Ten paces from him Obrien halted and returned the salute. The villagers watched silently.

"I greet you," Obrien said.

"Your greetings are as welcome as yourself," the Elder replied.

Obrien stepped forward, and they touched hands. This was not a native greeting, but he used it with some of the older men who were almost lifelong friends to him.

"I ordered a feast in the hope that you would come," the Elder said.

"I came in the hope there would be a feast," Obrien returned.

The formalities thus satisfied, the villagers drifted away murmuring approval. The Elder took Obrien's arm and led him to the grove at the top of the hill, where hammocks were hung. They stood facing each other.

"Many days have passed," the Elder said.

"Too many days," Obrien agreed.

The Elder's tall, gaunt frame seemed as sturdy

as ever, but his hair was silvery white. The years had etched lines in his face, and more years had deepened them and dimmed the brightness is his eyes. Like Obrien, he was old. He was dying.

"The way is long," the Elder said, "but at the end is a soft hammock, a full gourd, and a village of friends. Rest!"

They settled into two hammocks hung in a V, where they could lie with their heads close together, and a girl brought drinking gourds. They sipped in silence as darkness slowly settled on the village.

"The Langri is no longer a traveler," the Elder observed finally.

"The Langri travels when the need arises."

"Let us then talk of that need."

"Later. After we have eaten. Or tomorrow. Tomorrow would be better."

"Tomorrow, then," the Elder agreed. He pushed Obrien's gourd toward him.

Below them, the village was girding itself for the feast. New fires had been kindled—the oval blazed with them—and each of the village's most skilled chefs had brought out the piece of koluf meat that he or she had long been curing, or aging, or marinating, or smoking, or drying for just such an auspicious occasion as a visit from the Langri. The koluf was an authentic sea monster—one of them filled a hunting boat—and Obrien often wondered how many of the natives' ancestors had died before they found a way to capture this virulently poisonous creature and render it edible. Once found, the meat proved delectable beyond human powers of description. Obrien had tasted thousands of koluf dishes, because each chef had his own technique of seasoning and preparation, and each one tasted more delicious than any of the others.

Fires also leaped high on the distant beach, and soon Obrien heard the thum . . . thum . . . thum of the nabs. Like the smaller nabuls, they were stringed instruments fashioned of gourds, but the enormous nabs towered over the musicians who played them.

The thumming continued. Soon a raln, a type of

gourd used as a drum, added its resonant thuds, and then the twanging nabuls were heard. Already the dancing had begun, for the young natives needed no persuasion to perform a festive dance. They were circling the musicians with torches, and soon they would peel off in a sinuous dance line that would weave through the village and summon the guests of honor. The rippling night breeze blended savory odors of the coming feast with the crisp tartness of the sea that heaved tirelessly just beyond the mouth of the bay. Blended words of chant and song were flung up to them as the dance line gained momentum and began its progress through the village.

Obrien felt exhausted—had there been time, he gladly would have slept—but when the Elder touched his arm he dutifully swung to his feet. Escorted by the jubilantly singing dancers, the two walked to their places of honor on the beach.

Except for the chefs and the escorting dancers, the entire village had assembled there. Around the fires, enormous, elongated gourds had been placed in circles, and these served as platforms for the dancing. In the position of honor amidst the waiting villagers was a triple throne with a high seat in the center and lower seats on either side.

Obrien and the Elder took the two lower places, and the dancers returned to the village oval and began to escort the chefs to the beach. They came a few at a time, each carefully carrying his culinary masterpiece on a gourd platter that was lined with colorful leaves and encircled with flowers. The natives' existence depended absolutely on the whims of the koluf. When they caught enough, they ate well; when they didn't, they went hungry. But no matter how much or how little food they had, they lavished on it all of the care and skill at their command.

The chefs formed a line at the edge of the beach, and the dancers took the dishes, one at a time, and with great ceremony they moved to the place of honor and presented them to Obrien. The thumming, twanging music and rhythm continued; dancing about the beach fires was now a contortion of violent movement; now a sedate gliding; now a vigorous leaping from gourd to gourd.

Obrien inspected each dish in turn, broke off a crumb of meat, tasted solemnly, meditated, shook his head. The dish was passed to the waiting villagers, and its hopeful author retired in disappointment. Another took his place at the head of the line, and the dancers brought the next dish for Obrien's approval. Obrien tasted, rejected, and turned his attention to the dancing until another dish arrived.

The villagers watched avidly as Obrien tasted dish after dish. The Langri was no novice, and the chef who prepared the portion he found out of the ordinary would be honored indeed.

Suddenly Obrien, having tasted a crumb of koluf, tilted his head thoughtfully and broke off a larger morsel. He tasted again, smiled, nodded, and offered some to the Elder, who tasted it and smiled his own approval. Obrien accepted the platter of meat from the dancers, who returned to the line of waiting chefs to proclaim the winner. They escorted her to the throne, a plump, middle-aged woman delirious with delight. Obrien and the Elder arose and handed her up to the highest seat while around them the villagers slapped bare legs in enthusiastic approval. For with the natives, as with any people revering good food, the ultimate place of honor at any feast belonged to the cook.

In the morning, Obrien and the Elder walked together along the shore and seated themselves on a knoll overlooking the sea. Sweet-scented blossoms crowded up about them, nodding in the breeze. The morning light sparkled on the leaping water. Brightly colored sails of the hunting fleet were pinned flowerlike to the horizon. To their left, the village rested sleepily on its hillside, with a single thin plume of smoke wafting skyward. Children of both sexes romped in the surf or walked timidly along the shore to stare up at the Elder and the Langri.

"I am on old man," Obrien observed wearily.

"The oldest of old men," the Elder agreed promptly.

Obrien smiled wanly. To a native, "old" meant "wise." The Elder had paid him the highest of compliments, and he felt only bitterness and frustration. "I am an old man," he said, "and I am dying."

The Elder turned quickly and looked at him with concern.

"No man lives forever, my friend," Obrien said, "and you and I have been cheating the fire of death for a long time."

"The fire of death never lacks for fuel. Let those cheat it who can. You spoke of a need."

"Your need. The need of all of your people and of my people."

The Elder nodded thoughtfully. "As always, we listen well when the Langri speaks."

Obrien got to his feet, walked forward a few paces, and stood looking at the sea. "You remember that I came from afar and stayed because the skyship that brought me could fly no longer. I came to this land by chance and because I had lost my way and my skyship had a serious sickness."

"I remember."

"Others will come," Obrien said, "and then more others. There will be good men and bad, but all will have strange weapons."

"I remember. I was there when you slew the maf."

"Strange weapons," Obrien repeated. "Our people will be helpless. The men from the sky will take this land—whatever they want of it. They will take the hills and the forests and the beaches and even the sea, the mother of life. There will be boats that sail above and below the waters and poison them, and the koluf, the staple of life, will be driven into deep waters where the hunters can't find it. Our people will be pushed back into the mountains where there is no food. The strangers will bring strange sicknesses, and entire villages will lie in the fire of death. They will lay waste to the shores, they will hunt the waters and swim, and their dwellings will be taller than the tallest trees and their numbers on the beaches thicker than the marnl at hatching. Our own people will be no more."

The Elder was silent for a time. Then he said, "You know this to be true?"

"It will not happen this day or the next, but it will happen."

"It is indeed a terrible need," the Elder said quietly.

Obrien looked at the awesome beauty of the curving shore and thought, *"This beautiful, unspoiled land, this wonderful, generous, beautiful people—"* A man was so damned helpless when he was dying.

The Elder got to his feet, and for a time they stood side by side in silence, two old men in bright sunlight waiting for darkness. The Elder placed his hand gently on Obrien's shoulder. "Cannot the Langri prevent this thing?"

Obrien walked a short distance down the slope and knelt in the lush vegetation. He plucked the flowers, one at a time, and as each glistening, multicolored blossom turned dark in his hand he crushed it, tossed it aside, and plucked another.

The Elder followed and knelt beside him. "Cannot the Langri—"

"The Langri can prevent it—I think—if the men from the sky come this day or the next. If they delay longer the Langri cannot prevent it because the Langri is dying."

"Now I understand. The Langri must show us the way."

"The way is strange and difficult."

"What we must do shall be done. The Langri's wisdom will light the way."

"Strange and difficult," Obrien repeated. "Our people may not be able to follow it, or the path the Langri chooses may be the wrong one."

"What does the Langri require?"

Obrien got to his feet. "Send the young people to me, two hands at a time. I will make my choices. There must be a village for them, in a place apart. They must eat, though they neither hunt nor gather, and the burden of their food and its preparation must be fairly divided among all the villages."

"The first will come to you this day, and your wishes will be my wishes."

They touched hands. Obrien turned and walked away quickly. Fornri and the young paddlers were waiting for him on the beach, and they pushed off at once and hoisted a sail, because the wind was at their back for the return voyage. They moved swiftly out of the bay, and Obrien, looking backward, saw the Elder still standing motionless on the knoll with arm uplifted.

2

Cerne Obrien had been knocking about in space since he was twelve, and when he got sufficiently tired of being the top name on everyone's duty list, he saved a little money and acquired a battered government surplus survey ship. The sale—at discounted salvage value —was contingent on his junking the ship, but he scraped together some supplies and paid a dispatcher to be looking the other way when he took off.

He was only a dumb mechanic—though a good one—and he had no license to be touching anything at all on a spaceship forward of the retron cells; but he'd seen one piloted often enough to think he knew the fundamentals. The ship had a perverse streak that matched his own, but after he exercised his rich vocabulary of profanity and kicked the control panel a few times it would settle down and behave itself. Pointing it in the right direction was another matter. Probably any bright school kid knew more about celestial navigation than he did, and his only support came from an obsolete *Simplified Astrogation for the Layman*. He was lost ninety per cent of the time and only vaguely aware of his whereabouts for the other ten, but it didn't matter.

He wanted to see some places that were off the usual space lanes and maybe do a little illegal prospecting, but especially he wanted to be his own boss and make his own decisions. When supplies got low he looked for a small, privately owned port where there would be no authorities asking to see his non-existent license. Good mechanics were always in demand, and he could slip in for a night landing, work until he'd earned enough to replenish his fuel and supplies, and slip back into space without exciting anyone.

He went through the motions of prospecting, too, nosing about on dozens of asteroids and moons and small planets that either were undiscovered or forgotten. He would have been reluctant to admit even to himself that the prospecting was in reality an excuse that enabled him to enjoy the contorted strangeness of a stark lunar landscape or experience the awesome thrill of riding a barren, spinning asteroid through an unending procession of glowing dawns and precipitant sunsets.

No one could have been more amazed than Obrien when he actually struck it rich. An asteroid of solid platinum he would have overlooked, but a rich deposit of retron crystals made his ship's instrumentation misbehave so radically that eventually he got the message. He started back to civilization with a wealth so enormous and so unexpected that he had no notion of what he would do with it.

He had nothing with which to blanket the massive retron emissions from his cargo hold. He was lost when he started, and his erratically functioning instrumentation quickly lost him much more thoroughly while he fought a losing battle to conserve fuel and keep his worn engines operating. Finally he selected the world that seemed to offer his best chance for survival and pointed his ship at it. It was in fact his last chance, because his misbehaving fuel gauge had misled him. He ran out of fuel and crashed while attempting to land.

The natives made him welcome. He became a hero by turning his las pistol on an obnoxious, leathery-skinned flying creature that dove into the sea to tear its food from the living koluf. The maf had become so numerous that the natives' principal source of food was threatened. Obrien used up all of his magazines, shooting the creatures in flight and destroying chrysalides and young in the high, inaccessible lairs, and he rendered the maf virtually extinct.

Obrien then explored the lone continent end to end and found nothing more significant than scant deposits of coal and a few metals. Any serious prospector would have scorned them, but they sufficed to lead the natives immediately into a bronze age and give them the metal points they so desperately needed for their hunting spears. He next turned his attention to the sea and added an outrigger to the hunting boats for stability in the furious battles waged with the koluf.

He had lost interest in being rescued. He was the Langri; he had his family and his own growing village and a position of tremendous prestige. He could have been the Elder at a relatively young age, but the idea of him, an alien, ruling these people seemed repugnant to him. His refusal enhanced the natives' respect for him. He was happy.

He also was worried. The planet had such meager natural resources that no one would be attracted to it by prospective plunder. It was so inhospitable to humans that the natives could not have survived without the koluf and the many species of gourds. There were few material things that they needed that could not be made in whole or in part from gourds, but the koluf crop barely sufficed to feed them. Fortunately for the natives, there was no galactic market for gourds. Unfortunately, the world had another potential resource that rendered it priceless.

It was a beautiful world. Its beaches were smooth and sandy, its waters warm, its climate admirable. It would make a magnificent vacation resort, a world-wide vacation resort, and those paradoxical features that made life so difficult for the natives would become assets where tourists were concerned.

Man was the alien on this world, and these natives had to be descended from a space expedition or colonization party that had gone astray hundreds of years before. Except for the koluf—after a lavish purification process—and a few roots and berries, the world's flora and fauna were virulently poisonous to man. Fortunately, man was equally poisonous to the native animals. He could swim in the sea with perfect safety as long as he avoided drowning, for not even the most voracious monster would dare to molest him. A drop of his blood, a scrap of his flesh, meant sickness or death, and in that violent arena the first was rapidly followed by the second.

Man paid dearly for his safety, because there was so little that he could eat. The edible roots could be pounded into a barely palatable flour. A few specimens of bitter fruit and leaves were excellent for seasoning koluf meat, and there was a small, pulpy berry that was tasteless but contained juices that could be blended into an excellent fermented drink. That was all.

But if man brought his own food, avoided poisonous thorns and nettles, and guarded against those forms of the world's distressingly potent bacteria to which man was susceptible—and a well-ordered resort would take the necessary precautions—this world would become his playground. To the people of the myriads of harsh environments whose natural resources attracted large populations—dry worlds, barren worlds, airless worlds—it would be paradise. Those who could leave their bleak atmosphere domes, or underground caverns, or sand-blown villages for a few days in this sweet-smelling, oxygen-rich atmosphere could return to their rigorous environments with renewed courage.

Luxury hotels would crowd the beaches. Lesser hotels, boardinghouses, rental cottages would press back into the hills where magnificent forests now flaunted their lavishly colored leaves. Millionaires would indulge in spirited bidding for choice stretches of beach on which to locate their mansions. The shores would be clotted with vacationers. Ships would offer relaxing sea cruises, undersea craft would introduce their passengers to the world's fantastically rich and incredibly strange marine life, and crowded wharves would harbor fishing boats for hire—for though the sea creatures were inedible, catching such repulsive monsters would constitute rare sport. It would be a year-round business because the climate was delightful the year around: a multibillion credit business.

The natives, of course, would be crowded out. Exterminated. There were laws to protect them, and an impressive Colonial Bureau to enforce the laws, but Obrien knew only too well how such governmental bureaucracies functioned. The little freebooters such as himself, who tried to pick up a few quick credits, received stiff fines and prison terms. The big-money operators incorporated, applied for charters, and if charters weren't available they found the required legal loophole or paid the necessary bribe. Then they went after their spoils under the protection of the laws that were supposed to protect the natives.

The tourists' water recreations would drive the koluf to new feeding grounds, and unless the natives were able to follow it—continuously—or effect radical changes in their diet, their social structure, and their manner of living, they would starve. Obrien doubted that they could do any of those. And a century or two later, scholars, always worrying deeply about yesterday's tragedies while blithely ignoring today's, would bemoan the loss. "They'd achieved a splendid civilization. Some of its facets were highly original and even unique. It's a pity, really it is. One would think there'd be a law about that kind of thing."

The young people came from all of the villages. They swung lightly down the coast with flashing paddles and rollicking songs—ten at a time they came, handsome boys and lovely girls bronzed from their days in the sun, all of them equally experienced at the koluf hunt and the loom, for in this society either sex did the work it preferred.

Theirs was the age of carefree happiness, the age the natives called the Time of Joy, for they were granted the leisure for singing and dancing, for courtship, for—if they chose—doing nothing at all, before assuming their adult responsibilities. And though they solemnly beached their boats along the point and came into the august presence of the Langri with appropriate reverence, he knew that no talk about tomorrow's doom would easily divert their thoughts from today's delights.

His questions startled them. They grappled awkwardly with strange concepts. They struggled to repeat unutterable sounds. They underwent bewildering tests of strength and endurance, of memory, of comprehension. Obrien tested and rejected, and others took their places, and finally he had chosen fifty.

In the forest, remote from the attractions of sea and shore and village, Obrien had a small village constructed. He moved in with his fifty students, and he worked them from dawn until darkness and often far into the night, while other natives loyally brought food, and the villages in turn sent help to prepare it. Fornri stood by alertly to do whatever was needed, and Dalla waited patiently with a cool drink and a damp leaf for Obrien's brow when he tired, and an entire people watched and waited. The pain in Obrien's abdomen came and went. When he was able, he ignored it. When he could not ignore it, he dismissed his students until he felt better.

His own formal education had ended the moment he became large enough to outrun his school's attendance officer, but he had never stopped learning, and in his wandering he had acquired a smattering of all sorts of knowledge. Not until this moment did he realize what a scant thing a smattering amounted to, nor had he been aware that he could know something well and still have no notion of how to explain it.

He knew nothing at all about teaching.

He stood at one end of a forest clearing. Behind

him was an improvised writing board, a fiber mat stretched between two trees with a layer of moist clay smoothed across it. With a pointed stick Obrien had written the numbers one through ten, and below that he had carefully inscribed what he considered the beginning of an education in arithmetic:

$$1 + 1 = 2$$
$$1 + 1 + 1 = 3$$

His fifty students sat on the ground before him in varying stages of inattention or perplexity. Around the edges of the clearing children peered out curiously, for native children were ubiquitous, and their curiosity was insatiable. Behind his class, at the far end of the clearing, stood the village.

"One means one of anything," Obrien announced. "One dwelling, one spear, one koluf, one boat. One and one are two—two dwellings, two spears, two koluf. You, Banu!"

A youth in the front row started, and as Obrien continued to talk, his face assumed the contortions of total bafflement. "If you have a spear," Obrien said, "and I give you another spear, how many spears do you have?"

"Why would you give me a spear if I already have one?" Banu blurted.

Eddies of discussion and comment swirled about the class and merged into larger eddies. Obrien took a heroic grip on his patience. "You're hunting koluf, Banu, and your friend gives you his spear to hold while he secures the bait. How many spears do you have?"

"One," Banu said confidently.

"You at the back—pay attention here!" Obrien shouted. He turned to Banu. "Banu—you have *two* spears. One and one are two!"

"But one of them is my friend's," Banu protested. "*I* only have one. I always have one. Why would I want two?"

Obrien took a deep breath and tried again. "Look

at your fingers. On each hand you have one plus one plus one plus one plus one. Five. Five fingers on each hand. If a koluf bit off one of your fingers, how many would you have left?" He held up his hand, fingers outspread. Then he folded one finger down. "Four! Five take away one leaves four. Count!"

The entire class sat staring intently at outspread fingers. Banu had ahold of one of his, wiggling it back and forth. "I can't take away one," he announced finally. "I still have five."

"Damn it, can't you understand? Five of anything take away one leaves four. Five koluf, you eat one, you have four left."

A student seated at the side of the clearing got to his feet and absently ambled forward, keeping his eyes on the writing board. Obrien went to meet him. "What is it, Larno?"

"What happens after ten?" Larno asked.

Obrien showed him, writing the numbers eleven to twenty as he spoke them.

"Yes, yes!" Larno exclaimed. "And after twenty?"

Obrien patiently went on writing numbers and pronouncing them. The class had lost interest. Talk became louder; a girl squealed; some youths began playing a game with a small gourd. Obrien, sensing Larno's intense interest, ignored the disturbances and continued with the numbers until he had filled the writing board.

"Yes, yes!" Larno exclaimed. "And after ninety-nine?"

"One hundred. One hundred one. One hundred two. One hundred—"

"And after one hundred ninety-nine?"

"Two hundred."

"And after two hundred ninety-nine is three hundred?" Larno asked. "Yes, yes! And four hundred? And five hundred? Yes, yes! And if one and one are two, then eleven and eleven are twenty-two, and one hundred and one hundred are two hundred. Yes, yes! And if five take away one is four, then five hundred take away one hundred is four hundred. And if each of us has ten fingers, then two of us have twenty fingers, and all fifty of us have five hundred fingers, not including you and Fornri and Dalla. Yes, yes!"

Obrien turned grimly and walked away. "Yes, yes!" he muttered. "Now tell me how a dumb mechanic like me can teach arithmetic to a class with one mathematical genius and forty-nine nitwits."

He taught language. That much was all right. Through some freakish tradition this small population of isolated natives practiced bilingualism—they had a speech that was like nothing Obrien had ever encountered, but they also had a ceremonial speech that was a bastardized derivative of the galaxy's one universal tongue that men everywhere called Galactic. Obrien had grown up speaking Galactic, and a man who couldn't teach his own language was a fool. He had been teaching it ever since he arrived on this world, and many of the other natives had learned fairly good Galactic from him and passed it along to family or village. All of these young people already knew Galactic or something very close to it, and they easily mastered as much spoken language as Obrien wanted them to know.

Obrien taught science, and any spacer who didn't have a pragmatic grasp of basic principles rarely lived long enough to be able to inflict his ignorance on others. But Obrien also had to teach subjects that had been no more than faint academic rumors to him, subjects such as economics and sociology and government. He taught political science, and he stirred and sifted the dregs of his memory for facts that might have stuck there concerning constitutions and compacts and articles of confederation; and socialism and communism and fascism; and theocracies and oligarchies and meritocracies and as many of the variegated modifications and adaptations as he could remember.

He taught military discipline and guerrilla warfare and colonial procedure, and he brought his class together under the stars and taught the history of the people of the galaxy. He expected these young natives to stare openmouthed while he described flaming space wars, and fantastic creatures, and worlds beyond worlds, and suns more numerous than the leaves of the forest; but their attention spans seemed even shorter at night than during the day.

"There!" he said, using a hunting spear to point with. "See those two bright stars and that dim one? Aim a spear between those stars, and if it had its own power, like the skyships I was telling you about, eventually it'd reach the sun Sol, which you can't see without a large telescope. According to history or legend or maybe someone's fancy rumor, that's the system all of our ancestors came from.

"The bright stars are Tartta and Rologne, and long ago their planets had a war. The skyships fought it— so many ships on each side that you wouldn't be able to understand the number."

He paused to scowl his whispering students into momentary silence. "Thousands and thousands of ships, but so far apart that you have no number for the distance because space is so vast. And the ships shot bolts of fire at each other, and metal harder than your spear points became blobs of boiling liquid, and the crews were like charred sticks, and in every battle a few ships broke through on each side to shoot their bolts of fire at the mother worlds, and villages larger than this entire forest, with houses taller than the tallest, were boiled into liquid along with all of their people. Now no one lives on those worlds. Over there—"

He turned and pointed his spear in another direction. "Over there is a world called Watorno, and there's a creature that lives in its seas that would make your koluf seem like a child's toy. It's a hundred times as big, and it could swallow one of your hunting boats with one gulp."

As he paused, he heard a whispered voice from the shadowy fringe of the class. "Someone should tell the Elder. The Langri has a serious head sickness."

Probably it was inevitable; his class began to drift

away. Each morning he would search the faces anxiously to see how many more were missing, and then he would determinedly struggle on.

He taught as much as he could and improvised when he had to, which was often. While he talked to the class, Larno stood at one side of the clearing and worked mathematical problems on his own private writing board. Obrien, with the uncertain support of his *Simplified Astrogation for the Layman,* would sketch out a problem, following which Larno would gleefully fill all the available space with mathematical symbols, to the bafflement of those in the class who bothered to watch. Finally Larno would interrupt Obrien. "I've finished this problem. May I have another?"

Obrien would reach for his *Simplified Astrogation.* "All right. Your ship's velocity is fifty thousand units and the position is the same as before. Calculate the amount of fuel needed to reach Planet X and go into orbit."

"Yes, yes! And—this problem? Is my solution correct?"

"How the devil would I know?" Obrien would mutter as he returned to his lecture.

Whenever he caught Banu alseep, which was often, he would snarl at him, "Banu! What are those attorneys' names?"

Banu would blink himself awake and recite flawlessly: "Klarouse, Hraanl, Picrawley, McLindorffer and Webluston, city of Schwalofro, world of Schwala, Sector 9138."

Obrien fervently offered thanks for small favors. He had a mathematical genius who solved problems he didn't understand, and a mnemonic genius who remembered things spoken while he was asleep—which was fortunate, because sleeping was what he did the most of. Banu seemed never to forget anything, though he understood so little of what he remembered that mining his memory could be an involved and frustrating process.

The rest of his students were uncomplicated morons.

"Attorneys—" Obrien began.

He doubled up suddenly, clutching his abdomen. Fornri and Dalla hurried to him, but he shook them off, straightened up, wiped the perspiration from his face, and continued.

"One day you're going to need attorneys more than you need air to breathe, and that law firm wasn't afraid to take on a world government for me. It won't be afraid to take on a Federation of Worlds for you, but you may have trouble finding it—it's been a long time, and the names may have changed.

"Attorneys cost money, which you don't understand, but you may understand this. Look!"

He unwrapped a piece of cloth and displayed a handful of magnificent crystals. "Take a good look," he told the gaping class. "They're retron crystals. They make interstellar travel possible, and they're rare enough and valuable enough so they can be changed for monetary credits at any financial center in the galaxy."

An altercation broke out at the rear of the class, and he paused until it was resolved, to the accompaniment of much whispering and some squealing. Some boys persisted in teasing the girls, most of whom enjoyed it, and some couples overtly carried on their courtships during class. Obrien had not quite forgotten that he once was young himself.

"Monetary credits are money," he went on, "and attorneys require a lot of it. There are enough crystals packed away in my wreck of a spaceship to buy you a lot of legal service. They'll have to be buried in a safe place—deep in the cave under the double hill would be best. A wrecked ship will be the first thing that'll get looked at when the skymen come, and if the crystals aren't buried deeply there are instruments that will detect them.

"I was talking about governments. The other worlds won't understand a system like yours, where leaders just happen instead of being elected or appointed, so this world will have to—"

The stabbing pain returned, and this time he dismissed the class and weakly allowed Fornri and Dalla to help him into his hammock. He lay with eyes closed, face perspiring, hands clutching his abdomen, and he said softly, "So much to do and so little time. Law and government and economics and colonial administration and all the rest, and I'm only a dumb mechanic and I'm dying." Suddenly his eyes opened and he jerked erect. "Five more were gone today. Where are they?"

Fornri and Dalla exchanged uneasy glances. "Perhaps their villages needed them," Fornri said apologetically. "The hunting—"

"The hunting! What's an empty belly compared with slavery or death? Can't they understand that there won't be any hunting if they don't have a Plan?"

"They don't understand what you want them to do," Fornri said. "Perhaps if you told them the Plan—"

"They aren't ready for it. I should have started sooner."

He sank back into the hammock and closed his eyes. He heard Dalla whisper, "Can't the Elder help?" And Fornri answered, "He helps as much as he can, but it is difficult for him to make them stay here if they think they are needed elsewhere. Tomorrow will be worse."

The pain returned.

One day he had a class of fifteen, and the next day there were eleven. The pain came more frequently, and he ignored it when he could and doggedly continued. "You've got to understand the government of the Federation. There are independent member worlds and independent non-member worlds, and dependent worlds that are virtually the property of other worlds."

They were bored; most of them seemed asleep. He knew the problem—part of the problem—was that he was a lousy teacher, but he couldn't think of any other way to do it, and time was so short.

"You've got to start as an independent non-member and qualify for membership in the Federation or, so help me, you'll end up as somebody's property. I don't know the requirements for membership—that's one of the reasons you'll need those attorneys. Banu?"

Banu tonelessly recited the names and address.

"I do know you'll have to read and write," Obrien went on. "Everyone. The whole population, even the children, those that are old enough. It helps that you already know Galactic, but being able to speak it isn't enough. If you can't read and write, you'll never know what's going on in the galaxy and you won't be able to look after your own interests. Anyway, there's a literacy requirement of maybe ninety per cent for Federation membership. This afternoon we'll start writing lessons, and when you've learned you'll have to teach others, every day, whenever you get a chance. Everyone has to learn.

"You've got to know about bureaucracies. Every government has them. The bigger the government, the bigger the bureaucracies. What the government gives, the bureaucracy takes away and may not even know it's doing it. If you don't know how to fight back, it'll steal this world right out from under you. There's a Colonial Bureau that's supposed to oversee the administration of dependent worlds, but what actually happens—"

The pain struck relentlessly, and he clutched his abdomen and sobbed, "What's the use?"

Fornri and Dalla hurried to his side, and Obrien, rigid with agony, gasped, "Won't any of them come back?"

"They all say maybe tomorow," Fornri said.

"Tomorrow I may be dead. All of us may be dead."

He shook off Fornri's arm, staggered to a log at the edge of the clearing, and sat down. "I waited too long and now there isn't time. I can't make you see the danger."

All of the students were awake now, and some of them were standing.

"This is a poor world," Obrien said, "but it's got something that's priceless. It's a paradise. The beaches and ocean are wonderful. The climate is wonderful. Everything is beautiful."

He lurched to his feet. Fornri hurried to keep him

from falling, but Obrien recovered his balance and
jerked away. He said with terrible earnestness, "The
moment it occurs to *anyone* to put a vacation resort
on this world, you're doomed. That man is your enemy,
and you've got to fight him to the death. If you let him
build just one resort, there"ll be ten or a hundred more
before you know what's happening. You'll have to
move your villages back into the forest, and even if
you're allowed to use the sea there'll be no more hunting. The resorts will drive away the koluf, and you'll
starve. And I can't make you understand."

He staggered back to the log. The students had not
moved. "And this is what I have to work with," Obrien
said resignedly. "Banu, who remembers but never understands. Fornri, my great-great-grandson, who is being loyal even though he'd rather be hunting, and who
understands but rarely remembers."

Fornri was blinking back tears.

"And Dalla." Obrien struggled to his feet and
placed his arm about her affectionately, and she hid her
face on his shoulder and wept. "She's not here to learn,
but to keep me from making myself sick, and I'm already sick beyond any of your understanding." He
turned. "And the rest of you, who'll stay with me loyally until you find an excuse to leave. It's all I have, and
I'll do my damnedest with it. Come here, all of you."

He sat down on the log, and they gathered around
him. He nodded to Fornri, who brought Obrien the
smashed spaceship's battered logbook. Sporadically,
down through the years, Obrien had used it as a journal.
Now it contained the laborious working out of a world's
one hope for survival.

"I'm going to give you the Plan," he said. "You
aren't ready for it, and it's long and complicated, and
most of it you won't understand. I can only hope that
when you need it you'll be able to figure out what I
was talking about. If you can't pay attention, at least
keep Banu awake. *Someone* has got to hear this and remember it.

"I'll give it to you over and over, with all of the
details I can think of, and then I'll give it to you over

and over again. As long as I'm able to speak, I'll tell you the Plan.

"And then, before God—before my God and yours—I'll have done my best."

3

From Fornri's earliest memories the Langri had terrified him.

Few children possessed living great-great-grandfathers, and those who did had to care for doddering, decrepit oldsters who thought only of the fire of death.

The Langri was—the Langri. His was the rope spear in the koluf hunt, and his stroke never missed. He it was who launched the boat into one of the world's rare storms to rescue the children caught out in it. When all feared to cross a swollen stream, it was the Langri who found a ford and went first to test it. Those who had broken arms or legs were brought to him, for only the Langri had the skill to deal with such tragedies.

All manner of adults came to ask his counsel, from a woman whose marriage was troubled to the village leaders and even the Elder; and when the Langri said, "Do this," entire villages leaped to his bidding. Where the Langri led, everyone followed.

Such a great-great-grandfather was a frightful burden for a small boy. The Langri would say, "Why do you go upstream to cross the river? Why don't you swim it here, like the older boys?" Or "The older boys dive from the cliff. Why do you walk down?" Fornri was terrified, but he swam, and he dived.

And when the Langri said, "Spearing marnl is child's play. You should be hunting koluf," Fornri joined the hunters—the youngest person by far in his boat, perhaps the youngest who had ever joined a koluf hunt. The others did not know until afterward that the Langri had sent him, but the custom was for an empty place to be filled by anyone who wanted it, so they did not turn him away. Instead, they mocked him. "Look at the mighty hunter who honors us! Surely our boat is destined for greatness on this day! His will be the rope spear—if he can stop trembling long enough to throw it!"

But Fornri's trembling was from rage, not fear—rage at the Langri, for sending him, and at the hunters, for their mocking. He flung the rope spear with such fury that he fell overboard. The jeers stopped abruptly as the spear struck solidly in the best place of all, the notch just back of the head; and because Fornri was already in the water, he took the trailing rope and made the first loop about the koluf's knifelike, threshing tail, and the others thought he had gone into the water purposely. No one ever mocked Fornri again, about anything.

As the Langri grew older, still first in anything he felt like doing, more and more frequently he felt like doing nothing at all except lie in his hammock in his favorite grove on the point and sip the drink of intoxication. This brought new responsibilities for Fornri. Whatever the Langri did not care to do, he sent Fornri to do for him. And when Fornri came to his Time of Joy, when his peers could devote whole days and nights to music and dancing to song, to the tender turmoil of love and courtship, Fornri was merely the personal servant of a tyrannical old man. Other boys envied him, the great-great-grandson and support of the Langri's declining years, and Fornri could not understand why.

Then the Langri's health began to fail. The Elder wisely concluded that Fornri's talents were more suitable to hunting than nursing, and he sent Dalla to the Langri. Her mother, a widow, had died of the Hot

Sickness that sometimes followed the smallest cut or scratch and was invariably fatal, and Dalla and a young sister were left without relatives.

Fornri had never had a sweetheart. He could have had his choice of many—not only was he a young man of fire, but he was the Langri's heir, already famed for his bravery and his many skills, and there was no village that did not have maidens pining for the great-great-grandson of the Langri.

But the Langri, lounging in his hammock, demanding that his gourd be refilled, or that the leader of the next village be reminded that it was his turn to conduct the berry harvest, or that Fornri carry the Langri's acceptance to a feasting invitation—the Langri seemed unaware that Fornri had reached the Time of Joy. One of the most sublime of joys was young love and courtship, for which long-established customs required freedom and leisure and which could not be managed at all between errands run for a demanding and temperamental old man. The loveliest of maidens might sigh when Fornri passed her, but a youth entrusted with an urgent message from the Langri, with instructions to hurry back with the reply, had no time to suggest an assignation, or even the sharing of a song, and anyway no respectable maiden would have accepted the degradation of a hasty courtship.

Then Dalla came. No maiden surpassed her in loveliness, and they could conduct their courtship with proper leisure despite the Langri's demands because their very bondage brought them together constantly.

Because the Langri was sometimes seriously ill and racked with frightful stomach pains, it was decided that he needed more mature care. The adults took charge of him in spite of his objections, and they sympathetically gave Fornri and Dalla as much freedom as possible and found a younger boy to run the Langri's infrequent errands.

At last Fornri and Dalla had the full pleasure of their Times of Joy. They sang and danced with the other youths, and they passed both days and nights of sweetness on the Bower Hills, the hills reserved for courtship. Most who had Fornri's years were already betrothed. Because Dalla had not yet reached the age of betrothal, he was forced to wait; but in his belated pleasure of his Time of Joy he did not mind.

Yet even the sweetness was bitter-flavored when Fornri reflected that he possessed it only because the Langri suffered a serious illness and was growing old. He understood, now, that even though his great-great-grandfather possessed years far beyond those attained by ordinary men, he could not live always.

And he knew, too, that he loved him.

Then came the journey to the Elder, followed by the building of the Forest Village. Many joys suffered long interruptions because of the Langri's school, and those of Fornri and Dalla most of all. Fornri again had the Langri's errands to run, and both had to care for a sick old man who was trying to do more than his strength would allow. Even when the Langri's illness confined him to his hammock they could not escape, for then they had to trek wearily from village to village trying vainly to persuade former students to return to class.

Rarely did they find time for the pleasures of the Bower Hills, and when they did, Fornri's conscience troubled him severely. He could not understand the need for a Plan, or what the Plan would accomplish, but when the Langri said there would be no hunting, Fornri, at least, believed him. And if his world and his people were threatened, he knew he must put the Time of Joy behind him and do something about it. He only wished he could understand what it was he had to do.

With the class reduced to a mere two hands of students, the Langri finally began to teach them the Plan. All found it bewildering, and some flatly refused to believe it. If—as the Langri said—the skies were filled with worlds, why should anyone want theirs? It was known that the Langri was extremely old, and sometimes the minds of the aged imagined strange things. No one would willingly disrespect the Langri, but what he spoke was not believable.

Fornri would protest hotly, but even those who wanted to believe could make little sense of what the Langri told them. If this happens, he would say, that must be done. If the other thing happens, then something else must be done. If both happen . . . Banu sat with eyes closed and a dazed look on his face, but whenever the Langri asked him he could repeat what was said, word for word.

There would be a ship-from-the-sky, the Langri told them, and they might as well start calling such things spaceships, because that's what they were. Compared with other ships, this one would be small. And then—

But the Plan seemed interminable, and when it was finished the Langri started over again. And over again. And over again.

Each day he grew weaker, and his pains became more racking. When he no longer could leave his hammock, he gathered them about him and once more started at the beginning. There would be a spaceship, a small spaceship, and then—

And then the day came when his words grew incoherent, and finally he could no longer speak. The class wandered off; Fornri and Dalla remained with the women who came to see what could be done to ease his pain.

"His face is dreadfully hot," Dalla said. "Shouldn't we call the healers?"

"They would only anger him," Fornri told her. "The last time, he chased them away. He said there is no way to heal a body worn out by age, and I fear that he is right."

The women massaged the Langri's swollen limbs and applied damp leaves to his hot face. Fornri, watching with helpless concern, became aware of a faint, whistling sound. He puzzled over it for a moment and then set off at a lope toward the nearest village. He saw Dalla start after him, and he motioned her to go back. He broke into a run when he noticed that the sound became steadily louder.

At the edge of the forest he stopped abruptly. The

sound had grown to an earsplitting shriek, and the
villagers, all of them, were in panicky flight. They
raced past him, panting with terror, and beyond the
village he saw a spaceship slowly settling groundward.
He recognized it at once—it was just as the Langri
had described it.

"Stop!" he called to the villagers. "The Langri was
right! We must use his Plan!"

They paid him no heed. The ship had vanished
behind a hill, so he advanced cautiously to the hilltop
and scurried from bush to bush until he found a hiding
place from which he could observe this strange object.

It had come ponderously to rest in a seaside
meadow, and after an interminable wait the hatch
folded out and a man swung to the ground by his
hands. The strange costume that covered him from
ears to toenails was exactly what the Langri had foretold. Fornri made himself comfortable in his hiding
place and watched delightedly.

Once on the ground, the man stretched his limbs
luxuriously and then ran a finger down his chest, opening up his garment. Another man appeared in the airlock and shouted down to him, "Get back in here!
They haven't finished checking the atmosphere."

The man on the ground took an enormously deep
breath and exhaled slowly. "The atmosphere's fine," he
shouted back. "I just checked it myself."

Finally the walkway dropped from the opened
hatch, and the ship's company began to descend. The
Langri had said there would be both men and women,
but because of the strange costumes they wore, Fornri
had difficulty in distinguishing them.

He picked out the leader at once: a short, fat man
to whom others came for instructions. As the leader
surveyed the scene about him, to Fornri's gaping astonishment he blew a cloud of red smoke from his
mouth.

"It *is* a pretty place," he said.

"Pretty?" one of the others exclaimed. "It's a
paradise. Look at that beach!"

A slender man with bushy hair on his face came

down the ramp and began to talk with the leader. They walked back and forth together with so much arm movement that Fornri wondered if this was part of their language.

The sea breeze carried their spoken words to him clearly. Bushy-face said, "We *can't* leave without investigating those natives. Crystals only make you rich. Something like this would make you famous. Primitive humans! How could they have got to this out-of-the-way corner of the galaxy? I *must* have a look at that village!"

"Have a look, then," the leader said. "Since I'm chartered as a scientific expedition, it wouldn't hurt to have a few scientific results just in case someone asks what we've been doing. You can have an hour."

The leader turned to another man, who was performing mysterious rites with a strange black object that he held in his two hands. "I wish you wouldn't wear that gold tooth when I'm taking readings," the man said. "For a moment I thought I had a gold strike."

"No metals at all?" the leader asked.

The other shrugged. "Oh well—those natives may use copper spear points, but no one will ever run a mining concession on this world."

"How come you picked up retron interference?"

"I told you there couldn't possibly be retron crystals on this type of planet unless someone brought them here. I did pick up the interference. Maybe it's still there and the terrain is masking it. Or maybe the meters burped when they shouldn't have."

The leader turned away disgustedly. "Another landing shot on nothing. For your information, setting this crate down and taking off again costs money." He raised hs voice. "Captain?"

A man in a different type of clothing appeared in the airlock. "Yes, Mr. Wembling?"

"We'll lift in an hour. Break out the stun guns. Those wanting to stretch their legs are to stay in groups, and they're not to get out of hailing distance of the ship. I want one stun gun with every group, and that's an order. I also want an armed sentry here at the ship." He turned to the others, most of whom were looking longingly at the sea. "And no swimming. An unknown world can be damned dangerous. You've seen the list of precautions. Follow it."

The captain waved a hand and ducked back into the ship. The leader spoke to the man with the black object. "Take a group and scout around with that hand detector—just in case the retron interference was real."

Groups began to form and head off in different directions. The bushy-faced man led one toward the village. It passed quite near to Fornri, who studied its members carefully and puzzled over the strangely shaped weapon one of them carried. The Langri had described such things, but none of his students believed what he told them.

Twenty strides toward the village, one of the group turned aside suddenly, leaped into a clump of bushes, and dragged out—Dalla, kicking and screaming. Fornri leaped to his feet in consternation and then quickly dropped out of sight. He had not known Dalla had followed him, and it was a contingency the Langri's Plan did not provide for, but Fornri did not hesitate. While Dalla continued to struggle and occupied the men's full attention, he moved stealthily toward them.

The man who captured her was laughing. "I like this world better and better. I hope there's enough of these to go around."

"Let's take her to the ship," Bushy-face said. "I want to see what sort of language she speaks."

The other answered, "That isn't what I want to see."

Fornri was near enough to charge. He crashed into the man holding Dalla and knocked him sprawling. The others immediately grappled with Fornri, and all of them tumbled into a heap while Dalla quickly vanished into the forest. Three of the men pulled Fornri to his feet and held him, and another restrained Dalla's captor, who was furiously angry and attempting to assault Fornri.

"Never mind," Bushy-face said. "He'll do as well as the woman."

"Not for me, he won't!"

"Let's take him to the ship," Bushy-face said. "We can look at the village later."

As they approached the ship, the leader came to meet them. "What do you want with a native?" he asked disgustedly.

"I want to find out something about him," the bushy-faced man said. "His features are Abdolynian, and I think I have some language keys."

"With all the interesting things crawling in that ocean, you shouldn't be wasting your time on humans. There are life forms there I don't believe even when I'm looking at them. I didn't need to worry about anyone sneaking a swim." He turned to a man who was quietly following him about. "Hirus, what are the chances those freaks might be worth money?"

"The only ones interested would be museums and animalariums," the other said. "They haven't got money. If you donated a few of them, no doubt they'd be pleased to name a choice specimen after you. That thing with all the legs and the long neck—how'd you like to have it called genus *Wemblous?*"

The fat man shuddered.

Bushy-face had darted up the walkway to the ship while the others held onto Fornri. Now he returned with another sort of strange black object. He held it in front of Fornri, pressed some of the gleaming protuberances —and the thing spoke! It said, "Fraugh, villick, lascrouf, boumarl, caciss, denlibdra."

Bushy-face was watching Fornri intently. "Those are key words," he said. "If he's Abdolynian, he ought to be able to understand at least one of them."

Fornri, comprehending that he'd been expected to make meaning of the strange sounds, suppressed a smile.

One of the men exclaimed, "Look at the puggard! He's laughing at you! He understands Galactic!"

Suddenly Fornri bolted, slipping from their grasps, knocking over the sentry who was pacing an aimless circle about the ship, and getting away cleanly. He outdistanced the pursuit and reached the forest safely.

Dalla had been watching. She was waiting for him just inside the forest, and the two of them quickly placed its comfortably thick vegetation between themselves and the strangers' weapons. They hurried toward the Forest Village.

There a crowd of terrified adults clustered about the Langri's hammock. Women and men were wailing in turn, "Langri, a thing-from-the-sky! What shall we do?"

The Langri lay deathly still, but as Fornri and Dalla pushed through to him, his eyes opened and he muttered, "Too late."

"The Langri won't help us," a woman said reproachfully.

"The Langri is very sick," Dalla said. "You shouldn't bother him."

The Langri muttered again, "Go away. I'm dying."

"He won't tell us what to do," the woman said.

"He's already told us what to do," Fornri said. "He taught us his Plan. Now we'll follow it." He spoke quietly to the man beside him. "Sound the signal gourds. Summon all the villages." The man stared at Fornri for a moment. Then he smiled, nodded, and hurried away.

"We must capture the skymen," Fornri told the others. "We have to do it without spears or knives, because we dare not injure them. The Langri said that is very important. Even if they injure or kill us, we must capture them without harming them. Do you understand?"

"How?" a man demanded.

Fornri smiled. "The Langri has told us how."

The panic was lifting slowly. This descent of a thing-from-the-sky was the most terrifying event of their lifetimes, but if someone would tell them what to do, they would go and do it. Fornri divided them into two groups and sent them east and west to meet those coming from the other villages.

After he got them started, he turned again to the Langri. The staring eyes did not recognize him. "Should have taught the children," the Langri muttered. "Children were interested. Older ones in a hurry to grow up. Should have started sooner and taught the children." His body went rigid. "Hide the crystals!" he gasped.

Fornri clasped the Langri's hand. Then his eyes sought Dalla's. "Come," he said.

They turned away. Only a few women, the Langri's nurses, remained with him. Already a signal gourd was sending out patterns of deep honks, and the gourds of nearby villages were answering.

They had not reached the first bend in the forest path when they heard, behind them, the women's voices raised in the lament of death. They did not look back. The most important thing in the Langri's life had been his Plan; he surely would understand if they also made it the most important thing in his death.

The Langri had told them how, and they did exactly as he said. One group of skymen had blundered into the forest after Fornri. They advanced boldly, with one of their strange weapons in the lead, until one of them stepped off the path to pick fruit and ran a Death Thorn into his leg. The others argued as to whether the thorn should be left in his leg or pulled out at once with the chance of breaking it, because it was barbed, and he died before they could decide.

While they argued, Fornri surrounded them with the first villagers to arrive. The skymen started a panicky retreat, carrying the body with them, and Fornri sprang his ambush on a curve of the path. He captured them one at a time, without injury to anyone—just as the Langri had foretold.

A short time later, villagers from the west dropped from trees onto the party of skymen worshiping the mysterious black object. One skyman suffered an injured ankle and had to be carried. Fornri's friend Tollof was struck by the mysterious force of a skyman's weapon. They thought he was dead, but a short time later he regained consciousness, though it was the following day before he could move his arms and legs. The black object was broken, but that was the fault of the skyman carrying it.

Capture of the remaining groups required complicated stalking. Finally the ship was rushed and those inside made prisoners before they were able to close the hatch. The skymen were marched to a remote stretch of beach by a meandering route deliberately chosen to confuse them. They were given food and told that on the morrow shelter would be built for them.

So helpless were they that they could not make their own fire. And when one was kindled for them, they huddled about it and listened to the whining reproaches of the leader Wembling until the distant drums of the Langri's death procession frightened him into silence.

The following day dwellings were raised for the prisoners, and boundaries marked out that they were not to pass, for that was the Plan.

And Fornri and Dalla, that morning after the Langri's death rites, led the fifty youths of the Langri's class back to the Forest Village, there to grapple doubtfully with the heritage the Langri had left to them.

4

The battle cruiser *Rirga* was outward bound on a routine patrol mission, and Captain Ernst Dallman was relaxing quietly in his quarters with his robot chess player. He was about to trap the robot's queen, a suspenseful move because this robot was programmed for eccentricity, and at a given moment it could be functioning on any level from idiot to genius. He never knew whether an apparent lapse was due to stupidity or the setting of a cunningly contrived trap.

At that crucial moment the *Rirga's* communications officer interrupted to hand Dallman a message. From his apologetic manner and the speed with which he departed, Dallman knew that the news was not good. The officer was dropping the door shut when a bellow of anger brought him scurrying back.

Dallman tapped the strip menacingly. "This is an order from the sector governor."

"Yes, sir."

"Ships of the fleet do not take orders from bureaucrats, politicians, or port authority waste disposal engineers. You will kindly inform His Highness that there is an entity known as Fleet Headquarters, and that it esteems the illusion that it has full control over its own ships. I am currently on a third-priority assignment, and the fact that I am passing through one corner of his alleged territory does not give a sector governor control over my movements."

The communications officer fumbled with a pocket flap and produced his memorator. "If you will dictate the message, sir—"

"I just gave you the message. You're a communications officer. Communicate. Surely you have sufficient command of language to tell the man in a flattering way that Space Navy orders must come through Space Navy channels. Do so. And tell Commander Protz I want to see him."

"Yes, sir."

The communications officer exited nervously. Commander Protz sauntered in a moment later, met Dallman's foreboding scowl with a grin, and calmly seated himself.

"How long are we going to be in this sector?" Dallman asked him.

Protz thought for a moment. "Roughly forty-eight hours."

Dallman slammed down the message. "That's twenty-four hours too long."

"Some colony in trouble?"

"It's worse than that. The sector governor has lost four scratchers."

Protz straightened up and swallowed his grin. "By all that's spaceworthy! *Four* of them? Look here—I have a leave due in two or three years. I'm sorry I won't be able to see you through this, but I wouldn't give up that leave if the Chancellor himself had lost four scratchers."

"Not only does this oaf of a governor lose four survey ships at one crack," Dallman went on, "but he has the insufferable nerve to order me to start looking for them. *Order,* mind you. I'm letting him know that we have a chain-of-command procedure in the Space Navy, but he'll have time to get through to headquarters and have the order issued there. And since the *Rirga* is on routine patrol, headquarters will be happy to oblige."

Protz reached over and took the strip. By the time he finished reading, he had recaptured his grin. "It could be worse. We just might find all of them in the same place. The W-439 turned up missing. What's the 'W' for?"

"Maybe it's privately owned. The others belong to the Sector Survey."

"To be sure. The W-439 turned up missing, so they sent the 1123 to look for it. Then they sent the 519 after the W-439 and the 1123, and the 1468 after the W-439 and the 1123 and the 519. Too bad we happened to be here. Now we'll never know how many ships the governor would have lost one at a time before he realized that isn't the way to do it."

Dallman nodded. "Seems curious, doesn't it?"

"We can rule out mechanical failure. Those scratchers are reliable, and four of them wouldn't bubble out at the same time."

"Right. And no more than a fifth of the worlds in this sector have even had space ranging. Probably fewer than a tenth have been surveyed. An unsurveyed world can offer some queer kinds of trouble. The odds are that we'll find all four on the same planet and that the same trouble that caught the first one caught the others. Go down to the chart room and see if you can lay out a search area. We might even be lucky."

Twenty-four hours later Fleet Headquarters made it official, and the *Rirga* altered course. Protz paced the control room, whistling cheerfully and making deft calculations on a three-dimensional slide rule. Technicians were verifying them on a battery of computers and having trouble keeping up.

Finally he produced a set of co-ordinates, and Dallman accepted it skeptically. "I asked for an area, not a star system."

"I'm betting we'll find them there," Protz said. He stepped to the chart. "The W–439 last reported in from here, on course—so. Obviously this is where it was heading, and there shouldn't be more than one habitable planet. We can wind this up in a couple of days."

Dallman nodded grimly. "And when we do—if we do—I'm going to see that this sector's surveying section overhauls its procedures. If you're right, four ships in a row landed on an unsurveyed planet, and not one of them bothered to let its headquarters know where it was and what it thought it was doing there. If the navy operated like that—" He turned on Protz. "Are you out of your mind? A couple of days to find four scratchers? You've been in space so long you've forgotten how large a world is!"

Protz shrugged cheerfully. "Like you said, we might even be lucky."

They were lucky. There was one habitable planet, with a single long, narrow subtropical continent. On their first orbit they sighted the four gleaming survey ships parked neatly in a row in a meadow overlooking the sea.

Dallman studied the observational data, squinted at the film strips, and exploded. "By the time we get back on course we'll be a month off schedule, and those fools have just taken time off to go fishing."

"We'll have to land," Protz said. "We can't be certain."

"Of course we'll land—but only after we've observed the entire prescribed procedure for landings on unsurveyed worlds. And as we complete each step we'll notify headquarters that we have done so, just in case we have to be rescued. If whatever caught those scratchers also catches us, we'd better have a damned good excuse."

"Right," Protz agreed. "We land, but we land by the book."

Dallman was still looking at the film strips. "Take a good look at these," he said with a smile. "After this is over with, and after I've kicked those scratcher crews in the pants, *I'm* going fishing."

Protz instituted USW landing procedure, and before he completed half the prescribed visual and instrument surveys, headquarters intervened and ordered them to land at once.

Protz read the order incredulously. "Who was on that privately owned ship? A Federation congressman's brother-in-law?"

"At least," Dallman said.

"Going to protest the order?"

Dallman shook his head. "I'd lose the argument, and what if something happened to this party while I was protesting? Obviously it's someone important enough to risk losing a battle cruiser."

The *Rirga* came gently to rest a thousand meters down the shore from the survey ships. After the routine scientific tests, a security unit made a meticulous search of the landing area, and Protz led a patrol to investigate the survey ships under the cover of alert *Rirga* gunners.

Dallman was waiting at the top of the ramp when he returned. "There's no sign of any trouble," Protz said. "It looks as if the scratchers' crews just parked the ships and walked off and left them."

"Notify headquarters," Dallman said. "If you want my opinion, either this is something very simple, or else we have a major space mystery on our hands."

Protz returned to the control room, and Dallman strolled down the ramp and headed for the beach, sniffing the sea air hungrily. "Beautiful!" he murmured. "Where has this world been all my life?"

His communications officer had trailed after him with portable equipment, mortally offended that a naval officer would conduct a military operation from anywhere but his ship's command station. He said, "Commander Protz, sir."

Dallman, who was admiring the sea, did not bother to turn around. "Let's hear it."

The officer said, "Go ahead, sir," and directed Protz's voice at Dallman.

"That native village is recently deserted, sir," Protz said. "I'd suggest consolidation of patrols for a probe in that direction. If the natives have captured the scratchers' crews, they'll have enough weapons to give a small patrol a nasty surprise."

"Do so," Dallman said.

He strolled along the beach until he reached the point where *Rirga* sentries had established a perimeter. The communications officer, still following after him, announced suddenly, "Sir—we've found a native!"

"The *Rirga* ought to be able to cope with one native without harassing its commanding officer," Dallman said pleasantly.

"Perhaps I should say he found us, sir. He walked right into the perimeter—none of the outposts saw him—and he says he wants to speak with the captain."

Dallman turned and stared at him. "He wants to speak—any particular language?"

"He speaks Galactic, sir. They want to know what they should do with him."

"I suppose we'll have to pretend that he's someone important. Tell them to set up some props, and I'll receive him formally. Does Commander Protz know about this?"

The communications officer flushed. "Commander Protz says it's probably the local game warden, come to complain because the scratcher crews went fishing without a license."

Dallman returned to the *Rirga* and donned a ribbon-bedecked dress uniform. Then he went to the control room to observe the native on the viewing screen before he stepped forth to meet him in person. The young man was intelligent-looking and a model of bodily perfection, though he wore only a loincloth of doubtful manufacture. If he felt any nervousness about meeting the *Rirga*'s captain, he was concealing it.

Protz entered and asked, "Ready to go, sir?"

"I'm having a look at the native," Dallman told him. "Odd to find humans already in residence on such a remote world, isn't it? Lost colonies forgotten because of war or some other catastrophe have always been favorite scope subjects, but I've never heard of it actually happening."

"This place is too remote for it anyway," Protz said.

"I don't know about that. Historians think none of the old suspended-animation colonies survived, but one of the ships could have run off course and deposited a colony here. Or a private expedition could have landed and been unwilling or unable to leave. The equipment it brought would wear out, the ship would be disassembled for the metal, and if the colony found no metals here or didn't have the know-how to mine and smelter them, its descendants would have to survive as a primitive society. After a few hundred years they'd be as much "natives" as an indigenous population would be. Anthropologists will be fascinated. Did you notify headquarters? Then let's go talk with him."

Dallman marched down the ramp, and as he approached the props he saw the members of the honor guard struggling to keep their faces straight. He had to restrain a smile of his own. A naval captain in full dress uniform ceremoniously receiving a native in loincloth offered a study in incongruities worth pondering.

The props were upholstered sections from the ship's lounge. They had been assembled into a circle in a shaded location a short distance from the ship. In the center were chairs and a conference table, the whole looking strangely out of place in that sylvan setting, but Dallman hoped that the native would be impressed into amicability if that happened to be what the situation required.

The honor guard presented arms as Dallman approached. The native stood calmly surrounded by grinning officers. Dallman scowled at them, and the grinning stopped.

The native stepped to meet him. "I greet you. I am Fornri."

"I'm Captain Dallman," Dallman responded. He came to attention and snapped off a full salute. Then he stepped aside and gestured graciously. An officer opened a door in the circle of props, and Fornri stepped through and turned as Dallman and Protz followed him.

He ignored the proffered chair and faced Dallman with splendid dignity. "It is my unfortunate duty to inform you that you and the personnel of your ship are under arrest," he announced.

Dallman sat down heavily. He looked blankly at Protz, who grinned and winked. The native had spoken in a firm tone of voice, and beyond the circle the waiting officers were struggling to contain their laughter.

A seminude native possessed of not so much as a dull spear had calmly walked in and placed the *Rirga* under arrest. It was a gag worth retelling—if anyone would believe it.

Dallman said angrily, "Stop it! This is a serious matter." The laughter stopped. Dallman turned to Fornri. "What are the charges?"

The native recited tonelessly, "Failure to land at a proper immigration point with official clearance, landing in a restricted area, avoidance of customs and quarantine, suspicion of smuggling, and bearing arms without legal authority. Follow me, please, and I'll lead you to your detention area."

Dallman turned on his officers again. "You will kindly stop that idiotic grinning," he snapped.

The grinning stopped.

"This man represents civil authority," Dallman went on. "Unless there are special arrangements to the contrary, military personnel are subject to civil law." He asked the native, "Does this world have a central government?"

"It does," the native said.

"Do you have the personnel of the survey ships under detention?"

"We do."

"May I have permission to inform my superiors as to the charges?"

"On two conditions. All weapons that have been brought from your ship are considered confiscated; and no one except yourself will be permitted to return to the ship."

"May I request an immediate court hearing?"

"Certainly."

Dallman turned to Protz. "Order the men to stack arms at whatever place he indicates."

"You can't be serious!" Protz exclaimed, a note of hysteria in his voice. "One native in a loincloth—what would happen if we just packed up and left?"

"Probably nothing," Dallman said, "but several hundred independent worlds would have convulsions if they found out about it. The Federation's obligations toward *every* independent world are written into a lot of treaties."

Dallman opened the gate to the circle of props and stepped through it. Turning, he said again, "Order the men to stack arms at whatever place he indicates."

The courtroom was a lovely hillside by the sea. The slope was crowded with natives, none of whom had the air of knowing what was happening. At the bottom, seated behind something that looked suspiciously like an enormous, elongated gourd, were the justices: a girl and two young men. The chairs occupied by the defense and the prosecution also were fashioned from gourds, and Dallman was so impressed with the comfort of his that he considered trying to buy it.

The verdict, of course, was predetermined. Not only that, but the courtroom scene had all the blundering overtones of a drama badly rehearsed by amateur actors. Lines were bungled. The defense seemingly was expected to play dead, because every query or objection produced stark consternation on the part of both prosecution and court. The native Fornri, the arresting officer, also functioned as chief prosecutor. He addressed the young lady first justice as "Your Eminence" except when he absently called her Dalla. Fornri's assistant, a native called Banu, seemed to sleep through the proceedings, but when either prosecution or court was stumped on a legal point, Fornri would nudge him, whisper a question, and—after a searching meditation —receive a whispered response.

At one side and to the rear of the justices, a native named Larno sat beside a stretched matting that had been plastered with clay. When Dallman first saw this, he nudged his counsel, the *Rirga*'s young legal officer, Lieutenant Darnsel, and whispered jokingly, "The court recorder." He was only partly wrong. Larno's function, they eventually discovered, was to record the fines as they were assessed.

Lieutenant Darnsel had no more illusion as to the outcome than Dallman had, but as long as he had to be there he was determined to enjoy himself. His performance displayed a skill in histrionics and a gift for inspired improvisation that Dallman would not have suspected of him. The vibrant indignation with which he now leaped to his feet to shout, "Exception!" was sheer dramatic art.

The natives again displayed signs of consternation. Dallman could not understand why. They had bested Lieutenant Darnsel easily on every point he raised.

"State your exception," the first justice responded.

"We cannot be convicted on any of those charges —willfully disregarding landing regulations, avoidance of customs, landing in a restricted area, and so on, when you have failed to inform approaching ships as to what your regulations are."

Prosecution and court listened with deepening anxiety.

Darnsel continued, "You are *required* to so inform approaching ships, and the failure to do so places the burden of negligence on you."

The justices exchanged apprehensive glances.

"Does the distinguished world's advocate have any comment?" the first justice asked.

Fornri again turned to the dozing Banu, who eventually whispered a reply. Fornri nodded, got to his feet, and faced Lieutenant Darnsel. "Please tell the court what steps you took to obtain the necessary regulations prior to landing."

"We monitored the SCC, the Standard Communications Channel, which is required of any ship approaching a planet. The same regulations require every planet to broadcast its regulations in the common Galactic language and to state the communications channel to be used to obtain landing instructions and clearance. Obviously you failed to do so, and your negligence leaves this world open to severe penalties."

Fornri conferred with Banu again, and then he asked, "Where is this requirement of which you speak? Where is it stated? We are an independent world. Who requires this of us?"

"It is contained in every interworld treaty and in every commercial and communications agreement," Lieutenant Darnsel said.

"We have no such treaty or agreement," Fornri told him.

Darnsel reflected for a moment, shrugged wearily, and murmured, "Touché." He took a step toward his chair and then turned to Fornri again. "Would you mind if I consulted your lawbook?"

Fornri's expression was one of sheer bafflement, but he said politely, "Not at all."

Darnsel marched over to Banu, and they engaged in a whispered conference while court and audience gaped at them. Finally Darnsel straightened up and addressed the court. "No further questions."

The first justice said, "Will the court's recorder kindly tabulate the fines?"

"Certainly, Your Eminence," Larno said. "Five counts of failure to land at proper immigration points with official clearance." He turned to Darnsel and Dallman and added, with engaging apology, "That's one for each ship."

They watched intently as he wrote, and as he finished Darnsel leaped to his feet with a cry of anguish. He was no longer acting. "A hundred and twenty-five thousand credits!" he screamed.

"Next charge, please," the first justice said.

Darnsel stood with arms outstretched pleadingly. Fornri ignored him. "The next charge, Your Eminence, is 'Willful avoidance of customs and quarantine.' On this date, representing the fifth in a series of flagrant and willful acts, a ship of the Space Navy of the Galactic Federation of Independent Worlds did violate our sovereign territory—"

Darnsel continued his exhibition of dramatic pantomime, but neither court nor prosecutor paid the slightest attention.

Nor, in the end, did it have the least effect on the outcome.

As they marched back from the court hearing, with natives escorting them at a discreet distance, Darnsel remarked, "I've heard of piracy, sir, and I've had some experience with extortion, but this—half a million credits in fines—I don't know what to call this."

Dallman said philosophically, "They knocked off thirty thousand to make it a round number, which was nice of them."

"The government won't pay it. It'll let us rot here."

"It'll pay it," Dallman said confidently. "It'll have to, to avoid political complications."

"Where does it get the money, sir? Out of our wages for the next century?"

"Hardly. We were ordered to land immediately, and we followed orders. If the fine comes out of anyone's wages it won't be ours. What was it you asked the young chap who functions as a lawbook?"

"I asked him about the age of majority on this world. All of the justices looked suspiciously young to me—in fact, I thought I had sound basis for a mistrial."

"So what did you find out?"

"I had some trouble making him understand what I meant by 'age of majority,' and then he claimed it

was up to the individual to decide when he was an
adult. I didn't pursue the matter. What will you do
now, sir?"

"Communicate with headquarters and ask for instructions," Dallman said. He smiled wryly. "It could
only happen in Paradise."

5

It required eight days of frenzied communication
with his headquarters before Dallman finally was able to
complete negotiations with the natives. Before the last
conference started he asked to confer with the navy
men and scratcher crews under detention, and Fornri
led him on a fast-paced march along meandering forest
trails. He was fully convinced that the detention camp
was buried at the center of the continent when suddenly they emerged on the seashore again. For all Dallman knew, they were a couple of kilometers and a
short boat ride down the coast from where they had
started.

"They don't quite trust me," he mused. "But then
—why should they?"

A small village had been constructed in a sloping
meadow just above the beach. He had not been close
to a native village, and the dwellings startled him—the
brilliantly colored, precisely shaped roofs looked like
molded plastic.

But the village was deserted. Its entire population
was on the beach, either cavorting or relaxing. Some
prisoners were swimming, some sprawled in the sun,
and some were playing games with native boys. One

young native was giving juggling lessons wih oddly shaped balls that had color patterns similar to the roofs of the dwellings. In the water just offshore, an older youth was teaching some prisoners to spear sea creatures. A nav jabbed with his spear; the boy cried, "No, no!" He thrust with his own spear and brought up a squirming nightmare of a meter-long sea monster. Farther offshore was a boat race between Space Navy men and native boys. The boys, more of them convulsed with laughter than paddling, were have a difficult time making the race look close. The navy men were working furiously and accomplishing very little, and all were having a hilariously good time.

Fornri smiled and gestured, indicating to Dallman that he had the freedom of the place, and seated himself at the edge of the forest to wait. Dallman walked down to the beach and stopped beside one of his men who lay among the sun bathers. At first the nav had difficulty in recognizing his commanding officer. Belatedly he attempted to lurch to his feet, and Dallman put him at ease.

The nav grinned sheepishly. "I'm almost sorry to see you, sir. I suppose the leave is over."

"How have you been treated?"

"Perfectly. Couldn't ask for better treatment. The food is wonderful. They have a drink I'll swear is the best thing in the galaxy. Those huts they built for us are very comfortable, and each of us has a hammock. They told us where we could go and what we could do and left us alone. We hardly see any natives except for the boys. They bring our food, and they're around all the time. Look—" He pointed to the boat race, now fading into the distance. "It's been a riot."

"Three native women apiece, I suppose," Dallman said dryly.

"Well, no. The women haven't come near us. Otherwise, if you're thinking of naming this planet, sir, you can call it Paradise."

The men in the scratchers' crews had much the same story to tell. "You weren't harmed?" Dallman asked.

"No, sir. They took us by surprise and used just enough force to disarm us. One of the crewmen of Wembling's ship died from running a poison thorn in his leg, but that wasn't the natives' fault. He was out exploring, or something."

Eventually Dallman located Commander Protz, and the two of them sat down apart from the others and talked.

Protz said, "Half a million credits! The government will never pay it!"

"The money's already been transferred. What have you found out about this character Wembling?"

"More than he wanted me to know. Obviously he's a Very Important Big Businessman with plenty of political pull."

"What's the man doing out here?" Dallman asked.

"Neither he nor his crew is talking much about that. From an occasional careless remark, I gather that Wembling is speculating in bankrupt mining corporations. If he can find new sources of ore for them, he'll make a billion, so he's batting about this unsurveyed zone looking for worlds to plunder. In other words, the situation is shady."

"Very shady," Dallman agreed. "In fact, illegal."

"A Very Important Big Businessman with political pull isn't handicapped by legalities. Wembling has a right-hand man named Hirus Ayns who's as slick an expert in dirty manipulations as you'll ever meet. He offered to make me an admiral in two years for unspecified considerations, and I think he meant it. Anyway, Wembling got around the law by chartering himself as a scientific expedition, but with one exception all of his scientists are geologists and mineralogists."

"The one exception being the grain of truth in case he's caught? I'm sorry to hear that. I'm about to negotiate a treaty recognizing this place as an independent world, and guess whom the sector governor has nominated as the first ambassador."

Protz stared at him. "Not—*Wembling?*"

"I feel sorry for the natives, who seem to be a remarkably fine people, but I have my orders." Dallman got to his feet. "I'll talk with Wembling now, and then we'll wind this thing up." ·

Dallman found Wembling and the man Ayns seated on boulders near the water, and the beginning of their conversation was interrupted by the boat race, now on its return lap. It swept past them just offshore, and Wembling turned to scowl at it until the racket receded. When he could make himself heard, he asked incredulously, "What was that you said? *Ambassador?*"

"The sector governor wants to appoint one immediately so he won't be embarrassed by the loss of more ships."

Wembling chuckled. "Nonsense! That may be what he told you, but I know that cheap twiddler. He just wants to save transportation expenses. I'm here, and if I don't take the job he'll have to send someone. Tell him I haven't got time right now for playing ambassador."

"He instructed me to tell you that you already have more money than you know how to spend, and if you serve as ambassador, even temporarily, forever afterward you'll be able to refer to yourself as the Eminent H. Harlow Wembling."

Wembling guffawed heartily. "How about that? The Eminent H. Harlow Wembling! Not bad for the son of a jet swabber that had to drop out of school to support his family. Not bad! But no, I just haven't the time—"

Ayns's foot moved two centimeters and nudged Wembling's ankle. Wembling turned, and Ayns's head moved an almost imperceptible two millimeters down, two millimeters up. A nod.

"Maybe I better think it over," Wembling said.

"You can have half an hour. If you decide to stay, I'm authorized to let you have some prefab buildings for an embassy, equipment for a communications center, and enough supplies to last until a courier ship gets here. If you want to keep some of your own people with you, the governor will give diplomatic appointments to a reasonable number. Let me know as soon as you decide."

The props, with the central conference table and chairs, still stood in the shady grove near the *Rirga*. Dallman and Protz met Fornri there. With Fornri was the girl Dalla, formerly first justice, and the boy Banu, who had been Fornri's lawbook. The officers saluted; the natives responded with upraised arms. Then they seated themselves on opposite sides of the conference table.

"I now have my final instructions," Dallman announced. "I am authorized to accept unconditionally your listing of fines and penalties. The half million credits will be deposited to the credit of your government in the Bank of the Galaxy as soon as my government is notified that these negotiations have been successfully completed. In accepting it, you agree to return all confiscated equipment and weapons, to release all detained personnel, and to give departure clearance to all ships."

He passed the credit memo across the table. The natives glanced at it indifferently. Dallman found himself wondering what a half million credits—a modest fortune on any civilized world—could possibly mean on this one.

"Your planet's status as an independent world will be recognized," Dallman went on. "Its laws will be respected by the Galactic Federation and enforceable in Federation courts whenever Federation citizens or governments are involved. My government will maintain a representative in residence with the rank of ambassador, and his embassy will operate a communications center for contact with his government and with ships wishing to obtain landing clearance."

"That is satisfactory," Fornri said. "Provided, of course, that the terms of the agreement are in writing."

"Certainly." Dallman hesitated. "You understand—this means that you must return all of the weapons that you've confiscated, not only from the *Rirga*, but also from the survey ships."

"We understand," Fornri said with a smile. "We are a peaceful people. We have no need for weapons."

For some reason Dallman had expected negotiations to collapse over that point. He paused for a deep breath and said, "Very well. I'll have the treaty drawn up for signature."

"May we have copy reproductions for our district archives?" Fornri asked.

Dallman blinked at him; the very word "archive" seemed incongruous on this lush, primitive world, but he resisted the temptation to inquire as to whether the archives were kept in woven-walled huts or hollow trees. "You can have as many copies as you like," he said. "There is one more thing. In order to draw up the treaty, we'll need an official name for your world. What do you call it?"

The natives gazed at him blankly. "Official—*name?*" Fornri repeated.

"Until now your world has been a set of chart co-ordinates. It must have a name, and if you don't name it someone else will and you probably won't like his choice. The name can be a native word that means 'world,' or the name of a legendary hero, or a description—anything you like, really, but it's wise to make it short and euphonious. What do you want to call it?"

Fornri hesitated. "Perhaps we should discuss this."

"Certainly. It's extremely important, not only for the treaty, but for your relations with other worlds. Worlds have names for much the same reason that men have names—to identify them, to describe them, and so on. We can't even deposit the half million credits for you unless your world has a name with which to identify its account. But one word of caution. Once you choose a name, it will become a matter of record in all sorts of places and virtually impossible to change."

"I understand."

"As soon as you decide on the name, then, we'll draw up the treaty."

The natives withdrew. Dallman relaxed and poured himself a tumbler of the natives' fermented drink. It was all that the nav had claimed, and the food Dallman had eaten when the natives invited him to a festival the night before—something called koluf—was a delicacy any member of the Galactic League of Culinary

Artists would have been proud to assign his mark to.

All of this beauty, and gastronomical delights as well. "Perhaps Paradise *would* be the proper name for the place," he mused aloud.

Protz raised his own tumbler, took a long draft, and sighed deeply. "Agreed, but we'd best leave the choice to them. Their idea of Paradise might be a very different sort of place. Anyway, all kinds of complications arise when worlds are named by outsiders."

Dallman smiled, remembering the famous story of the survey ship calling for help from a swamp on a strange planet. "Where are you?" its base had asked. The survey ship gave its co-ordinates and then added, quite unnecessarily, "It's a helluva place." The people of that planet had been trying for centuries to have its name changed, but on all the official charts it was still Helluvaplace.

Three hours later the *Rirga* was in space, and Protz and Dallman stood in the control room watching the receding disk of a planet they always would remember as Paradise.

"I'd feel a lot better about this if the ambassador was anyone but Wembling," Protz said.

"That couldn't be helped," Dallman said, looking dreamily at the viewer. "What a lovely world it was, though. I wonder if we'll ever see it again."

"And they call it 'Langri,'" Protz mused. "What do you suppose that means?"

6

Young Mr. Yorlon was purring landing data into the courier ship's intercom. Talitha Warr listened with a half-smile as she worked on an unruly lock of hair. The performance was exclusively for her benefit, since she was the only passenger aboard; but then, the purser had been purring for her ever since she took passage, and the only difference now was the desperate note of sadness in his voice.

"World of Langri in fifty seconds, Miss Warr. Surface temperature, twenty-six; humidity, fifty-one; gravity, ninety-four per cent normal; atmosphere, twenty-four per cent oxygen. World of Langri in thirty seconds—"

She said, "Drat it," stepped around the pile of luggage in the center of her cramped passage quarters, and threw herself into the cushioned landing chair. The warning light was already on; at her elbow, her diffracto softly played music that matched Mr. Yorlon's mood. She despised it, but she was too preoccupied with dressing to change the grating.

Mr. Yorlon's voice purred on. "Landing in ten seconds; landing!"

The ship settled to ground with a gentle lurch that produced a squalk from the diffracto. The warning light faded. Talitha bounded back to her mirror and resumed the fussing with her hair. Finally she switched the mirror to full length and stepped back to inspect herself: immaculately gowned, tiara in place, coiffure elegantly sculpted except for the one dratted lock.

57

The gong sounded, and the intercom crackled again. This time it was the captain. "Clear for disembarking, Miss Warr."

She moved closer to the mirror for a last try at that hair. "Thank you, Captain. I'll be ready in a moment."

Finally satisfied, she retracted the mirror, closed the diffracto and placed it with her other luggage, and picked up a wrap. The captain was waiting outside her door. His greeting was a wide-eyed stare, but she thought nothing of that. She was quite accustomed to being stared at.

"Ready to disembark?" he asked.

"Yes, thank you."

She handed her wrap to him, and he helped her into it. Then she moved along the corridor toward the airlock. Up ahead, a door dropped open. Two eyes surmounted by a bald head peered out at her. The purring, lovesick Mr. Yorlon was memorizing her for his garden of regrets. She decided that the kindest thing she could do would be to ignore him. She said over her shoulder, "Is the limousine here? I told Mr. Yorlon to ask the embassy to send one."

"Limousine?" the captain exclaimed. "There aren't any ground vehicles on Langri. Anyway, the landing field is the embassy's back yard."

"No ground vehicles? How do they get about?"

"By boat, mostly."

"You mean—it's a water world?"

The captain did not answer. They had reached the airlock. He handed her through, and the two of them stood at the top of the ship's ramp while she looked about her in consternation. "This—*this* is the world of Langri?"

A cluster of shoddy prefab buildings stood on a rise at the end of the landing field. They looked as though they'd been dumped wherever a machine tired of carrying them. They stood, or floated, in an undulating sea of flowers. The gigantic, vividly colored blooms, along with the fantastic colors of the surrounding forest, made the view breath-taking despite the blight imposed on the scene by the buildings.

She could not comprehend, let alone believe. She looked again at the shoddy prefabs the captain had called the embassy. "You mean—Uncle Harlow is ambassador—to *that?*"

The captain regarded her with amusement. "The citizens of Langri offered to build an embassy for him, but your uncle was afraid his status would suffer. Native buildings are made of woven grass."

"But—" Again she looked about her bewilderedly. "But—where's the capital city?"

"There aren't any cities," the captain said. "Just native villages with grass huts."

Talitha burst into laughter. She still hadn't grasped what had happened, but she knew that the joke was on her—and no wonder the captain had stared at her, attired in the latest soiree gown to land in a wilderness! "I came because I thought Uncle would need a hostess," she gasped. "I brought a special wardrobe for the embassy receptions and soirees and dinners. I spent all my savings on it. And look!"

She moved down the ramp a short distance. "It *is* beautiful," she said.

She walked to the bottom of the ramp and looked about her. The tossing, floating flowers seemed to beckon, and suddenly she broke into a run. Gown flapping, coiffure completely forgotten, she dashed buoyantly through the flowers, and as she ran she reached out and snatched a handful. Then, glancing down at them, she came to an abrupt halt. They had wilted in her hand and turned brown. She puzzled over this, and finally she plucked another flower and watched its glistening petals fade as though she were holding a flame to them. She dropped it and thoughtfully walked toward the buildings.

They were connected by muddy paths, and paths led away from them in several directions, one of them curving toward the beach. The ocean had not been visible from the landing field; from the hilltop it could be seen spanning the horizon, a shimmering, sparkling, incredibly lovely blue-green sea under a blue-green sky.

She looked into the buildings. One contained a communications center and offices. Three were divided into sleeping quarters. One had a dining room, library, and game room. One was a storage building. All were as immaculately clean and tidy as a properly programmed housekeeper could make them, and all of them were deserted. As she examined them, she had the panicky sensation of trying to convince herself that this world of Langri was in fact inhabited.

Finally she returned to the building with the offices, and a short time later the ship's captain dropped the door open and came in swinging a mail pouch. He tossed it onto a desk and took another from its hook by the door.

"Your luggage in on the way," he told Talitha. "Is there anything else I can do for you?"

"Prove to me that someone lives on this stupid world."

He stepped to the window and pointed. On the watery horizon she could just make out specks of color. "Native hunting boats," the captain said. "Can you see the sails? The creatures they catch are the most hideous monsters imaginable, and one of them completely fills a boat." He grinned at her. "Great place, Langri. You'll have a wonderful time here."

"Doing what?" she demanded scornfully.

"Swimming, playing games with the natives—go have a look at that beach."

They turned as three perspiring crewmen entered with Talitha's luggage. The captain picked up his mail pouch and started for the door, and the crewmen awkwardly moved aside for him.

"I'm tempted to leave with you," Talitha said.

"Nonsense. Have a nice vacation, like everyone else on Langri. *Then* if you want to leave, I'll be back in two or three months."

He nodded, smiled, and went out swinging the pouch.

The crewmen were still holding her luggage.

"Please excuse me," she said. "Just set everything down here. I don't know where my quarters will be. Thank you. It's a warm day for carrying loads."

One of them said bitterly, "I don't know what the blasted hurry is. We're never on schedule anyway, and I could do with a swim."

They nodded at her and went out. She hesitated for a moment, and then she followed them and stood watching the ship. The supplies had been stacked haphazardly just beyond the ship's landing perimeter. The captain had been willing to deliver luggage for a lady in distress, but obviously he would not transport supplies a centimeter farther than was absolutely necessary for an embassy staff that did nothing but swim and play games with the natives. She watched the ship until it lifted, and then, feeling very lonely, she returned to the embassy.

But she did not go inside. After a moment's hesitation she chose the path to the beach, walked for a short distance along the water's edge, and retraced her steps. Another path led from the buildings across a flower-spangled meadow to the magnificently colored forest. She hesitated once more, and then she shrugged and followed it. Crossing the meadow, she stooped over to look closely at the strangely fragile flowers. Her breath was even more corrosive than her touch—it blackened them instantly. She straightened up in consternation and walked on.

Not until she found the trees looming directly in front of her did she pause. The path obviously was not much used. The forest seemed very dark.

Off to her right, a flash of color caught her attention. She hurried to it and leaned over it in utter fascination. It was the most magnificent flower she had ever seen. Instinctively she stretched out her hand—and the flower ran off, scurrying over blossoms, leaping from leaf to leaf, and finally dropping to the ground and disappearing into the long vegetation.

As she stared after it, Talitha was vaguely aware of a slight movement above her head. Before she could move, before she had time even to feel alarmed, a cluster of wreathing vines fell upon her. In an instant they swarmed over her and began to tighten. She screamed and clawed at them, but almost before she could struggle they whipped away, twisting and threshing, and slowly began to hoist back into the brilliant canopy of leaves. She staggered backward. Her bare arms were laced with networks of tiny blood spots where the vines had seized her. Otherwise, she seemed unharmed. Panting, she stared up at the tree, which held numerous clusters of vines poised for dropping on the unwary.

Then she noticed that the forest floor under the tree was thickly strewn with the skeletal structures of small animals. She screamed again, louder. Pounding footsteps approached her, and a man burst from the forest. He was heavily bearded, his skin beautifully bronzed by the sun, and he wore only a loincloth. She immediately took him for a native. While she stared at him, he was looking about for the cause of her scream. Then he noticed her costume and stared at her with a rare frankness.

"What's the matter?" he asked.

"The vines," she said, pointing. "They grabbed me."

"And then they ungrabbed you. Look."

The vines were still wreathing just overhead, and he strode forward and deliberately extended a hand toward them. They retreated, threshing violently.

"Humans are poisonous to it, and to all the other insidious life forms on the planet," he said. "For which we all offer thanks daily. Actually, it knows better than to attack humans, but your gown and light complexion probably fooled it. Come back in a couple of weeks, when you've got yourself a good coat of tan, and it won't pay any attention to you." He paused, looking at her with puzzled admiration. "Going to a party, or something?"

Talitha burst into laughter. "It must seem like an odd costume for exploring!"

He spoke very seriously. "Don't do that. Not in any costume. It's a lovely world, but it can be deadly.

Excuse me. Things are rather informal on Langri. I'm
Aric Hort. I'm an anthropologist. I'm supposed to be
studying the natives, but I don't make much progress
because they'd rather I didn't."

"I'm Talitha Warr," she said. "My uncle is ambassador to this place, or so he said, and I decided to
pay him a surprise visit. Thus far I'm the one surprised."

"Better wait for your uncle at the embassy. I'll
walk back with you."

She said stiffly, "I'm sure I can find the way myself."

"I'm sure you can, and I can't think of any danger
you might encounter along the way, but I'll go with
you anyway."

He took her arm firmly and turned her toward the
embassy, and they walked side by side through the
flower-clustered meadow.

"What's so deadly about Langri?" she asked him.

"The world isn't compatible with humans. The
first colonists must have had a horrible struggle for
survival, because there's so little here that humans can
eat. In compensation, there's nothing here that wants to
eat us, but there are a number of things that can cause
unpleasant sickness or death.

She reached out and plucked a flower and watched
it turn brown. "Then the flowers are allergic to humans?"

Some are. Some the natives can wear as orna-
ments. Some are poisonous to everything that comes
near them. Better not touch anything at all without
asking first."

"What's Uncle Harlow doing in a place like this?"

"Playing ambassador," he answered indifferently.

"That doesn't sound at all like him. He's a dear,
and he can move mountains, but usually he won't stir a
muscle until he counts the profit."

"Being able to put the word 'ambassador' in front
of one's name is a kind of profit," Hort said.

"I suppose, but it still doesn't sound like Uncle
Harlow."

They were approaching the embassy buildings.

Hort touched her arm and pointed, and she saw her uncle approaching from another direction. He seemed to be leading an army, but she quickly picked out familiar faces: Hirus Ayns, her uncle's executive assistant, and two of her uncle's secretaries. Ayns had noticed her. He spoke to Wembling, who turned. His mouth dropped open. Then he bellowed, "Talitha!"

She dashed into his arms. A moment of ponderous embrace, and then she backed off and looked at him. "Uncle Harlow!" she exclaimed. "You look wonderful! You've lost weight, and what a marvelous tan you have!"

"You're looking pretty good yourself, Tal. But you're supposed to be in medical school. Vacation time?"

She ignored the question. "I thought I'd find you lording it over a big embassy staff in some glamorous world capital. What are you doing here?"

He glanced over his shoulder at the natives, and then he drew her aside and spoke quietly. "Frankly, I'm working on the biggest deal of my life. I fell into this appointment, and if I use it properly—" He broke off. "Why aren't you in medical school?" he asked sternly.

"Because I quit. I wanted to help suffering humanity. Know what they were making of me? A computer technician."

"Medical computation is a damned good job," he said. "Good pay, and you can always— Look here. Wemblings don't quit. I'm sending you back on the next ship."

He stomped away. The natives and his staff respectfully fell in behind him. No one looked back, but she shouted after him furiously, "You won't have to! I'm leaving on the next ship!"

She glared at Aric Hort, who was looking on innocently. "I like that. The nerve!"

She flounced toward the nearest building, dropped a door open, entered, and dropped it closed again, leaving him staring blankly after her.

7

Her next impression of Langri was of the peering eyes of children. Whenever she left the embassy there were native children watching her. They stared at her from behind bushes, they trailed after her, they anticipated her movements and were there ahead of her wherever she went. The only sounds they uttered were suppressed giggles.

On the morning following her arrival she lay drowsily on the beach, acquiring a first installment of sun tan, and already she was so accustomed to children slyly circling around her that when Aric Hort approached she did not even open her eyes until he spoke.

He told her good morning, and she answered politely and closed her eyes again.

He sat down beside her. "Do you like Langri any better than you did yesterday?"

"Worlds usually don't change much overnight," she murmured.

She was silent for a time, and when she looked up at him she found him grinning at her. She said testily, "The ocean is the nicest blue-green I've ever seen, except for the sky, and the forest colors are magnificent, and the flowers are wonderfully fragrant and lovely until you pick them, and if you take away this world's blatant prettiness what have you got?"

"At least you're enjoying the beach," Hort observed.

She picked up a handful of sand and flung it aside.

"I tried to go swimming, but there are things out there I don't care to share an ocean with."

"They feel the same way about you. If you know how to swim, the ocean is the safest place on Langri."

She pushed herself into a sitting position. "Tell me," she said seriously. "Just what *is* Uncle doing here?"

"Yesterday he was laying out a drainage system for a native village. I don't know what he's doing to-day. Let's find him and see."

He helped her to her feet, and they walked off along the beach. She looked back once and saw a group of children scurrying to keep up with them.

"I wanted to ask you something," Hort said. "Yesterday your uncle said you'd been in medical school."

"I had one year of medical school, and it was ten per cent physiology and ninety per cent electronics, and I'd rather not think about it. You'll have to take your aches somewhere else."

He grinned at her. "No, no—I'm not after free medical advice. I'm worried about the natives. They're a healthy people, which is fortunate—they have no medical science at all. When one of them *is* sick or in-jured, he's in deep trouble."

"If I tried to look after him, he'd be in worse trouble. Anyway, nursing a bunch of ignorant savages wouldn't appeal to me."

He said sharply, "Don't call them ignorant! On this world they're much more knowledgeable than you are."

"Then they're knowledgeable enough to nurse themselves."

They walked on in silence.

The shore curved into an inlet, and a native village came into view, built on a gently sloping side of a hill above the sea. The dwellings stood in concentric circles, with a broad avenue pointing straight up the hill to bisect the village, and other avenues radiating out from the central oval. Children were playing along the beach, and older children were swimming and spearing sea creatures. The moment they saw Hort all of them headed for him at a rush, the younger children flocking along the beach and the older ones quickly swimming to shore and chasing after them. All of them shouted, "Airk! Airk!"

The younger children made faces at him, and the contorted expressions he produced in return convulsed them. The older children circled around him playing some kind of complicated hitting game that he invariably lost, and his expressions and gestures of feigned pain dissolved all of them in hilarity. Even the quivering gloom of his scowl set them squealing with merriment.

Plainly they loved this man, and his very presence was a delight to them. Talitha looked at Hort with interest for the first time and found that he had the kindest eyes she had ever seen, and that his face, behind its ridiculous façade of beard, radiated compassion and good humor.

She also thought that something was troubling him deeply.

Hort picked up one small girl and introduced her. "This is Dabbi. My prize student. Dabbi, this is Miss Warr."

Dabbi smiled charmingly and spoke an unintelligible greeting.

Hort answered her unspoken question. "They're bilingual. It's a very strange situation. They have a language that I can't make anything of, and then many of them are quite fluent in Galactic and almost all of them understand it—some of the young people even use fairly up-to-date slang expressions."

He put Dabbi down and directed Talitha's attention to the sea.

A hunting boat was rapidly approaching shore below the village. The crew, which consisted of both men and women, was standing poised on the edges of the boat. Hort waved, and all of them waved back.

"Why do they call them hunting boats?" Talitha asked.

"Come and see what they catch, and you'll understand."

He took her hand, and they ran along the beach with the children trailing after them. When they reached the village, the crew already had dragged the boat ashore. Hort led her over to it.

She looked once, briefly, and felt a wave of revulsion and horror such as she never before had experienced. She reeled backward with averted face, not believing, not wanting to remember, trying not to be sick.

The koluf was an enormous creature that completely filled the boat. It had a double row of clawing legs and a hideous, mottled, threshing, multitudinously jointed body that swiveled obnoxiously and formed strangely contorted curves. The vast head was slashed from front to rear by a gaping mouth with huge, protruding, curved teeth that snapped viciously. It was held in place in the narrow boat by poles and lashings.

Talitha turned and looked out to sea, where the colorful sails were just visible on the horizon. "Did they come all that distance with *that* in the boat?"

"It makes for a lively ride," Hort said with a smile, but it's the only way it can be done. If they tried to tow it in, either it would haul them out to sea, or its friends and relatives would tear it to pieces. They have to get it into the boat as quickly as possible."

"What do the women do?" she asked.

"The same thing the men do. They hunt koluf."

The natives were hauling the koluf from the boat. They dragged it far up onto the beach, pulling it by its long, stringy, lashing fins and deftly avoiding the slashing teeth, clawing legs, and threshing, knifelike tail. By the time the hunters had finished, men and women of the village were gathered about them. The hunters turned at once, launched their boat, reefed in the sail, and paddled away.

The koluf continued to twist and thresh violently, and the villagers began to push sand over it with long-handled scrapers. As they worked, they shouted a rhythmic song in the native language. The koluf's violent movements increased and several times it broke free, but they continued to push the sand. Finally they built a mound from which it could not escape, though its struggle made the sand heave and jerk.

A few villagers remained, putting finishing touches on the mound and watching to make certain that the koluf did not break free. The others returned to the village.

Talitha said incredulously, "And Uncle says it's the most delicious meat he's ever eaten!"

"If there were pantheons of gods in the Langrian religion," Hort said solemnly, "that creature would be their ambrosia. It's delectable beyond mere human comprehension."

"I wish I'd tasted it before I saw it," Talitha said. She counted eight widely spaced mounds along the beach and shuddered.

They walked on, skirting the village but passing close to the outlying dwellings, and Talitha stopped to examine one of them. She ran a finger over the brilliant color design of the roof and then rapped on it. "What's it made of?"

"It's a segment of a gourd. Beautiful, isn't it?"

"It is." She rapped again. "A *gourd?* If this is only a segment, they must be *huge.*"

"Enormous," Hort agreed. "And when the shell is soaked in sea water and dried it becomes as tough and durable as plastic. Did you notice the lovely symmetry these dwellings have? They're a fitting ornament for a beautiful world, and they're also the best sort of housing that could be devised for this climate. Look at the walls—they're a fine mesh woven of fiber, and they not only keep out pests, but they also breathe. They're incredibly durable. Interestingly enough, the fiber is made from threads extracted from gourd stems, and the natives also use it for a rope—"

Talitha had lost interest. She saw her uncle approaching the village, followed by his usual incongruous escort. One of his two secretaries, Sela Thillow, carried an electronic gadget for note taking. The other, Kaol Renold, seemed to be waiting to be told to do something. Hirus Ayns followed along at the rear, sharp-eyed as usual, saying little but missing nothing. What the natives were doing she couldn't fathom at all.

"Here's Uncle," she said.

Hort turned off his lecture, and they went to meet him. As they approached, the grinning natives suddenly scattered in all directions, and Wembling shouted a final admonition after them. *"Big* logs, mind you!"

"What are you doing?" Talitha asked him.

"Trying to get the natives to build a raft," he said.

"What do they need a raft for?" Hort demanded. Talitha turned and stared at him. Few men spoke to her uncle in that tone of voice.

Wembling seemed not to notice. "They need a raft to hunt with," he said.

"They seem to be doing quite well without one," Talitha observed.

Wembling shook his head. "Have you seen the way they hunt? Whenever they catch one of those monsters, a crew has to bring it all the way to shore. Every catch costs them up to an hour of prime hunting time. Look at that!" He was counting the mounds on the beach. "Six, seven, eight. That's a good start on the day's hunt, but it means the boats already have made eight round trips from the hunting grounds. That's the loss of a boat and crew for eight hours of hunting, and while one boat is bringing a koluf to shore, the fleet is less efficient. It takes every crew available to haul one of those monsters out of the water. If they could anchor a big raft close to the hunting grounds they could transfer the koluf to the raft, and then in the evening they could tow in the day's catch all at once. A village this size would save a couple of hundred man-hours of work a day and hunt much more efficiently. That would make it possible to catch more koluf and get off their subsistence diet. Got that, Sela?"

"Got it," she said, fingers playing rapidly on the electronic keyboard.

"Did you say *subsistence* diet?" Talitha asked. "I've never seen a healthier-looking people."

"They're healthy enough now, but they have very

little food reserve. Whenever the hunting falls off, they come close to starvation. It takes a lot of koluf to feed a world population, even when it's a small population. I wanted to teach them some ways to preserve their surplus meat. Couldn't get them to understand what I was talking about. Turned out the reason they couldn't understand was because they have so little surplus. A raft would increase the daily catch and let them store an emergency reserve. Well, Hort?"

"I've told you what I think," Hort said. "The natives lead a precarious existence in the ecology of a hostile environment. Any tampering at all might upset the balance and exterminate them."

Wembling grinned at him and spoke in conversational tones. "Hort, you're fired. You can't see beyond your textbooks. Increased efficiency in hunting will put them on the safe side of that precarious balance."

"Increased efficiency in hunting could change the koluf's feeding habits or reduce the breeding stock. The result would be fewer koluf and starving natives."

"Long before that happened, we'd think of something else. Here's Fornri."

A group of young natives approached them, and one, obviously their leader, strode up to Wembling and wasted no time in coming to the point. "Excellency, this *raft*. It could not be used."

"Why not?" Wembling asked.

"The koluf must be buried in sand."

Wembling turned questioningly to Hort. "Some religious quirk?"

"It's probably vital," Hort said. "Most things on this world are poisonous to humans. Burying the koluf in sand must do something to neutralize the poison."

"It must be buried as soon as possible after it is caught," Fornri said, "and it must be kept buried for a day and a night. Otherwise, the meat cannot be eaten."

Wembling nodded thoughtfully. "I see. Couldn't we load the raft with sand and bury the koluf there?"

"The sand must be dry. Would that be possible on a raft at sea? And burying the koluf is dangerous. Much room is needed for the burying."

Wembling nodded again. He was bitterly disappointed and trying not to show it. "I'll have to think about it. A dying koluf does thresh about a bit. As for keeping the sand dry—I'll think about it."

He turned and marched away, and his entourage formed up and followed him. Fornri and a young woman remained behind, and Hort performed introductions. "Fornri, this is Talitha Warr, sister-daughter of the ambassador."

Fornri smiled and raised his arm in the native greeting. Talitha hesitated and then awkwardly tried to imitate him.

"And this is Dalla," Hort said.

The native woman greeted her warmly.

Fornri said to Hort, "It is a very interesting suggestion. Is the ambassador angry?"

"Frustrated, perhaps. You might consider building a small raft just to show him that it wouldn't work."

"But then he would say the failure was because the raft was too small," Fornri said with a polite smile. "And it would not work no matter how large the raft was. Every time a new koluf was taken onto this raft much water would go with it, and such a small amount of sand would quickly become wet even if it did not wash away. And the sand must be dry, or the koluf cannot be eaten. So I think we won't build the raft."

The two of them took their farewells with upraised arms and disappeared into the forest.

Hort said thoughtfully, "Among all the records of primitive peoples I can remember, it was the elders who ruled and made the decisions. Here it seems to be the young people who lead, but actually they're doing what Fornri tells them to do. He reflects, he speaks, and that's the law. If it's really complicated he asks for time, and then he probably consults with others, but even so he carries an enormous responsibility for one so young."

"They're a handsome couple," Talitha said. "Are they married?"

"That's another mystery. They aren't. Other youths Fornri's age are married, and many of them have a child. I'd suspect that he's a youthful high priest with a rule of celibacy if it weren't for the fact that he and Dalla obviously are sweethearts. They behave like a betrothed couple."

Wembling had been talking with a group of natives on the beach, and now he called to them, "We're going back by boat. Want to come?"

Talitha turned questioningly to Hort.

"Go ahead," he said. "I have a class of native children to teach."

"Really? What are you teaching them?"

"Reading and writing."

She stared for a moment and then burst into laughter. "What for? Once they've learned, what possible use could they have for it?"

"Who knows? They're exceptionally bright children. Maybe someday Langri will create its own great literature. You go with your uncle. I'll walk back after my class."

She joined her uncle on the beach. He was finishing his conversation with the natives—something about drainage ditches—and while she waited she watched Aric Hort. The children were dashing to meet him, the girl called Dabbi in the lead. "Airk!" they shouted. "Airk!"

Hort knelt on a level stretch of packed sand near the village. "Proud," he said. The children repeated the word. "Proud."

He spelled it. "P - R - O - U - D. Proud." They spelled it after him, and he wrote the word in the sand. Then he stalked about on his knees, nose in the air, acting out the word "proud." The children, in convulsions of merriment, imitated him.

"Strong," Hort said.

"Strong," the children repeated.

Wembling patted Talitha on the arm. "Ready to go, Tal?"

He helped her into a boat, and the paddlers, young native boys, pushed off. Looking back, she saw Aric Hort, surrounded by his mob of children, acting out the word "strong."

"What a dear man!" she exclaimed.

Wembling grunted skeptically. "I'd say he acts rather silly."

She smiled. "Yes. He certainly does."

8

She swam in the gentle surf, she lounged on the beach, and sometimes she flirted mischievously with an unlikely-looking animal that eyed her warily from the forest or, at dusk, scurried along the water's edge on scavenger patrol. Dusk came too soon on this world of Langri, and no one lay abed mornings because the dawn touched the bulging clouds with a drama of color to set in motion a renewed procession of ever changing facets of beauty.

The beach sand was the finest she had ever seen. She poured it, powderlike, from one hand to another, and to her amazement she saw that it, too, was composed of myriad grains of color. The sun, warming but never burning, so relaxed her that she had to will herself not to sleep.

She rarely saw Aric Hort. His days were filled with teaching and learning, and on the infrequent occasions when they met she could not refrain from mocking his preoccupation with Langrian trivialities. The things that elated him—that an elderly native accidentally revealed a memory of a time when there were no metal spear points, or his new theory that the poor quality of clay was as much responsible for the absence of pottery on Langri as were the easily available multitudes of gourds, or the list of a hundred and seventeen words that proved some kind of interworld contacts for the natives no more than seventy years before—Talitha failed to see anything universe-shattering about such discoveries.

But as time passed, and Langri's beauty became cloying, even a Langrian triviality eased her boredom somewhat, and she occasionally accepted Hort's invitation to look at something or other that he found remarkable.

Returning from swimming one day, she stopped at the embassy's office and found her uncle talking guardedly with Hirus Ayns. She would have withdrawn without disturbing them, but her uncle waved and invited her in.

"Well, Tal," he said, "you seem to be keeping busy."

"I'm keeping busy the way a tourist keeps busy," she said bitterly. "The beach until it gets boring, and then sightseeing until I can't stand that any longer. Tomorrow Aric is taking me to see some gourds that are supposed to be fascinating. Dangerous trip, that—into the forest. Tomorrow night we're to be entertained and fed by the natives, songs and dances, gourmet dishes that will make me sick because I've seen what they're made of, everything certified authentic and uncorrupted. It reminds me of that vacation I took on Mallorr. I didn't like it there, either."

"The natives' food will make you forget what you saw, and their dancing and singing are lovely." Wembling strode to the window and looked out absently. Obviously he had a few problems of his own to cope with, so she said nothing more to him. "The natives are a fine people," he announced finally, "but I wish they weren't so confounded stubborn. I think maybe I ought to fire Hort—really fire him. He encourages them."

He served himself a smoke capsule, exhaled a cloud of lavender smoke, and started for the door. "I'll see if Sela has those messages transcribed," he said to Ayns.

Talitha looked after him affectionately. "Poor Uncle. The biggest deal of his life, and the stupid natives won't co-operate. By the way, what is this big deal?"

Ayns eyed her calculatingly. When she was younger, that look had disturbed her; but now she knew that he eyed everyone calculatingly. "Ambassador to Binoris," he said.

She straightened up in astonishment. "Wow! That's quite a deal! How does an ambassador get promoted from a nothing world like this to the most important independent world in the galaxy?"

Ayns leaned back, transferred his gaze to the ceiling, and spoke meditatively. "It's tricky. For that matter, getting appointed ambassador to anything is tricky these days. We fell into this, so the question is what we can make of it."

"I knew Uncle wasn't just 'playing ambassador.' "

Ayns nodded. "We've got the political pull, but that isn't enough, not in the diplomatic service, certainly not for a choice appointment like Binoris. We've got to make a sensational record here, and we have less than two years to do it. The ambassador to Binoris retires next year."

"Ah! So that's why the drainage ditches and the rafts."

Ayns nodded again. "We have to transform this world and make vital improvements in the people's living standard, and we have to do it in ways that make good copy for the diplomatic press. We have very little time. And the natives give us no cooperation whatsoever."

"But what a prize if you can bring it off!" Talitha enthused. "High-class society, the arts—"

"Nonsense!" Ayns scowled at her. "Binoris has huge mineral reserves, and no one is in a better position to influence mining concessions than the Federation ambassador. The appointment is worth a minimum hundred million a year."

Wembling returned carrying a sheaf of papers, and Talitha said sympathetically, "Poor Uncle! So much at stake and the natives won't co-operate. Haven't they accepted *any* of your suggestions?"

He sputtered indignantly. "Of course they have!

Haven't you seen my ferries? Solved their river-crossing problems—like that. Come on. I'll show you."

He rushed her out of the building and across the flower-choked meadow toward the forest. At first she was too startled to protest, but when she found herself dashing along a forest path she began to eye the trees uneasily, looking for clusters of vines. "How far is it?" she panted.

Her uncle did not even break stride. "Another kilometer or two."

"So what's the hurry?" she demanded. "It'll still be there if we walk, won't it?"

He slowed his pace, and they moved along the meandering forest path at a fast walk. It ended at a riverbank, where Wembling turned, beaming with pride, to study her reaction.

Nearby was a native boat, and at each end was an inverted V over an overhead rope. Other ropes were tied to trees on either side of the stream. To cross, one simply pulled on the appropriate rope and coiled it into the boat. The other rope payed out as the boat made its crossing. The overhead rope kept it at the crossing site.

Wembling handed Talitha into the boat, pulled it across the narrow stream, pulled it back again. "Well, what do you think of it?" he demanded.

"It's very—clever," she murmured.

"We've got them at all the main crossings," he said. "I've had real good publicity on it—action photos made the news transmissions on eight worlds, including Binoris, and—"

He broke off, staring at her. "Tal—you can help me! Pose for some pictures. A picture of this thing with you in it in that bathing costume would make the news transmissions on a hundred worlds. Drat it—I should have brought my camera. What d'ya say?"

She was too indignant to speak. Fortunately Aric Hort called to them from the bank before the silence became embarrassing.

"I wondered where you two were going in such a rush," he said. "There's a delegation of natives at the embassy waiting to see the ambassador."

"That'll be the official invitation to the festival," Wembling said. "I'll have to hurry back."

Hort helped him out of the boat, and as he scrambled ashore he said, "Give her a ride, Aric, if she wants it. Let her try it out as much as she likes." He trotted off along the forest path, and a moment later, before either of them had moved, he was back again. "Let her pull the rope herself, Aric."

"I will," Hort promised. "Both ways."

Wembling grinned, nodded, and turned away with a wave of his hand.

"Gracious! Isn't he proud of it!" Talitha exclaimed.

"Come out of there! Quickly!" Hort snapped.

Startled, she scrambled ashore, and he helped her from the boat and into a place of concealment behind some bushes. An instant later two natives emerged from the forest on the opposite bank. Without breaking stride they walked through the river, which was only waist-deep, and disappeared into the forest.

"Don't they use it at all?" she asked bewilderedly, when the natives had passed out of hearing.

"Only when they think one of us is watching," Hort said. He led her back to the boat, and so that she could wax properly enthusiastic about it without an uncomfortable amount of lying, she gave herself a round-trip crossing while Hort watched from the bank.

"You know—he really is trying to help the natives," she said when she'd returned to him. "But I suppose it's human nature to resist change."

"There's much more to it than that. At one time this must have been a horribly dangerous world for humans. The first settlers probably survived by an eyelash. There are still plenty of ways humans can die on this world, but it's a relatively safe place because over a long period of time the natives found out by trial and error what the dangers are and how to avoid them. No outsider can come in and instantly know better ways of doing things than the natives have learned from generations of costly experience."

He got into the boat and took a seat at the opposite end. "I'm worried about the natives. Your uncle is being wonderfully patient, but that won't last forever. Eventually he'll start maneuvering to make them do what he tells them, and he has the influence and the political and legal connections to find ways to force them. If he does, he stands an excellent chance of destroying them."

She stared at him. *"Destroying* them? Nonsense! Uncle is no monster."

"Have you noticed anything unusual about the feet of those on the embassy staff?"

"They're all badly scarred," she said. "I've wondered about that."

"Your uncle had this notion of eliminating the muddy village streets. He tried to talk Fornri into paving them with gravel. Fornri nixed the idea emphatically. So your uncle demonstrated his wisdom by having the staff members bring in enough gravel to pave the paths between the embassy buildings—just to show the natives how it ought to be done. It turns out that there's a fungus that thrives in gravel and has an unfortunate affinity for human feet. Now the entire staff has scarred feet, and the paths between embassy buildings are muddy again."

"The entire staff except you," she remarked, inspecting his feet.

"Well—I suspected something like that, so when your uncle graveled the paths, I didn't walk on them. The natives know this world and we don't, and when they say something shouldn't be done, I'm not going to do it. Look at this."

He pointed to the strangely convoluted lashings by which the ferry apparatus was attached to the boat.

"What about it?" she asked.

"I thought that knot was so interesting I was going to send an example to the Anthropological Institute. While I was writing my report, one of the crewmen from the courier ship happened by, and he laughed himself silly over it. This is a very common knot. It was developed to secure wires in spaceship construction to avoid problems caused by vibrations in faster-than-light travel. Anyone who's had much to do with ships will know this knot. Obviously our expedition wasn't the first to discover these natives."

He paused and looked expectantly at her. She resented being treated like a backward child in one of his classes, and she said icily, "If you expect me to believe that this knot is somehow connected with the fungus—"

"Think. The natives have such a perilous struggle for survival that they have to use every available weapon. They're bright. If they happen onto a more efficient way of doing things, they'll adopt it. No one knows how many visitors they've had, down through the centuries, and out of all the knowledge that those visitors brought here, the only item I can positively identify that the natives found useful was that knot."

Before she could comment, he changed the subject abruptly. "As long as you've walked this far, why don't we see the gourds now?"

"Why not?" she murmured. "By an incredible coincidence, I have no other engagement."

They used the ferry to cross the river, and when they reached the other side he told her, "The one rule is to go single file and keep to the center of the path. There's no danger there, or there wouldn't be a path."

They moved off into the forest. Several times vegetation along the path drew back from them as they passed, alarming her, but Hort paid no attention to it. She followed him silently. They passed trees with enormous, multicolored flowers, and they splashed through a small stream just downstream from a towering waterfall in which a strange flying creature, magnificently colored but unspeakably hideous in appearance, was enjoying a shower bath. The creature suddenly became aware of them and soared away squalking, dripping water on them as it passed overhead.

Abruptly they came to another river and another of Wembling's ferries, and this one was in use. A crowd of extremely happy children were playing in it, hauling back and forth across the river. Now and then a child tumbled overboard and found that hilarious, too. With whoops of joy they ran the ferry to shore, made room for Hort and Talitha, and gave them swift passage.

Hort helped Talitha to disembark, and then the two of them stood with arms uplifted, and the children, giggling delightedly, responded as they pulled the boat back across the river.

"I forgot about that," Hoyt said. "The children think the ferries are absolutely scrumptious playthings. If they want to cross a river, though, they'll swim."

A short distance beyond the river, Hort stopped abruptly and pointed. "There's one of them."

Talitha gazed blankly at the enormous, looming thing that vanished from sight among the branches of the surrounding trees. She said, "It *grew* that big?"

"Some of them do," Hort said. "Probably the natives pick most of them when they're smaller, because they have so many uses for them. A gourd this size must be many years old. What I can't figure out is how the things reproduce. There are dozens of them here. Look."

He moved along the path, parting leaves and showing her gourds of various sizes. "All of them come from one plant," he said. "Wherever you see gourds, whatever the species, there's always one plant. I can't figure out how a thing like this can scatter seeds or spores so widely—and in a forest, too."

"Are they edible?" she asked.

"No, but they're used for everything else. Roofs of houses, containers, hammocks, furniture, and they make really splendid drums and musical instruments. Children play all sorts of games with gourd toys. They're platforms for native dances, and the end of a small one can be painted to make a splendid mask. The vines yield a thread that makes excellent rope and cloth. Remarkable, aren't they?"

He leaned over and thumped on one, and it gave off deep, booming thuds.

"Is that all there is to see?" she asked.

"That's all," he said cheerfully.

"They certainly are remarkable. I'm glad I didn't wait until tomorrow to see them. Two such tremendous thrills like gourds and a native festival on the same day would be more than my nervous system could stand."

She turned and walked away. Where the path curved, she was able to glance back at him without turning her head, and she saw him still standing in the path looking after her.

9

There were two fires on the beach, and they produced an enormous halo of light that not only illuminated the spectators crowding the hillside but also touched off spectacular flashes in the breaking wave caps. Between the fires a musician had set up his instrument. A nab, Aric Hort called it, and it was constructed of a gourd twice as tall as the musician and of tremendous circumference. Talitha's first incredulous conclusion was that it took one musician to play the thing and two to hold it down, because two members of the audience were seated atop the gourd. Later, when they began to stomp their feet, she learned that they were drummers.

The musician struck his first tones, and the native festival was under way. For a time nothing happened but the rhythmic thum . . . thum . . . thum of the nab strings. Then another musician joined him.

He played the same instrument.

Sets of strings were stretched from a yoke near the top to a wood collar near the bottom. The nab was not an instrument; it was many instruments. More musicians joined in, each on another set of strings, until Talitha counted eight playing one nab. Probably there were others hidden by the instrument. The rhythm took on fantastic complexities.

Then the drummers began punctuating the thums

with their vigorous stomping, marking off new rhythmic complexities with a thud . . . thud . . . thud. An orchestra began to assemble about the nab, and smaller drums and stringed instruments joined in. Then the colorfully costumed dancers entered. The young men circled one fire, the young women the other.

The lines broke off and interwove as the groups changed fires. The lines broke off again and began to weave through the spectators. Several of the young women tried to coax Talitha into the dance as they passed her.

She shook her head. "I don't know how."

Hort, seated beside her, got up and tried to pull her to her feet. "Go ahead," he said. "It's the custom—they're making an honored guest of you. Just do what they do."

Her uncle, seated nearby, was smiling encouragement at her. The natives around her seemed delighted. The movements did not look difficult, so she succumbed and let the girls lead her away.

For a time she thought she was not doing badly, though the steps quickly became more intricate. They circled a fire and broke off to weave through the line of young men. Aric Hort smiled at her as they passed; the young men had pulled him into the dance.

The men returned to form a circle around the girls, and she found herself paired off with Hort. The dance picked up speed, the steps became more and more difficult, but they blundered along until they were exhausted. Laughing, gasping for breath, they staggered back to their places.

When she had caught her breath, Talitha looked about her at the rapt audience of natives. She nudged Hort. "Why aren't Fornri and Dalla dancing?"

"It's like I told you—Fornri is the leader. He seems to have forsworn marriage. He and Dalla are sweethearts, but they aren't dancing. Dalla isn't happy about that, but she's not accepting any other offers."

"What's that got to do with dancing?" Talitha demanded.

"It's a betrothal dance."

She stared at him. *"Betrothal* dance? You mean—you and I—"

"Only on Langri," he said with superb nonchalance.

Angrily she slapped his face and dashed off into the night. At the top of the slope she looked back. The throbbing pulse of the music, the blend of color and intricate movement, gripped and exhilarated her.

Then she saw Aric Hort anxiously looking about for her, and she laughed merrily.

Lying on the beach, hand cupping her chin, looking thoughtfully out to sea, she made up her mind. Ahead of her she could anticipate only dreamy, lethargic days too frequently interrupted by long monologues from her uncle and Aric Hort. Her uncle was preoccupied with the brilliant new projects he was devising. Hort was obsessed with one trivial mystery after another.

Her uncle was determined to help the natives, and obviously they didn't want to be helped. Hort was intent on studying them, and they didn't want to be studied. What they did want was to be left alone, and that was perfectly satisfactory to her.

She heard her uncle's booming voice and the usual chorus of farewell from his native retinue. Resignedly she got to her feet, gathered up the robe she'd been lying on, and walked determinedly toward the embassy office.

As she dropped the door open, they turned toward her: her uncle, Hirus Ayns, and Aric Hort. They were about to drink a toast, and they held tumblers raised.

Her uncle greeted her with a smile. "You're just in time, Tal." He filled another tumbler. "Join our celebration. Fornri has accepted my suggestion about the drainage ditches. They'll start work on them in the morning."

He offered her the tumbler, and in a sudden burst of anger she struck it to the floor. "You fools!" she exclaimed.

Ayns and Hort stood frozen with tumblers raised. Her uncle stared at her dumfoundedly.

"Can't you see the natives are laughing at you?" she demanded. "You work from dawn to dark just tramping about trying to help them, and when they condescend to accept a suggestion, like your precious ferries, they give it to the children to play with. Now I suppose you'll expect me to pose for pictures in your drainage ditches!"

She marched to the window and stood there with her back to them, looking out. "Langri is a lovely world," she said. "The singing and dancing are charming, and the food is delicious, and it's a nice place for a vacation, and I've had one. I'm leaving on the next courier ship."

Her uncle said quietly, "You're free to leave whenever you like, Tal."

She turned and faced them. Hort was struggling to conceal his embarrassment. He suddenly became aware that he still held a drink in his hand, and he downed it. Wembling and Ayns did the same.

Talitha, looking past them through another window, asked, "What's this?"

Natives had landed a boat just below the embassy, and they were walking up from the beach carrying a segment of gourd with what looked like a pile of blankets on it. Fornri led the way. Dalla, weeping, walked at one side.

Aric Hort dashed to meet them, with Wembling and Ayns following on his heels. Talitha, after long hesitation, trailed after them. When she finally reached them, the procession of natives had halted, and Hort was bending over the segment of gourd.

He peeled back the blankets and gazed down at an unconscious child.

Dabbi.

Her eyes were closed. Her small, pinched face looked violently feverish. Her breathing was rapid and shallow.

Hort spoke incredulously, and his agony throbbed in every syllable. "Not—the Hot Sickness?"

Fornri said gravely, "She cut her foot. On a sharp rock, we think. And now—"

His voice broke. Hort turned away, brushing his eyes with a gesture, and the procession followed him. They turned off and took the path to the rear, where Hort's quarters were located. He hurried on ahead, dropped the door open, and stood waiting for them.

When Talitha entered the room at the end of the procession, Hort had folded out a bed and lifted the child onto it. The natives, except for Fornri and Dalla, took the gourd stretcher and left at once. Hort knelt beside the bed and gently loosened the blankets, exposing Dabbi's foot and leg.

Talitha gasped. Both were hideously swollen to twice, three times their normal size.

Hort straightened up slowly. "I can try something different," he said. "We might possibly learn from it, but I'm afraid she's going to die."

Dalla knelt at the head of the bed and continued to weep soundlessly. Fornri, still grave and courteous despite his obvious grief, and politely, "We understand. The Hot Sickness always brings death, and we are grateful for your attempts to find a cure. Please do what you can."

He bent over the bed, placed his hand for a moment on Dabbi's forehead, and then he turned and left the room. As he did so, Wembling stepped forward and spoke to Hort, who stood looking down at the sick child.

"How long are they going to be here?" Wembling demanded.

"Only until the child dies."

Wembling shrugged resignedly. "Well—keep them quiet."

He went out. Hort moved a chair into position beside the bed and started to examine Dabbi's leg again. Now Talitha edged forward. "Why did they wait so long?" she asked angrily.

Hort looked up at her blankly. "This probably didn't happen much over an hour ago."

"What is it?"

"Some kind of blood poisoning. Our antibiotics have no effect on it. I've been trying them in combination, and the last pair kept the victim alive for eight days, but he died just as certainly as if I'd left him alone, and a great deal more painfully. The only thing I can do now is try a stronger dose of the same thing and see how she reacts."

Talitha knelt beside the bed and conducted her own examination, but she could draw no conclusion except that the infection was appallingly virulent. "How do you administer your antibiotics?" she asked.

"By mouth if the patient is conscious. Otherwise, by absorption. I've been afraid to use the injector."

"When an infection has spread this much, it's too late for oral or absorbent applications," she said dryly. "Let me see your medical kit."

Hort wheeled the kit from the closet. She noted with relief that it was prime rated and had been renewed within the past year. She quickly rolled it into position, clipped a surgical mask to her nostrils, sprayed on a pair of gloves, and began a quick but thorough examination of the patient. She drew a blood sample by palm osmosis, and while the kit analyzed it she taped a cardiosensor to Dabbi's chest and monitored the faltering heartbeat.

"What did you give the last patient—the one that lived eight days?" she asked.

"Kornox Four and Cybolithon."

"Dosage?"

"Half normal for each. I figured mixing the medicines was experiment enough, and two halves made a whole."

While the cardiograph continued to click its appallingly irregular pictures of Dabbi's heartbeat, the blood analysis data drifted across the screen: WBC 18,440 [] ZYN 9+ [] W3W 7.5 [] BUN 38 [] CPK 790 [] BROS 1,125 [] GAMMA GT 2,220 [] XRX 8.4 [] PY4 0— [] SGOT 57 [] RRR 190 [] SGPT 55 [] EBD 440 [] BILIRUBIN 3.5 [] MIC 99 [] DQS...

Her memory of blood analysis norms was fuzzy, but even without the red warning tabs she would have recognized the scientific confirmation of what Hort al-

ready had said: this was a dying child. She turned off
the cardiograph and punched the code for the antibiotics chart. She read the data on Kornox Four and
Cybolithon, read it again, read it a third time. She
had been working quickly and confidently, but thus far
she had followed a routine practiced countless times.

Now, with a dying patient before her, she was
forced to make a medical decision light-years beyond
her competence, and she was frightened.

She dared not hesitate. A delayed decision, even if
right, could be as fatal as a wrong decision. "Unless
we act quickly, she won't live an hour," she said quietly
to Hort. "Is it possible to consult her parents?"

"Her parents are dead," Hort said. "Dalla is her
sister. You can consult her."

Dalla was still kneeling at the head of the bed.
Talitha knelt beside her. "If we do nothing, she'll die
quickly. If we give her too much medicine, we may
cure the disease and kill her with the medicine. I can
only guess and hope. Are you willing for me to try?"

Dalla's face was tear-stained, her expression agonized, but she did not hesitate. She said calmly, "Yes.
Please."

Talitha swung the injector over Dabbi's leg,
radiated it, punched the code for .55 of the specified
dosages of the two antibiotics, mixed them, and threw
the switch. She examined Dabbi's leg immediately to
make certain that the injection had not filtered im-
properly; but the puffy flesh was unbroken, and she
could not even find the usual upwelling of fluid. She
radiated the leg again and pushed the medical kit aside.

"Now all we can do is try to control the fever and
wait," she announced.

"Is there anything I can do?" Dalla asked.

"I'll fix a vol solution. We'll have to keep spraying
her to get the fever down. Otherwise, if your religion
has any gods that are well disposed, you might try
praying. That's what I'm going to do."

She mixed the solution and set Della and Hort to
spraying the patient. Then she stripped off her gloves,
returned the mask to the sterilizer, and went to stand

at the window. She'd thought her medical career long
since washed out; unexpectedly she'd drawn her first
and probably her last patient, and she was forced to
search her mind for deliberately forgotten data and
dicta while frantically reviewing her performance for
fatal errors committed and crucial procedures overlooked.

Outside the building, the natives who had brought
Dabbi, Fornri with them, sat on the ground in a circle
in prayerlike meditation. None of them moved a
muscle. It was dusk now, and her uncle, walking from
his office to the commissary, had to circle them. He
paid no attention to the natives, and their attention was
fixed on the infinite.

She returned to her patient, took Dabbi's hand, and
watched the small, flushed face. The sprayers hissed
continuously, but the fever was not dropping. The
child's breathing seemed more labored. Certainly they
were too late, and yet—and yet—

With all of the fervor her mind could command
she willed the child to live. It came to her as a revela-
tion that this small creature was not a semihuman animal from the most uncivilized of worlds. She belonged
to the universe of children, and no sick child, anywhere,
was significantly different from any other sick child.

Looking at Dalla's agonized face, Talitha suddenly wondered if there was also a universe of people.

The room was growing dark, and Hort got up and
adjusted the illumination to a subdued glow. As the
night wore on, Dalla finally succumbed to sleep and
huddled on the floor by the bed. Eventually Hort followed her. With Dabbi's fever finally in check, Talitha
stopped the spraying and covered her lightly. She continued to watch, leaving her patient only when she
moved quietly about the room in an attempt to keep
herself awake. And whenever she looked from the
window, the natives, dimly visible in the pale light
that seeped from the sickroom, sat unmoving in their
circle.

At dawn, dozing in her chair, she snapped to instant wakefulness and bent over Dabbi in alarm. The

child's eyes were open. She was looking about the room bewilderedly and attempting to sit up.

Dalla awakened with a cry. Hort sprang up, and as he did so the door dropped open and Fornri bounded into the room. All watched tensely while Talitha examined her patient.

The swelling in the leg and foot was miraculously reduced, and she no longer was feverish. Hort exclaimed incredulously, "Then—she's going to be all right!"

Talitha was anxiously watching the cardiograph. Finally she pushed the medical kit aside. Dabbi sat up, smiling, and Dalla leaned over and embraced her. Fornri stood beaming down on them.

Talitha said quietly to Hort, "Her heart action is very erratic. I should have studied the literature before I administered the medicine. Combinations of medications can be terribly dangerous. Do you have a medical referencer?"

"In the office," Hort said. "But it's a small one, and it hasn't a thing about pairing antibiotics. Believe me, I checked every shred of information available. I thought I might as well gamble, because the patients were going to die anyway. What's the matter with her heart?"

"I don't know," Talitha said. She felt so weary, so indescribably weary. She had been fighting for a child's life, and now she did not know what to do, and her fight was merely to hold back her tears. "I'll have a look at the referencer anyway," she said. "No, I'll go. If I don't move around a bit I'll collapse." She said to Dalla, "Keep her covered. She might catch a chill—though what that means in terms of Langri's viruses I have no idea."

"Nor does anyone else," Hort growled.

The natives no longer were sitting in their circle. They were excitedly peering through the windows. Talitha plodded slowly to the office building, found the medical referencer, and began to punch out questions. Finally she slumped back in the chair, eyes closed. Perhaps the question was too complex for this machine's programming, or perhaps the pairing of antibiotics was such a medical blunder that the programmer thought it unnecessary to mention it.

She buried her face in her hands and wept tearlessly—wept from exhaustion and frustration. Then, with a wrench of determination, she stonily got to her feet and started back to the sickroom. She was almost there when she heard Dalla's scream.

Dalla was on her knees by the bed, face buried in the blankets, sobbing. Fornri stood with head bowed. Hort turned toward her as she entered, an expression of stunned grief on his face.

Talitha rushed to the bed and bent over Dabbi. Then she straightened up, shaking her head.

"It was her heart," she said bitterly. "The medicine killed her."

10

Talitha and Aric Hort despondently faced each other across a table in the embassy's dining room. The autoserver loomed nearby, but nothing it could offer on this morning tempted either of them.

Finally Tilitha burst out angrily, "A biological research laboratory could develop a specific for that disease in a couple of hours."

Hort's response matched her bitterness. "I don't happen to have one with me."

"Any competent doctor with training in bioanalysis—"

"If you run into one on the beach, send him up here and I'll put him to work."

"Does it cause many deaths?"

"Dabbi's is the third this month. The last two months there weren't any; the month before that, eight. Not many in terms of the total population. The bacteria has to be present, and there has to be a fairly deep flesh wound. When the two happen together, the mortality is a hundred per cent."

Wembling entered. He nodded pleasantly, and when they did not respond, he suddenly remembered. "The child died?" Neither of them answered. "Pity," he said. "Too bad they've no conception of medical science."

He strode to the autoserver, consulted the breakfast list, punched buttons, and accepted a steaming tray. He carried it to their table and seated himself, and he was taking his first mouthful of food when he noticed that they weren't eating. He asked, "Finished breakfast already?"

"I may never eat again," Talitha said.

The rest of the staff strolled in, gave them a chorus of greetings, and gathered about the autoserver.

"Isn't it time you reprogrammed this thing?" Sela Thillow asked Renold. "Everything is starting to taste the same, and it was a lousy menu to begin with."

"See if you can coax it into putting out some of that native koluf," Hirus Ayns said.

They took their trays to another table. Talitha said to her uncle, "Did you ever have the agony of watching a child die?" He stared at her. "A death like that is absolutely unnecessary," she went on.

Wembling nodded. "Of course. Health always is a problem where medical facilities are primitive. Living on such a world is dangerous—something like that could happen to any of us." He shrugged to show how oblivious he was to danger and went on spooning his breakfast.

"Uncle Harlow!" Talitha exclaimed. "You're wasting your time trying to build a reputation with drainage ditches. Give the natives a medical center!"

Wembling shook his head. "That'd only give me a reputation for being rich—which I already have. Anyway, it'd cost more than the publicity would be worth."

"What's so expensive about a small clinic?"

"The staff. No medic is going to leave a comfortable situation to work on a primitive world unless he's offered an enormous salary. He'll also want lavish support in the way of assistants and laboratory and research facilities. It'd cost a fortune annually to finance that kind of operation. Hirus?"

Ayns had been listening. He always was listening. He said, "Depends on what you want to accomplish. The kind of medical center found on civilized worlds would be impossibly expensive to duplicate here. On the other hand, a small clinic, bring in an unsuccessful doctor who'd jump at a steady salary—"

Wembling was shaking his head. "No good. That kind of setup wouldn't accomplish a thing except find alternate ways of killing the natives. To do the job adequately would cost a fortune. It'd certainly cost a lot more than I'd be willing to spend."

"Then get governmental support," Talitha said.

"Can't be done. Langri is an independent world, which means that its health problems are its own business. If it were dependent, the government might be coaxed into putting a medical station here."

"Then change its classification."

"Perhaps the natives think their independence worth more than a medical station," Hort remarked.

Talitha ignored him. "Why not offer those doctors and technicians a free vacation if they'll work part time in the medical center? 'Vacation in Paradise'—that ought to fetch a few doctors."

Wembling found that amusing. "A long trip with a part-time job at the end is no vacation. No, there won't be a medical station on Langri until the government can support one, and I can't imagine where it would get the money. A world can't amass exchange credits unless it has something someone else wants, and Langri—"

For a suspenseful moment Wembling stared at Talitha. Then he scrambled to his feet and dashed for the door. Talitha hesitated, exchanged glances with Aric Hort, and then she followed her uncle. Hort hurried after her. The staff had left off eating for a moment when Wembling got to his feet, but none of them moved to follow him. When Wembling wanted his staff, he let them know it.

Talitha and Hort caught up with Wembling on the beach. He was standing where the gentle surf lapped at his sandals, waving his arms excitedly. "That's the answer, Tal!" he exclaimed. "The people of Langri can operate a vacation resort, and the profits will finance a medical center and anything else they want. And setting it up for them will make my reputation."

"I don't think the natives would want their world cluttered up with tourists," Hort said.

Wembling grinned at him. "Hort, you're fired." He turned toward the sea and raised his arms, a man with a vision. "Langri—even the name sounds like a vacation paradise. There are plenty of barren worlds in this sector where life is either difficult or monotonous, and their peoples would pay a soul's ransom for a vacation on a world like this. Look at the ocean. The forests. The natural beauties of every kind. The word 'paradise' is an understatement. How could I have been so blind?"

Now Hort was genuinely concerned. "I don't think the natives—"

"Don't talk nonsense," Wembling told him. "Giving up a stretch of the beach to a tourist resort won't affect the natives at all. Unless they want to work in the resort and get rich. If they don't want to, we'll import labor and they'll get rich anyway." He paced back and forth excitedly. "How could I have been so blind? This will make my reputation, Tal, and you'll be able to play hostess in the Binoris Embassy." He turned to Hort. "Get Fornri."

Hort hesitated a moment, shrugged, and trotted off along the beach.

Wembling resumed his pacing. He said over his shoulder, "What do you think?"

"I think it's a wonderful idea," Talitha said. "Anything that gets these people the medical help they need—"

Wembling wasn't listening. "We can leave the

landing field where it is. Lay out a village on the embassy site for employees. What a resort it'll be!" He waved his hands rapturously. "Fleets of pleasure craft at the wharves!"

"Undersea craft, too," Talitha suggested.

"All kinds of water recreation. Fishing—those weird things in the ocean ought to provide plenty of excitement. Never know what you'll catch when you fish on Langri. A native festival every night. Gourmet feasts of native-prepared food. I've been blind. You kept saying this was like a vacation world, and I never saw it that way. This is the kind of thing Binoris will understand—developing a resource a world never knew it had. It'll make my reputation. The Binoris appointment—"

He broke off and muttered, "Now that was a fast trip."

Hort and Fornri were approaching along the beach. Wembling and Talitha walked to meet them.

"He was on his way to see you," Hort told Wembling. "He wants to invite us to attend Dabbi's death rites."

"Yes, yes, of course we'll come. Thank you. Fornri, I have a wonderful idea. All of Langri's problems are solved. We'll build a World Medical Center, and the Hot Sickness will never come again. We'll build schools for the children, and there'll be plenty of food and everything else Langri needs."

Fornri smiled politely. "This is welcome news. Where do the things come from?"

"We'll get them with money. I don't know how much you know about that—money's the one thing without which very little can be done. Medical centers and things like that require huge amounts of money, and we'll get it for the world of Langri by establishing a vacation resort."

Fornri's polite smile did not waver, but his tone of voice was firm beyond any possibility of appeal. "No, thank you. We would not care for that. We will expect you at darkness for the death rites." He took a backward step, delivered the native salute, and strode away.

Wembling stood looking after him. "You were right," he told Talitha. "They're laughing at me."

He marched back to the embassy.

Hort said to Talitha, "Now that's a puzzle. From the way Fornri turned it down he might have been expecting it. Whenever anything strange is offered, the natives ask highly astute questions and then they retire to think it over. He didn't take time to flick an eyelash —and how would he know what a vacation resort is?"

Hort wanted to observe the preparations for the death rites, so he followed Fornri back to the village. Talitha returned to the embassy and found her uncle and Hirus Ayns talking in the office.

Ayns said, "If the natives are that stupid, I don't suppose there's anything we can do."

"Why do you have to have their permission?" Talitha asked. "You're doing it for them, aren't you? You're offering something that will save lives, and what possible harm can come from that?"

"It's their world," Wembling said. "It's their decision to make, and they've made it."

"Maybe they don't understand what you're trying to do. We know 'medical center' means good health and lives saved, but it may be gibberish to them. When a primitive people can't understand, then the decisions should be made by someone who does."

"I think Fornri understood," Wembling said.

"He couldn't watch that child die and immediately afterward turn down something that would save children's lives. A vacation resort means the medical center, and schools, and a proper diet for his people with no risk of famine when those whatever-they-are can't be caught, and decent housing, and all the rest. How could he reject that if he understood what you were talking about?"

"He's the head of the government of the independent world of Langri," Wembling said. "Whether he understands or not, the decision is his to make." He turned to Ayns. "Do we have a copy of that treaty?"

Ayns pulled the general referencer toward him

and punched buttons. "Yes. Here it is. What about it?"

"How does one obtain concessions under it?"

Ayns took the time to read the treaty. "You'd have to obtain them from the government of Langri," he said finally.

Wembling strode to the window. He said over his shoulder, "How many places do you suppose that treaty is on file?"

"Not many. It isn't an important treaty."

"How many of them could you fix?"

"Some. Maybe half. It'd be much easier to fix the references so the computers would lose it for a few years. Would a few years be enough?"

"One year would be enough. What a fool I've been! All these months of work trying to peddle a few piddling ideas to these stupid natives and make myself ambassador to Binoris, and the mineral wealth of a dozen worlds couldn't buy Langri's vacation potential. I've had the financial coup of my life right under my nose and I never saw it."

"What about the medical center?" Talitha asked.

"They'll have their medical center. Right away. We'll have to solve Langri's health problems to protect our work force and the tourists, and the sooner we do that the better. You can go back on the next courier ship, Hirus, and get to work on that treaty. As soon as its taken care of we'll get the world reclassified and apply for a charter."

"It'll take time and money to lose the treaty," Ayns said.

"You can have all you need." Wembling returned to his desk, adjusted his chair, and faced Ayns. "While you're working on the treaty, you can set up an office for Wembling and Company and hire a sharp law firm. Look for some competent people in construction and resort planning. We can start stockpiling supplies immediately, so we'll be ready to move the moment the charter is issued."

"Won't the natives object to that?" Ayns asked.

"Probably." Wembling grinned at him. "I'll tell

them the stuff is for their medical center. Part of it will
be. We'll use the medical center as a pilot project."

"You'll need an expert in medical research," Talitha said.

"Not an expert. Just a competent technician. We'll
bring one in the moment facilities are ready. He can
give the world a routine going over and have the
medical problems solved before the resort opens. A
couple of cases of that Hot Sickness would destroy a
resort. I promise you, Tal—we'll solve all the natives'
medical problems. We'll have to. The medical center
will be a good investment in public relations, too, just
in case later on there's a stink about the treaty."

"If the resort is going to make that much money,
you should give the natives some of the profits," Talitha
said. "It's their world you'll be using."

Wembling cocked his head and looked at Ayns,
who nodded slowly. "Ten per cent?" Wembling asked.
Ayns nodded again. "Good idea," Wembling said.
"We'll put ten per cent of the profits in trust for them.
When the treaty tampering is discovered, it'll be more
than worth the cost. It'll make us look like humani-
tarians." He turned to Talitha. "All right, Tal. Your
natives will get their medical center and a thorough
study of their diseases. They'll also get ten per cent of
the resort profits, and eventually that'll be enough to
support the whole native population. In addition,
there'll be a lot of resort jobs they can handle if they
want them, and we'll pay them well for festivals and
koluf feasts for the tourists. They'll be doing very nicely for themselves. Satisfactory?"

Talitha smiled and nodded.

"There is one thing, though." He looked at her
calculatingly. "I'm going to have to get rid of Hort."

"Am I supposed to cry?" she asked belligerently.
"If you have to, then get rid of him."

"I thought you liked the guy."

"I don't dislike him. Away from Langri he might
be an interesting person, but one gets tired of lectures
about gourds and native hunting techniques."

"Firing him might make him suspicious," Ayns

said. "Let me find him a plush assignment somewhere else."

"Good idea. I won't fire him, I'll promote him. That all right with you, Tal?"

"Whatever you think best," she said. "How soon will our medical center be ready?"

11

Fornri ran.

He widely circled the village, where Dabbi's small body lay surrounded by mourners, and he moved at top speed along a forest path, forcing himself forward, ignoring protesting muscles and aching lungs, willing his body to respond to his desperate haste.

At a point where several paths intersected, he panted to a halt, looked about him carefully, and then burrowed onto the apparently impenetrable undergrowth that lined the path.

He emerged in a small clearing. Two native youths were lolling in front of a native dwelling, bored with waiting for nothing to happen. Banu sat cross-legged on the ground nearby, head bowed, eyes closed, sifting his recollections. At one side was a hammock, where the Elder lay resting. All of them leaped up when Fornri burst upon them, and they waited expectantly while he tried to catch his breath.

Finally he was able to speak. He gasped, "The ambassador is the enemy!"

The secret headquarters was but one of many parts of the Plan that they could not understand. It was a meeting place for those responsible for the Plan. It also was the center of a complicated arrangement for keeping track of every alien on Langri. The children were organized into an army of small patrols, and the moment the ambassador or one of his staff made a move, a child nipped off at top speed to the secret headquarters to report that fact. A map had been sketched on the level ground in front of the dwelling, and by means of stones the position of every alien was marked, and his every movement followed.

They did it even though it made no sense to them, because the Plan said they should do it. In the beginning the embassy staff had been larger, and many of its members wandered about with little to do; but very soon the ambassador decided that they weren't needed and sent them away. Of the four staff members remaining, three of them always accompanied the ambassador. Further, the ambassador had asked for natives to assist him and give him information when he needed it, and he never went anywhere without a large escort. The leadership council frequently debated why the children should bring reports about the ambassador when he always had adult natives with him.

Then there was Aric Hort, who very quickly became one of them, a genuine friend who was always willing to help them in disagreements with the ambassador. It seemed almost a breach of friendship to be following him about secretly when everything he did was done so openly.

The Plan said they must know where everyone was, all the time, and they followed the Plan. They had no choice.

The ambassador's sister-daughter introduced a complication that made the Plan's dictates more understandable. Everything she did was unpredictable. Worse, others reacted strangely to her. Aric Hort, having announced that he would go to a certain place, or do a certain thing, would meet her along the way and go elsewhere to do something entirely different.

That was bad enough, but the ambassador's unexpected dash into the forest to show his sister-daughter the ferry, along with Aric Hort's dash after them, left the council confounded. After weeks and months of painstaking care always to have the ferries in use when the ambassador passed that way, it was a shock to have their secret discovered by Miss Warr. Aric Hort had known, but they knew instinctively that Hort would not tell the ambassador. They knew nothing at all about Miss Warr.

The incident prompted a debate. Fornri sat on the ground before the map, scowling at the stones representing the ambassador, Miss Warr, and Aric Hort and attempting to fathom this turn of events that so swiftly and inexplicably moved them from embassy to forest. The Elder, who always was present in their deliberations but rarely spoke, looked on solemnly while others furiously argued the import of Miss Warr's seeing Rarnt and Mano cross a stream without using the ferry.

Finally Fornri said, "Banu?"

Banu was in his usual position, legs crossed, head bowed. He spoke without moving. "Nothing. She is not important."

"I think the sister-daughter of the ambassador is important," Fornri said.

Narrif, who frequently opposed Fornri, remarked lightly, "She laughs at us and our world. Soon she will leave. She has said so. How can she be important?"

Dalla asked, "What are the marriage customs of the ambassador's people? Airk is attracted to her, and he is our friend. If they were to marry—"

"Is she attracted to him?" Tollof asked. "Would Airk need her consent or the ambassador's?"

In the silence that followed, Fornri gave the boy who had brought the message a friendly pat and sent him away to rest. He said, "The next time Airk questions any of us concerning our customs, he should be asked about his own marriage customs."

In the end they did nothing, and if the ambassador's sister-daughter told him of the river crossing, he never mentioned it. But once again the wisdom of the

Langri's Plan stood starkly revealed to them, and never after that did anyone question the need for knowing where everyone was, always.

It worried Fornri desperately that there were so few questions they could resolve, and that a growing minority of the council advocated rash moves or—occasionally—disregarding the Plan. He knew that soon he would lose his leadership, for almost every decision he made was challenged by Narrif, and that worried him—not because Narrif was incapable, for he was very capable, but Fornri feared that he would not follow the Plan.

Everything the Plan predicted had happened, every instruction they had followed succeeded easily, and Fornri needed no further evidence of the Langri's infallibility. Either they followed the Plan, or they would lose their world and their lives.

The fate of his people depended on his leadership, and he found it increasingly difficult to lead. Even when the Plan clearly told them what should be done, it sometimes was impossible to say *when* it should be done.

Almost daily Narrif would ask Fornri, "Have you spoken to Airk about the message to the attorneys?"

And Fornri would reply, "I am asking him, one at a time, the questions the Langri suggested."

"Are you *still* testing his friendship?" Narrif would exclaim. "Surely Airk is a friend worthy of trust."

Fornri could only answer that he agreed, but when possible he preferred to follow the Langri's wisdom rather than his own; and then Banu would dredge up an appropriate recollection: "The Langri said—a friend worthy of trust won't object to proving his worthiness."

Then there were the crystals. The Langri had said that they should be converted into monetary credits as soon as possible, but they feared to mention them to anyone until they fully understood what must be done and had friends whose worthiness was tested. The Langri himself had told them, over and over, how strangers would prey upon them if they were not alert.

The most difficult thing of all was not knowing

whom the Plan was directed against. They could not identify their enemy. Some thought it was the ambassador, but there was no proof, and the ambassador seemed to be sincerely trying to help them. Further, the Langri himself had said that the enemy might not arrive for years after the first spaceship.

Fornri felt increasingly alienated from the other members of the council. That Dalla frequently joined his opponents hurt him most of all. It had been a long time since they shared their joy, and the burden of leadership grew heavier and heavier on him.

But now they knew the enemy.

The others listened, heard Banu recite tonelessly what the Langri had said about the first person who got the idea of building a vacation resort on their world, and doubtfully assented.

"What do we do?" Dalla asked.

Fornri did not know. He said slowly, "The Langri told us so much, and we understand so little."

"What will the ambassador do?" Dalla asked. "What *can* he do?"

No one knew.

"We must continue to watch with care," Fornri suggested, and at least no one could disagree with that.

They watched, and they waited, and nothing happened. One of the embassy staff, Hirus Ayns, left on the courier ship to visit his family. Their friend Aric Hort seemed increasingly preoccupied, but when Fornri asked him why he was troubled, he would only say, "There's something peculiar going on, and I can't find out what it is."

Nothing seemed to have changed. The ambassador marched about each day making suggestions that they usually declined with thanks. The ambassador's sister-daughter continued to spend her days on the beach, doing nothing at all, and that, too, they found incomprehensible. Aric Hort's somber mood puzzled them only until Dalla observed that he no longer was seen with Miss Warr.

Fornri, taking an overland short cut through the forest near the embassy, suddenly heard the faint, shrill whistle of an incoming spaceship. Perplexed, he halted and listened. The courier ship was not due for many weeks, and no other ship came to Langri.

A moment later he was able to distinguish a second whistle, and a third, and he broke into a run. By the time he reached the edge of the forest and stood looking down on the landing field, two ships had landed and a third was settling to ground. He paused a moment to stare at them, because they were the largest ships he has seen except for the navy battle cruiser.

Then he hurried down to them.

The man the ambassador was talking with wore a uniform that vaguely reminded Fornri of the clothing Captain Dallman had worn. The two of them were leafing through a thick stack of the plastic sheets the aliens used for records.

Fornri, still breathing deeply from his long run, slowed to a walk and tried to catch his breath as he approached. The ambassador greeted him with his usual broad smile.

"Captain," he said, "this is Fornri, the leader of the Langri Government."

"Honored," the captain murmured, snapping off a salute.

Fornri acknowledged it gravely before turning to the ambassador. "May I ask why these ships have landed without official clearance?"

The ambassador seemed astonished. "But you gave us permission to land routine supplies at any time!"

"The permission applied only to the courier ship," Fornri said. He hesitated; what he was about to do troubled him, but the Plan offered no alternative. "I must ask that these ships leave immediately."

The ambassador was smiling again. "Frankly, I wanted to surprise you, but I suppose I'll have to tell you about it. You may want to keep it as a surprise for your people, though. These ships have brought part of Langri's new medical center."

"Medical center?" Fornri echoed blankly.

"I'm also bringing in a doctor to study Langri's diseases, so no more children will have to share Dabbi's fate. This is a gift to the people of Langri from Wembling and Company."

Fornri stared at him. *"Wembling and Company?"*

They were angry. Often the council members had been resentful of Fornri, but now they were openly rebellious.

"I can't believe that an *enemy* would give us a medical center!" Narrif exclaimed.

Banu, seated as usual with bowed head and closed eyes, completed the search of his memory. "The Langri didn't mention a medical center," he said.

Fornri said stubbornly, "We must refuse this gift and ask the ships to leave."

Dalla turned on him furiously. "What harm can come of a medical center? How can it be bad to save lives?"

"The Langri said gifts always have a price," Fornri said slowly. "He said to beware of them, or we might learn too late that we have sold our world and ourselves."

"How can there be a price on something that is freely given?" Dalla demanded. "Are you too proud to admit that we need this medical center? Must we watch our children die while Fornri enjoys his pride?"

Fornri said wearily, "I ask your support. We must refuse this medical center and ask the ships to leave."

He looked about the circle of silent, hostile faces. "Very well," he said finally. "According to the Plan, you must choose a new leader."

He had intended merely to step down from the leadership and become a member of the council, but when he took a place beside Dalla, she deliberately turned her back to him. Slowly, feeling very tired, he pushed through the undergrowth and walked off into the forest.

Later the Elder found him, and after they had talked long together, they walked toward the embassy looking for Aric Hort. They came upon him at the edge of the landing field, talking with Talitha Warr, and at the sound of angry, raised voices they discreetly watched from the concealment of a convenient cluster of bushes.

"There's such a thing as too great a price!" Hort shouted.

"Too great a price for whom?" Miss Warr returned. "For Dabbi? Someone has to violate the natives' rights in order to save their lives!"

"It isn't that simple. You have to understand—"

"I understand that you can watch a child die without being affected," she said furiously. "I can't."

She stormed off, leaving Hort looking after her. Finally he walked a short distance to a group of boulders and sat down to watch the bustle of unloading around the ships.

He greeted Fornri and the Elder with a wan smile when they approached him. "My friends," he said, "I need your help. The ambassador wants to send me to another world. I'd rather stay here, so I'm no longer employed by him. Have I your permission to remain on Langri?"

"We implore you to remain," the Elder said. "I fear that my people are in serious trouble."

"That is my fear," Hort said soberly.

"We welcome your presence as a friend, and we need your counsel," Fornri said. "Now more than ever. Have you found a way to send a message to the attorneys?"

"The problem was to find a *safe* way to send a message," Hort said. "The answer is no. Every ship that lands here from now on will be owned or chartered by Wembling and Company—I have a hunch that we won't see the courier ship again. If we paid a crewman to smuggle out a message, he would guess that the ambassador would pay more to know what the message said, and he'd be right. It's a difficult problem."

"What if one of us were to go to see the attorneys?" the Elder asked.

Hort smiled at them. "You're asking whether it

would be easier to smuggle out a person than a message. Probably not. It might be possible to have someone leave openly, as a passenger; and when a passenger pays his passage there are laws protecting him and he's under no obligation to tell the captain his ultimate destination or why he's going. Whoever went would find it a frightening experience. Whom were you going to send?"

"Fornri," the Elder said. "Since he has lost his leadership—"

"*What?*"

Hort scrutinized their faces. "So that's how it is," he said finally. "Tried to get them to turn it down, did you? And they wouldn't. I don't know if it would have made any difference. I don't know—yet—just how Wembling means to do it and how he expects to get away with it, but obviously he intends to build a resort, whether you want one or not. By accepting the medical center, they're making it much easier for him. So you want to see the attorneys yourself."

"If that is possible," Fornri said.

"It may be much worse than a frightening experience. It may be worse than terrifying."

"If you will tell me what to expect and what I must do," Fornri said, "I will go in confidence."

"There won't be any trouble about the passage," Hort said. "I'll tell Wembling that I'm leaving, and he'll be so pleased he'll arrange it himself. Just before the ship lifts you can go aboard in my place. You'll need clothing. I'll see what I can buy from the crewmen."

"When would I go?" Fornri asked.

"There's a ship leaving tonight, but that's rather soon. I think on the last of these three, if I can arrange it. We'll need as much time as possible. I'll send you first to a friend of mine, who is also an anthropologist. He'll be delighted to give you lessons in civilization, and he'll help you find those attorneys. Or, if that firm no longer exists, perhaps he can help you find another."

"There is one thing more," Fornri said. "We have some retron crystals."

"Really?" Hort exclaimed. "You actually have some crystals? Now that's interesting!"

"We would like to convert them to monetary units. Should I take them with me?"

"Certainly not. Crystals have to be transported in special containers, or their emissions mess up a ship's instrumentation. You'd be asked to leave the ship before lift-off. Maybe the attorneys could help you find out how to do it."

The three of them sat for a time in silence, looking down at the ships. Finally Hort said to the Elder, "Has Langri developed any sayings about the fickleness of women?"

"Many," the Elder said. "But I think the word is 'contrariness.'"

Hort nodded. "Yes. That's the word."

12

In the background stood the geodesic frameworks for the clusters of small domes that were to constitute the medical center. A machine was at work leveling the top of the bluff on which the building was being erected. Talitha Warr strode about confidently, giving instructions; the foreman followed her, and Dalla followed the foreman, and both listened attentively.

"A sturdy wall," Talitha said. "We don't want anyone falling over the edge. Resident patients can come here and enjoy the breeze and the sea view."

The foreman scowled and scratched his head. "Resident patients? The plans don't call for no hospital accommodations."

"The hospital will be at the rear of the medical center," Talitha said. "As much as possible we'll keep the patients in native-style buildings. They'll be more comfortable in familiar surroundings. The center will house the various treatment and surgical and laboratory clinics."

"I see."

"Back there we'll put the children's playground," Talitha said, pointing. "Over here I want a formal park laid out, with a fountain and the most attractive Langrian flowers and shrubs we can find. Now—about the road down to the beach. I want the grade as easy as possible. Sick patients will have to climb it, or their friends will have to carry them up. I'd like to have a lift for them, but I'm afraid it'd be too expensive."

"Doesn't have to be," the foreman said. "We can cobble up something for you."

Talitha shook her head firmly. "Uncle offered me a platform pulled up by ropes and pulleys and things, and I turned it down. I'm not having my patients falling out of a lift. Let's just concentrate on making that road with the easiest grade possible."

Aric Hort and the Elder stood at the edge of the forest looking down at the medical center construction site and the lovely sweep of sea and shore beyond it. Hort lowered his binoculars. "Miss Warr is firmly in charge," he said. "They seem to be making good progress. It'll be an attractive building. I'm relieved about that—I was afraid they'd put up more of those hideous prefabs."

The Elder said nothing. Hort looked at him for a moment and then he raised his binoculars again. "So Dalla is going to study nursing," he remarked.

"Miss Warr will teach her," the Elder said. "It's all right, isn't it?"

"Of course. Hard to argue against health care and medical centers and the like, even when Wembling is importing a thousand times the supplies and materials the medical center will require. Has the council bothered to look at the landing field lately? The cargo holders are piled eight high and eight deep all along one side of the field."

"Narrif says he is tired of senseless complaints about the ambassador."

"That's unfortunate. They ought to have *some* notion of what a small building like the medical center requires. At a guess, ten cargo holders, and someone ought to ask the ambassador what he intends to do with the other six hundred. Let's hope that Fornri and the attorneys will be ready to act the moment the council's eyes are opened."

"Narrif feels that the attorneys aren't necessary. He talks of preventing Fornri from using Langri's money to pay them."

"Narrif is getting suspiciously friendly with the ambassador," Hort said. "I've noticed that he calls at the embassy every day."

"I, too, have noticed that."

The two men seated themselves on the board trunk of a fallen tree, and Hort continued to study the medical center site with his binoculars.

"I've noticed that Narrif is courting Dalla," Hort said. "Has she had a change of desire?"

The Elder smiled. "I think her desire will always be Fornri's."

"Too bad she didn't realize that before he left. Her turning against him hurt most of all."

"She did realize it," the Elder said. "She came to the ship. Perhaps she would have spoken to him if he'd been alone, but because we were with him she held back until it was too late. I saw her weeping in the forest above the landing field after the ship left." He paused. "She asked about him yesterday."

"By strange coincidence, so did Wembling. He hasn't quite figured out what's happening, but he's highly suspicious. We were wise to tell Fornri not to send any messages. Wembling passes my mail along to me, but he opens it first."

"Are you comfortable living alone in the forest?" the Elder asked anxiously. "Any village would be honored to be your host."

"Thank you, but I'm very comfortable. It gives me a sense of achievement, living in a dwelling I built myself—even if I never did get the walls woven right."

"You could have built your own dwelling in one of the villages."

"True, but I think I'm more useful where I am. I'm close enough to Wembling's iniquities to keep track of them, but not so close that he'll think me a nuisance. You can tell Dalla that we're confident Fornri's all right. My friend will look after him. What worries me is that Wembling may have his resort built and in operation before Fornri can get an appointment with the attorneys."

Hirus Ayns returned on one of Wembling and Company's freighters, and Wembling was waiting for him when he came down the ramp. He grabbed his hand anxiously and asked, "Well?"

"No problems," Ayns said. "I have your charter."

"I was getting worried."

"I told you it would take time, and you told me not to communicate."

"I know—any kind of a leak would have crimped the whole show. But I've got a fortune stacked up here, and if the natives had decided to confiscate the stuff I wouldn't have had a legal leg to stand on. You really got it?"

Ayns grinned and handed the document to him. Wembling read it eagerly. Then he turned and shouted, "It's all right. Break out the machines and let's get going." He turned back to Ayns. "What about the rest of my work force?"

"The ship should get in day after tomorrow."

"Good. Now we can stop this dratted acting and get to work."

Workers were removing tarps from the long rows of enormous cargo holders. At one end they pulled off dummy facings and removed blocks from the concealed construction machines. The first motor whirred, and an earth planer crept ponderously across the landing field. Others followed. The surveying crew was bustling about locating its hidden stakes and replacing them with visible ones. Wembling, watching with deep satisfaction, saw the first machine take its first deep bite of Langrian soil.

Dalla had been going from village to village talking about the medical center and recruiting young people to study nursing there. It was Miss Warr's idea that every village should have its own trained nurses.

Narrif offered to take her. He found a crew of boys willing to serve as paddlers, and they went down the coast by boat, stopping at every village. Then at dusk, when they reached the last village she planned to visit that day, he sent the boat back without telling her; and when she had finished he suggested that they walk.

She knew his wish—that they should go to a Bower Hill for the night—and she declined firmly. He had asked her often since Fornri left, but even had her desire changed, she could not have consented because she had not offered Fornri the broken branch. She had no intention of doing so—if the broken branch came between them, it would have to be his offering—but Narrif thought she had not offered it because Fornri left suddenly, and he tried to convince her that the offering was no longer necessary.

He followed her through the forest, arguing angrily and telling her that Fornri had fled like a coward because the council had refused his leadership. He was still making surly remarks as they passed along a forest path near the embassy, and a sudden awareness of strange sounds silenced him and halted both of them.

They turned aside, and—very cautiously, because the sounds were frighteningly strange—they made their way to the edge of the forest, parted the foliage, and looked out.

Between them and the sea the land had been carved with hideous slashes. There were strangely shaped monsters tearing at it, and others were smashing and devouring the trees. Near the beach stood a row of strange dwellings like those of the embassy, and while they watched a flat object suddenly flung up walls and roof and became another dwelling.

Staring down at the appalling devastation, frightened, angry, Dalla exclaimed, "Fornri was right! The ambassador is the enemy!"

13

The clothing Fornri wore chafed him awkwardly weeks after they said he would become accustomed to it. The marvels they promised to show him gave him a turmoil of impressions, some of which he would have preferred not to believe.

He worried about what might be happening to his own world, where the marvels were the colors of the forests, and the soft warmth of the beach sand, and the crisp, fragrant breeze off the sea. He missed Dalla enormously. He was lonely, confused, very tired, and frightened—for he had to make decisions that would affect the entire future of his people and his world, and the thought of a wrong choice terrified him.

This was another building of the stone that was not stone. Above the vaulted entrance were words he did not understand even after they were explained: HALL OF JVSTICE, and INTERWORLD DIVISION.

Fornri had arrived in one of the strange, bubble-like air boats that darted everywhere above the city's vast and intricate skyline. His companion was Jarvis Jarnes, of the firm of McLindorffer, Klarouse, Hraanl, Picrawley, Webluston, and Jarnes. As the Langri had foretold, its name had been changed.

Just inside the vast entrance, they stepped onto a floor-that-moved. This was one of the things Jarnes and his friends expected Fornri to marvel at, and he could only wonder why they did not walk, which would have been so much faster. On this day Jarnes went to a room called Interworld Law Library. He had explained what he would do—ask the strange machine-that-remembers about other legal actions that could have had to do with troubles like those of Langri's, and in Jarnes's notebook were long lists of questions that he thought might stir the machine's memory; but through all the questions the dark green panel that should have answered only flashed, at intervals, the symbol that said it did not know.

On the way out they stopped to pay the attendant for the use of the machine. Jarnes presented a circular token, which the attendant fitted into a machine that growled over it.

"Still no luck?" the attendant asked. "There couldn't possibly be a legal question with no references!"

Jarnes smiled wistfully and said, "Couldn't there?"

They rode the moving floor again and got off at a room marked REGISTRAR, INTERWORLD PACTS AND COMPACTS, where Jarnes talked with an attendant consulted his own machine-that-remembers and shook his head. The rode on, to a room marked EXTRA-FEDERATION REGISTRAR, with the same result.

Finally they rode to the Justice Arena.

They left the moving floor and followed a broad corridor that encircled the justice chambers. The curving outer wall of each chamber was transparent—a genuine marvel—and within it the two side walls narrowed almost to a point at the dais where opposing attorneys faced each other across the consoles of their machines-that-remember. Above them sat the clerk, and above and behind him sat the justice—except that the justice was not really there. His image appeared when the session opened and disappeared when it closed, and no amount of explaining by Jarnes could

but no one can locate it without knowing the magic word—just as I couldn't get you to stand up by saying 'chair' when someone had told you secretly that the word had been changed to 'table.' "

Fornri continued to regard him blankly, wondering whether Clerk Wyland actually wanted him to stand up and why.

"Of course the references are a bit more involved than the words 'chair' and 'table,' " Clerk Wyland said.

"Just a bit," Jarnes agreed, with a wistful smile.

"But something like that must have happened, and now we won't be able to find the Langri treaty officially until we figure out what the new reference is— just as I wouldn't have been able to make you stand up until I tried out a lot of words and found that you were now responding to 'table.' It shouldn't be possible to tamper with a reference—aside from the technical difficulties, there are all sorts of safeguards, and there are stiff penalties for even trying, but someone has done it."

"Someone was bribed to do it," Jarnes amended.

"Undoubtedly. And sooner or later—"

"Even 'sooner' will be much too late," Jarnes said grimly. "I told you—Fornri brought a complete report from Aric Hort, who is a competent anthropologist and a former employee of this man Wembling. The world of Langri is about to suffer an ecological catastrophe. The natives' food supply will be wiped out."

"Yes, indeed," Clerk Wyland said, with a side glance at Fornri. "The poor natives. Master McLindorffer informed me as to the urgency of the problem, and I consulted with Justice Laysoring, as I promised. He saw no hope at all for an action on the treaty. It's an extra-Federation matter. No Federation court would assume jurisdiction."

"The only other source of redress would be the legislature," Jarnes said glumly. "Since the party in power is also the party responsible for the injustice, the outlook is less than bright." Clerk Wyland gestured forlornly. "That leaves only one point of attack for us," Jarnes went on. "Wembling's charter. Rather, his use of his charter, since the courts would decline jurisdiction on any question concerning its legality."

Clerk Wyland nodded. "Justice Laysoring agrees that each of the points your Master McLindorffer listed has legal validity and should secure you a temporary injunction with a temporary restraining order stopping Wembling's work until the hearing. He also gives it as his opinion that none of the points would be sustained."

Jarnes turned to Fornri. "Do you understand all this? The copy of your treaty means nothing unless something official exists that it is a copy of. Wembling somehow managed to get the official version lost. Eventually it'll be found again, perhaps with appropriate scandal, but that may not happen for years. There are various legal questions we can raise, but the best we can hope for is to delay and harass Wembling and Company. We can make him stop work on his resort while the legal questions we raise are being decided—one week, two weeks, sometimes a little longer. There's very little chance that we could win one of these actions. They will be extremely expensive, and the most we can hope to gain for you is a little time."

"Time is what we need," Fornri said. "Time for the Plan."

"Do they have money?" the clerk asked.

"That's another peculiarity about this case. The Federation Office of External Affairs maintains that Langri is a dependent world. The Bank of the Galaxy has half a million credits, plus some interest, registered to a Government of Langri. Oddly enough, that half million credits was deposited to the Government of Langri by the same Federation Office of External Affairs that now maintains there is no such government. Would you care to comment?"

"You can't amaze me with governmental stupidities," Clerk Wyland said. "I've seen too many of them. You'll be able to stir things up a little with the half million—but only a little, unfortunately. A fortune doesn't buy much legal action on the interworld market."

"Yes. They also have a cache of retron crystals. From Fornri's description I'd estimate the value at a minimum million credits and possibly as much as two million. Enough to stir things up quite a bit. Problem is getting the crystals back here. Would it be feasible to have a couple of marshals sent to Langri when we make our first filing? They'd be on the scene to answer any court questions, and they could make certain that Wembling does in fact stop work when an injunction is issued."

Clerk Wyland nodded eagerly. "It would have to be done at your expense, but relatively the cost would be a pittance and well worth it. Otherwise Wembling might take no notice of your actions."

"When eventually the marshals returned, they could be instructed to bring sealed containers of records or other objects of value the natives wished to send to their attorneys. We could provide the necessary containers to mask the retron interference. Feasible?"

"Entirely feasible," the clerk agreed.

"Fornri could return to Langri with the marshals, and we'd send communications equipment with him. The natives won't be able to entrust any secrets to it, because Wembling certainly will intercept every message they send, but the fact that they are able to communicate will help us immensely and restrain Wembling a bit. Maybe we could arrange for the marshals to deputize this anthropologist Hort so there'll be someone permanently on the scene who can make official reports."

"Excellent idea," the clerk said. "If there's an observer on the scene who can report violations, Wembling will obey court orders scrupulously. He won't want the investigation that a contempt citation would provoke. How will you begin?"

"By questioning Wembling's use of his charter. The charter gives him the right to develop Langri's natural resources. Actually he's building a vacation resort, which should be, ipso facto, a violation of the charter."

Clerk Wyland flashed his smile and nodded approvingly. "Have you searched it?"

"Yes. There's no firm authority as to whether a vacation resort constitutes the development of natural resources. It would require a new point of law."

"Very good. That should give you a handsome delay—perhaps as much as three or four weeks."

"I hope so," Jarnes said. He turned to Fornri. "I'd feel better about this if I knew what your Plan is, but since you'd rather not say—and I can understand that the universe must seem like a rather bewildering place right now and you'd rather keep your own secrets until you know us better—I'll spend your money as wisely as I can and stop Wembling's work as often and as long as I can. At the moment that's the only thing I can do, but it will give you a little time for your Plan."

"Thank you," Fornri said. "We need all the time you can find for us."

"Then we'll do it that way. Since I haven't got a Plan, I might as well help you as much as I can with yours, whatever it is. In the meantime, I'm sure you're needed on Langri, so we'll send you back with the marshals and the communications equipment."

"May I give you some advice, Fornri?" Clerk Wyland asked. "This Plan of yours. Don't let it get you into trouble. Mr. H. Harlow Wembling has a charter, which is a very weighty document, and the law is on his side. If you try to interfere with him, except through the courts, you can do yourself substantially more harm than good. Leave that problem to Submaster Jarnes. He'll do the very best he can for you, and one careless act there on Langri might destroy everything he accomplishes here."

Fornri smiled politely and nodded.

14

H. Harlow Wembling had developed the habit of looking out of one particular window of his embassy office. Now his office was in a different location—all of the embassy buildings had been moved down the slope to the construction area, where dormitories, offices, and workshops made up a small village—but in his idle moment Wembling continued to look out of the same window.

It faced on the ocean, and now the beach was crowded the way he had anticipated when he envisioned his resort—except that it was crowded with Wembling and Company's idle work force. Men and women were cavorting in and out of the water and playing silly games, and Wembling glowered at them.

Hirus Ayns came in and seated himself. Wembling said, without turning around, "Any news?"

"About lifting the injunction, no. Otherwise, one small item. Fornri is back."

Wembling turned.

"Narrif told me," Ayns said. "He arrived with the marshals—he was the mysterious third passenger, and he managed to slip off the ship without being noticed. They've made him head of the council again."

"Pity," Wembling said. "I think we could have come to an agreement with Narrif, but we'll never manage it with Fornri. He's as smooth a scoundrel as I've ever met. So he came with the marshals." He paused for a moment. Then he exclaimed, "So it *was* Fornri that started the legal action!"

"Right. And until the natives spend that half million credits they collected in fines, you can count on more of the same. Let's cut to a token work force until the natives run out of money or their attorneys run out of arguments."

Wembling shook his head. "Time is much more important than money. We've got to get as much work done as possible before the blowup over the treaty. If we can only work between lawsuits, that's better than no work at all. Anyway, this morning I reached an agreement with the overseers. As long as the court stops work, they'll take half pay. They'll still be making food wages in addition to having a glorious vacation. They hardly put up an argument. They were afraid I'd close down completely. No, I'll keep everyone here. Did Narrif give you anything else?"

Ayns shook his head. "He's frightened. He bought your line about the medical center. So did the others, but he led the way, and of course now they have to blame someone. There was a move to kick him off the council, but Fornri squelched it—he said if they punished everyone who made a mistake, the world would soon run out of councilors. But from now on I don't think we'll see much of Narrif."

"Pity. He might have been useful." Wembling ambled back to the window. "Right now there's nothing we can do but wait."

Two days later Wembling discharged most of his work force. He had received from his attorneys, the eminent firm of Khorwiss, Qwaanti, Mllo, Bylym, and Alaffro, an astute analysis of his legal position with a projection of the probable future legal actions to be expected from the natives' attorneys. If all legal alternatives were explored, and if the natives' money held out, they estimated that Wembling would be doing no work at all for the next six months. Wembling ordered transportation for his work force, keeping only a maintenance crew and the surveyors. The court had ruled that surveying stakes in no way permanently damaged a world. Wembling was permitted to set as many as he wished, and the natives were enjoined from interfering with them. This pleased Wembling. He could proceed with his first-stage planning, and less time would be lost than he had anticipated.

The other information he received pleased him less. Aric Hort was designated a reporting deputy marshal. Hort himself brought the information in the form of a notice from the marshals, who would be leaving shortly.

Wembling exploded. "Now I suppose I have to worry about a dirty double-crosser sending in false reports!"

"Certainly not," Hort said with a grin. "True reports."

The workmen left; the waiting dragged on. Finally the question of whether a vacation resort constituted a development of natural resources was resolved in Wembling's favor. To the amazement of Wembling's attorneys, Submaster Jarnes brought no further actions. Wembling gleefully hired a new work force, transported it to Langri, and again began tearing up meadows and forests; whereupon Jarnes struck again. Abruptly he appealed the natural resource ruling to Higher Court, and he astutely avoided having to deposit bond by pointing out that Wembling had brought in his work force before the period of appeal had expired. Higher Court merely extended the injunction previously in force, and Wembling again found himself glaring out of his office window at an entire work force cavorting in Langri's enticing surf.

"So what do I do now?" Wembling demanded. "If I keep them here, he'll hit me with injunction after injunction. If I send them home, he'll wait with the next one until I bring in a new force."

"Then keep 'em here," Ayns said. "If time is more important than money, make him play his whole hand. Then you can get to work."

"Well—maybe. Except that I don't need to keep all of them here. Just enough so they'll think they have to keep me from using them."

Submaster Jarnes followed the suit that challenged Wembling's right to build a resort with another that questioned his right to run the resort after it was built. Wembling lost a week's work before Higher Court voided the injunction, dryly affirming that if Wembling wanted to exercise his legal right to construct a resort that he might not be able to use, he had the right to do so. While the courts were meditating that question, Jarnes followed with another action asking the courts to prevent Wembling and Company from destroying Langri's natural resources through the building of a resort, and to compensate the natives for those already destroyed. Construction was halted for five weeks, and a furious Wembling had to count each tree that had been removed, and tabulate cubic meters of soil redistributed, and tons of rock dumped into the ocean, and shrubs, herbs, and meadow grass crushed, dug up, or buried, and wild life driven away, knowing as he did so that the moment he won this idiotic suit Submaster Jarnes would have another ready.

Which he did.

The weeks became months and Wembling could only contemplate his mounting costs and wait. Finally the day came when Master Khorwiss notified him that Jarnes had no more cards to play. Further, the courts were becoming highly impatient of these well-reasoned but legally unsound requests for injunctions. Wembling enlarged the work force so he could employ double shifts the moment the last injunction was lifted.

Aric Hort brought the message, as he had so many times previously. Wembling already had been informed by way of his own communications center, and once again he grudgingly verified that Hort was just as prompt in delivering news of an injunction dissolved as he was of an injunction imposed.

"Well, that ends this farce," Wembling said, as Hort handed him the official release. "That was the last one."

"If you say so," Hort remarked agreeably.

Wembling eyed him suspiciously. "What infamies are the natives concocting now?"

"I've told you at least a dozen times that the natives don't confide in anyone. If they ever do decide to trust me, you'll be the last to know it."

Hort strolled away, and Wembling, bristling with anger, stepped to the nearest com unit and sent his work force into action.

A few minutes later he was watching with satisfaction while his gigantic machines carved Langri's soil and masticated its forest. Suddenly one of them leaned sideways at an unlikely, rakish angle and came to an abrupt stop. Wembling charged toward it and found the operator gazing bewilderedly at the left front wheel, which was firmly lodged in a deep hole.

"Of all the stupid things to do!" Wembling bellowed.

The operator protested that he hadn't seen the hole.

"Don't tell me you didn't see it. You can't drive a machine into a hole that big without seeing it. Don't just stand there—let's get it out, and fast, and next time look where you're going."

As Wembling turned to walk away, the ground dissolved beneath him. He landed with a thud and found himself standing waist-deep in a neatly incised hole. For a moment he ignored the helping hand extended by the operator and thought deeply. The hole obviously was freshly dug, and yet no dirt could be seen nearby. He could testify that it had been artfully hidden. It was, he reflected, of a size and depth nicely calculated to entrap the wheels of his machines.

"The natives did this!" he roared.

He shook off the operator's hand and climbed out by himself. Ayns came hurrying up, and Wembling exhibited the hole. "They must have sneaked in and done it during the night. I want the entire site ringed with lighted sentry posts."

"We don't have enough men," Ayns objected.

"We'll get enough men. I want those sentry posts operating tonight."

He turned to watch another machine lumbering past. Abruptly he leaped toward it, screaming, "Stop!"

The machine skidded to a halt a few centimeters from a native who had sprung out of nowhere to fling himself across its path. As Wembling charged up, the operator got out and bent over the native.

"There's nothing wrong with him," the operator said. "He just laid down there to interfere with the work. Let me run over him and put a stop to this nonsense."

"You fool!" Wembling bellowed. "That's the one thing that could cost me my charter. I don't dare harm a native, and they know it. They don't dare harm one of you, and they know that, too. Take him over to the forest and throw him in. Next time, be on the lookout for something like this."

He waved some workmen over, and they picked up the native and carried him away. The operator mounted his machine, and before he could get it in motion another native darted up and sprawled in front of it.

"I'm beginning not to like this job," the operator growled.

Wembling paid no attention. He had glimpsed a peculiar movement at the edge of the forest. He raised his binoculars, and then he broke into a run. By the time he arrived, one of his machines had raised itself into the air only to fall back with a crash as a tree collapsed on top of it.

The operator babbled excitedly. "Native was in that tree. He fed a vine into the winding drum. I didn't pay no attention—what's a little vine to a machine that big and heavy—and then, before I could get back to shut the thing off—"

Wembling turned on his heel and walked away. He was past anger. For the remainder of the day he watched without comment while the ground repeatedly collapsed under his machines and natives persistently halted the work; and at the end of the day he expressed no surprise whatsoever when Ayns came to report seven men missing.

"The natives are playing right into our hands," he said grimly. "This time they've gone much too far, and they're not going to get away with it."

"The men are alarmed," Ayns said. "If we don't light the dormitory area tonight and put a strong guard there, we'll lose our work force."

"If we do, we can't protect the construction site," Wembling protested. "The natives'll riddle it with holes and commit all kinds of deviltry."

Ayns repeated firmly, "We'll lose our work force."

Wembling raised his arms resignedly. "All right. Set the guard around the dormitories."

Looking out of his bedroom window, Wembling cursed the lights. They perfectly illuminated the area around the buildings, but beyond the bright swath they cut through the still Langrian night, he could see nothing at all. If the natives possessed any kind of a weapon that was effective from a distance, they would be helpless.

Seven of his men had disappeared without a trace. Each of them had been working alone near the edge of the forest, and in a matter of seconds he had vanished.

"Probably overpowered by a mob and carried off," Aynes said, but it made no difference whether it had been done by a mob or by sorcery. The entire work force was in a panic. Wembling had said the natives wouldn't dare, and they had dared. Probably they thought they had nothing to lose, and as far as Wembling could figure out, they were right. He dared not attempt any kind of retaliation.

Work procedures would have to be revised. In the future his men would have to work in groups, with the site guarded both day and night. The additional expense could be written off, but it would slow the work.

Abruptly the night erupted. Shouts, screams, the hellish thud, thud, thud of native drums, the deep honks of their signal gourds, all blended into a horrifying cacophony. Wembling raced to his door and looked out. Something enormous crashed and thudded across the construction site, and he took one glance at the monstrous, looming, shadowy form that suddenly roared into the circle of light and fled toward the rear of the building. It struck with a hollow, popping sound that made his ears ring, accompanied by a splintering crash. It was followed by another, and still another, and the fourth struck Wembling's office and skidded it sideways into the next building.

Silence rushed in for a moment, and then the shouts and curses of the work force rent the night. Wembling crawled out from under a table, shakily confirmed that he had no bones broken, and went to assess the damage.

Ayns, with several of the sentries, was outside studying the remains of the object that had struck the office. "The natives rolled some of those silly gourds down the slope," he said. Then he exclaimed sharply, *"What's that?"*

The sentries hauled a squirming figure from the slimy pulp. It was one of the missing men. Fumbling distastefully, they found another. Other sentries were performing similar rescues from the slimy remains of the other gourds.

"Are they all right?" Wembling demanded.

"We don't know yet," Ayns answered.

They had been bound and gagged and stuffed into the large gourds with protective small gourd helmets on their heads. Not only did they show no gratitude for their release, but they were, all of them, thunderingly angry—not at the natives, but at Wembling. While they flexed cramped limbs and stomped feeling into numbed feet, they poured torrents of abuse on Wembling and Company and all of its works.

"Now just a moment," Wembling said. "Maybe you had a rough time, but you don't seem any the worse for it, and I don't have to stand for that. Report in the morning for disciplinary action."

"I'll report in the morning for transportation," a worker snapped. "I quit."

"Now wait—"

"So do I," another said.

The onlookers shouted in chorus, "We all quit!" and sent up a cheer. Wembling turned and went back to his office. It had been pushed down a slope, and it stood at a crazy angle.

"I want this back on its foundation as soon as it's light," Wembling told Ayns, who had followed him. He grabbed a towel and began wiping the gourd pulp from his hands.

"I think they meant it about quitting," Ayns said. "What do we do now—issue weapons?"

"You know we don't dare. One injured native, and our friend the deputy marshal will turn in a report that'll cost us our charter. On the other hand, it's no concern of ours if someone else injures a native."

"What do you mean?"

"The Space Navy. We're citizens of the Federation. Our lives and property are threatened and our lawful endeavors have been interfered with. We're entitled to protection."

Ayns gave Wembling one of his rare smiles. "Now that you mention it, I'm sure that we are."

Wembling thumped on the sloping top of his desk. "H. Harlow Wembling has enough influence to get what he's entitled to."

15

An obsolete freighter, bound from Quiron to Yorlang on a seldom-used space route, mysteriously vanished. A thousand light-years away a bureaucrat with an overactive imagination thought of piracy. Orders

went out, and Commander James Vorish, captain of
the battle cruiser *Hiln*, changed course and resigned
himself to a monotonous six months of patrolling.

A week later his orders were canceled. He
changed course again and mulled over the new assignment with Lieutenant Commander Robert Smith, his
executive. "Someone's been stirring up an indigenous
population," Vorish said. "We're to take over and
protect Federation citizens and property."

"Peculiar assignment for a battle cruiser," Smith
observed. "Where the devil is Langri? I've never heard
of it."

Looking westward, Vorish thought it the most
beautiful world he'd ever seen. The forest stretched
back into the hills, its unbroken foliage an awesome
expanse of dazzling variegation. Flowers lifted deli-
cately beautiful, enormous petals to the lightly stirring
sea breeze. Waves rippled in lethargically from an indescribably magnificent sea, and the fine beach sand
caught the afternoon sun with a billion billion facets of
flashing color.

Behind him was the hideous, scarred, noisy, reek-
ing cauldron of the construction site. Motors whined,
machines shuffled back and forth, workmen scurried
hither and yon like a blighting invasion of mindless
insects.

Smith touched Vorish's arm and pointed. A clumsy
ground conveyance sped away from the clutter of prefab buildings and bounced toward them—the first official acknowledgment of their arrival. Vorish strode
down the *Hiln*'s ramp, inspected the sentries, and then
turned to see what that official acknowledgment would
consist of.

There were four men in the vehicle, and when one
vaulted out and hurried toward the *Hiln*, two of the
others, obviously personal bodyguards, sauntered after
him. Vorish appraised the short, rotund figure and
decided that it probably contained more muscle than
one would suspect. The agility with which the man had
left the vehicle was impressive, and obviously he

worked in the sun. His bronzed complexion was one the pale-faced inhabitants of frigid worlds would regard with envy.

"Glad to meet you, Commander," the man said. "I'm Wembling."

They touched hands.

"Seems peaceful here," Vorish remarked. "From my orders, I had the impression that the natives were keeping you under siege."

"They are," Wembling said bitterly. "They're pulling every dirty trick they can get away with."

Vorish murmured polite concern and looked about him again. He could see nothing that contradicted his first impression: Langri was a spectacularly beautiful, peaceful world.

Wembling chuckled, completely misinterpreting Vorish's scowl. "Don't let it worry you. We keep them pretty much under control in the daytime. Why don't you give your men a few hours of leave—let them enjoy the beach and shake off their space tremors. And as soon as you settle in, Commander, come down to my office and I'll show you what I want you to do."

He turned away, carelessly tossed a gesture of farewell over his shoulder, and boarded his conveyance. He was driven off at once, and the guards had to pile unceremoniously into the moving vehicle.

Vorish turned and found Lieutenant Commander Smith grinning down at him from the ramp. "Who was that?" Smith demanded. "The Grand Admiral? He certainly seems to know what you're supposed to be doing."

"I'm glad someone knows what I'm supposed to be doing. I certainly don't. Do you notice something peculiar about this situation?"

"I seem to detect a certain pronounced odoriferousness," Smith remarked.

"Tell Macklie to scout around and talk with Wembling's men and see if he can find out what's going on here. I suppose I'll have to go see the man. At a guess, he wants the entire crew of the *Hiln* for sentry duty. While I'm gone, take a patrol and circle the construction site. See what the security arrangements are and what problems we're likely to encounter."

One wall of Wembling's office was an enormous map, and Wembling, with energetic gesticulations, explained what it was he wanted. He wanted a solid wall of men around his construction site, though it took him twenty minutes to say so.

Vorish heard him out, and then he politely informed Wembling that it wasn't possible. "My men are capable," he said, "but there aren't enough of them, and thus far I haven't been able to teach them to function in seven different places at once."

"It's your solemn duty to protect the lives and property of citizens of the Federation!" Wembling snapped.

"If Fleet Headquarters had meant for me to stand guard duty over an entire continent," Vorish told him coldly, "it would have sent a larger force—say *two* ships. What you want would require ten divisions of troops and a billion credits' worth of equipment and even that wouldn't be foolproof. Why do you have sentries along the beach?"

"Sometimes the puggards sneak in from the sea. Can't trust the unprincipled scoundrels for an instant. My men won't work for me if they're all the time in terror of their lives."

Vorish turned in surprise. "I wasn't aware of that. How many men have you lost?"

"Well—none, but that isn't the natives' fault."

"Have they been damaging your equipment and materials?"

"Plenty. They manage to put two or three machines out of commission every day, and they keep sneaking in and stopping the work. It'd be a lot worse if I hadn't imported a double work force just to guard the site. Commander, I've met a lot of different kinds of people in my lifetime, but never before have I encountered this measure of ingratitude. My whole project was started just to finance projects the natives need, and the first thing I built was a medical center for them, and they're going to share in every penny of profit this place makes. In spite of that they've harassed us in every possible way right from the beginning. This is a multibillion-credit project, and I've backed it to the limit of my resources, and these ingrates are trying to ruin me. I resent that. Now—this is what I suggest. Each of us will assign a man to each sentry post on every shift. My men know what the natives are up to and how to handle them, and they'll show your men what to do. I'll tell my super to work out the details with you."

"Do you have another map?" Vorish asked.

"Why, yes—"

"With the sentry posts marked on it?"

Wembling shook his head. "Never needed more than one."

"That's all right. We'll probably want to shift them anyway. Send your super up to the *Hiln* with the map. We'll ask him what we need to know, and then we'll work out with him what we're prepared to do."

Smith returned from his inspection patrol and glumly remarked that it wasn't the Space Navy Wembling wanted, but the Space Army—all of it. Vorish turned Wembling's super over to him and left the two of them arguing about the sentry posts. He wanted to see the situation for himself.

He was standing on a lonely stretch of beach at the far end of the perimeter, looking out to sea, when Lieutenant Commander Macklie, his intelligence officer, caught up with him.

"You were right, sir," Macklie said. "It's a queer situation. These raids Wembling talked about—the natives usually sneak in one or two at a time. They lie down in front of a machine or grab ahold of something, and all the work has to stop until someone pries them loose and tosses them back into the forest."

"Have any natives been hurt?" Vorish asked.

"No, sir. The men say Wembling is very strict

about that. He knows that mistreating the natives, even when he thinks they deserve it, would bring him more trouble than he could handle."

"He knows correctly."

"Yes, sir. The natives may be aware of it, because they almost seem to be trying to get hurt. It's got on the workers' nerves—they never know when a native is going to pop up in front of them. They're afraid if one did get hurt the others would come after them with poisoned weapons. This world is reputed to have some very wicked poisons. There's a thorn that will kill a man almost instantly."

"Have any of the workers been injured?"

"Several were abducted before Wembling got the idea of making them work in groups. The natives returned them unharmed. They stuffed them into giant gourds and rolled the gourds down the slope at the prefabs. Scared everyone half to death, especially the workers inside the gourds, but no one was hurt."

"Sounds like some kind of childish prank," Vorish observed.

"Yes, sir. From what I've seen of Wembling, sir, my sympathy is with the natives."

"And mine. Unfortunately, I have orders. It's just as well that the natives have a sense of humor. I'm afraid they're going to need it."

"Smith asked me to tell you we'll have to assign the specialized ratings to guard duty or there won't be enough men."

"They'll howl, I suppose."

"No, sir, they won't. A couple of hours on this beach each day are worth four times that in guard duty. I'll scout around some more, sir."

He saluted and hurried away. Vorish strolled along the beach toward the landing field. As he passed the prefab dormitories and offices, a messenger hurried out to intercept him. "Excuse me, sir, but Mr. Wembling would like to use your ship's power plant to extend his lighting system. If you'll wait just a moment, his engineer—"

"Tell him to send his engineer to the *Hiln*," Vorish said. "He can arrange it with my engineer."

At the ship he okayed Smith's guard rosters, and then he went to have a look at the security arrangements. He inspected sentry posts, watched the engineers set up new lights, and listened in on some of the arguments between his men and the construction workers.

Smith was complaining to a foreman that the lights in Sector R were useless because the field of observation was cluttered up with large bushes. He wanted them cut; the foreman protested that he had neither the men nor the machines for bush cutting. Smith was perfectly free to do the job himself, though. Since devices for cutting bushes were not standard equipment on Space Navy battle cruisers, Vorish knew how this was going to end. He walked on. At the north end of the perimeter, a nav technician was insisting that the line of sentry posts be moved back from the forest. "You can't light up a forest," he kept saying. "There'll be a zillion shadows. Move the posts back, and the natives will have to come out of the trees to get at us." Vorish gave him high marks but left him to win his own argument, which he did. The line was moved back.

While Vorish made his rounds, a stream of messengers from Wembling plodded in his wake.

"If it wouldn't be too much trouble, sir, Mr. Wembling would like your Post Number Seven Two moved ten meters to the north. The light will fall on his bedroom window."

"Mr. Wembling's compliments, sir. It's a frozen tart for your mess. And if it wouldn't inconvenience you too much, would you mind spotting half a dozen more sentry posts at the head of the inlet?"

"Excuse me, sir, but Mr. Wembling would like to meet with your duty officer at seventeen hundred."

"At your earliest convenience, sir, Mr. Wembling requests that—"

"Damn Wembling!" Vorish exploded.

At dusk Smith reported the sentry arrangements completed and the first echelon posted. "I think we're in good shape," he said. "There isn't much to worry about anyway—outside Wembling's imagination. The natives have no weapons."

"Who says they don't?" Vorish demanded. "Just because they haven't *used* any doesn't mean they don't *have* any. These natives aren't fools. I have a dozen reports of them watching from cover while you were posting the sentries. If they have foolish ambitions, to-night is the night they'll try them out. They'll know that fifty per cent of the sentries are new here, and they may know that Space Navy men aren't accustomed to ground duty. Some of our men are going to be scared stiff standing out there with nothing between them and a dark forest, and the natives may know that, too. I want the off-duty echelons organized into platoons and bedded down where they'll be available the moment re-inforcements are needed anywhere. Have you talked with Macklie?"

Smith nodded. "Did he tell you the natives actually took Wembling to court over this?"

"No!"

"It's a fact. They hit him with one suit after an-other and held up his work for months. Wembling won every case, but he was enjoined from working while the cases were being decided."

"No wonder Wembling is in a foul mood!"

"That's just the half of it. Once the courts let him go back to work, the natives started harassing him with those silly pranks to slow down his work. It gets on the nerves of his work force, and he's had a tremendous turnover in personnel."

"Did you know that Wembling claims he's doing all this for the natives?"

Smith stared at him. "Then what are we doing here? Ours not to reason why, I suppose."

"Nonsense," Vorish said. "If a military man doesn't know why, his work will suffer while he tries to figure it out for himself. Anyway, there's no special secret why we're here. Wembling may toss the natives a few crumbs, but he's operating mainly for himself, and when he loses time he loses money. Whenever you encounter dirty politics, wherever you encounter it, it was caused by someone losing money, or someone trying to make money. Remember that."

Along with the night, silence descended on the construction site. At the landing field the *Hiln* stood in an oval of light, and there was an unbroken band of light in front of the sentry posts around the entire perimeter. The dormitories and offices were surrounded by another band of light, and revolving lights swept the site, briefly illuminating the beginning of a skeletal framework where the resort building would stand. In spite of the lavish lighting, Wembling did not dare to continue work at night. In the confused play of shadows, the natives that broke in might be injured; or they might contrive really serious damage.

As soon as darkness had settled in, Vorish made another inspection tour. His men were less tense than he'd expected. The bored aplomb of Wembling's veterans seems to have a tranquilizing effect on them. Vorish returned to the *Hiln* and worked on a report, and when the second echelon had been posted he made another inspection. He had resigned himself to a sleepless night, but his men seemed in good spirits, and the night seemed so peaceful that he thought to catch a couple of hours' sleep before inspecting the third echelon. He went to bed, and he was sound asleep when the explosion went off.

The enormous blast was still echoing in the distant hills when Vorish reached the ship's ramp. High-pitched buzzes sounded from several directions as jittery men discharged their weapons. A patrol working inside the perimeter had taken cover, and the men in sentry reserve had sprung to their feet and were jabbering nervously. Down on the construction site, workers were pouring from the dormitories, and Wembling's ground conveyance spun its rollers and lurched away toward the landing field. Vorish waited resignedly.

Another explosion sounded, and then another.

Smith was delivering a preliminary report when the conveyance arrived. Wembling, in his slippers and a flapping robe, scrambled out and ran toward the *Hiln,* his ever present guards close on his heels. Vorish went to the bottom of the ramp to meet him. The echoing *boom* of the explosions continued.

"The natives are using explosives!" Wembling gasped.

"It certainly sounds that way," Vorish agreed.

"We're being attacked!"

"Nonsense. None of the sentries has seen a thing."

"Remember those poison thorns I told you about? What if they have some kind of weapon that shoots them into the construction site?"

"If they were shooting anything at all into the construction site, it would have landed by now," Vorish said dryly. "Nothing has."

Wembling stood silently for a moment, and the two of them listened to the booming explosions. They ranged the full arc of the surrounding forest, but obviously they came from widely varied distances. If there was a pattern, Vorish couldn't detect it.

"I want the sentries reinforced," Wembling said.

"That'd be silly. I'd be left without a reserve."

"I'm relying on you to take charge of the situation," Wembling proclaimed oracularly.

"I've already done so."

Trailing his guards, Wembling shuffled back to his conveyance and was driven away. Smith had loped off into the night while they were talking, so Vorish returned to the *Hiln*'s control room to wait for his report. The explosions continued.

Finally Smith returned. "No one has even seen a flash," he said. "That's maybe understandable considering how thick the forest is, but no one has smelled anything, either, and the wind is in our direction. I think the explosions are taking place a long way off. Nothing like this has ever happened before, and Wembling's people haven't an inkling of what's going on. They say there's only one man on Langri who's likely to know anything about it—an anthropologist named Hort. He was on Wembling's staff, and Wembling fired him because he stood up for the natives. He's living by himself in a native-style dwelling back in the forest. Interestingly enough, he's now a deputy marshal."

Vorish arched his brows. "With what authority?"

"I don't know."

"See him tomorrow and put him on the staff," Vorish said. "I don't mind if he takes the natives' part. It's time someone did."

"I want to see him tonight and ask him what the natives are up to."

"How far?"

"A few kilometers."

"How large a patrol?"

"Three men and myself—just enough to carry lights and com equipment."

Vorish silently pondered the specter of a small patrol of his men taking a stroll along a narrow path in a thick, possibly hostile forest. It seemed a strange midnight occupation for the Space Navy, but he'd seen stranger things, and worlds far weirder than this one.

"I know about the thorns," Smith said. "It's perfectly safe as long as we keep to the center of the path. The paths were made by the natives, and they wouldn't pass that way often enough to make a path if it wasn't safe. Also, they're too bright to be ambushing a patrol from a ship that could incinerate every one of their villages on one pass around the planet."

"We don't know that," Vorish said. "On the other hand, since they haven't harmed anyone yet, I'll risk the assumption that they'd rather start with Wembling than us. Go ahead, then. And before *you* shoot anything, be damned certain it's something you want to kill."

Smith waved a salute and hurried away.

Vorish told a technician to give Smith's patrol a special channel, and then he began to monitor the sentry posts. His men were nervous about the explosions, but they seemed to be holding up well. He caught bits of conversation. A nav muttered, "Whatever they're blowing up, they've got a lot of the stuff," and Wembling's hammerhead replied, "You can't trust the pug-gards as far as you can spit. Let me tell you about the time—"

An officer called in a suggestion that the beach sentries be moved to the forest side of the perimeter. "The natives would like that," Vorish told him dryly. "Especially if the explosions are a diversion to keep our attention on the forest while they attack from the sea."

By that time the technician had Smith's patrol tuned in, and Vorish watched them in three-dimensional projection as they moved along a path, their lights poking holes in the forest's blackness. Several of the explosions sounded alarmingly close by, but Smith, when Vorish asked him, chuckled and said they were kilometers away.

Finally the patrol rounded a bend and came upon a small clearing with a native hut. A bearded man stood in its doorway scowling fiercely at the intruders.

Smith marched up to him. "Aric Hort? I'm Lieutenant Commander Smith. Space Navy. What's causing the explosions?"

"If I had the faintest idea, is there any reason why I should tell you?"

"Do the natives have explosives?" Smith asked.

At that moment one went off close by, with an enormous charge, and both Hort and Smith winced. "You deaf, or something?" Hort demanded. "Of course they do. Not that it's any of your business—or is Wembling claiming sovereignty over the entire continent?"

"Wembling is hiding under his bed," Smith said. "I have no intention of interfering with the natives. I'm just curious about what woke me up."

Suddenly Hort grinned. "If you put it that way, so am I. Let's go have a look."

They moved off into the forest, with Hort leading the way. Explosions continued to sound. Smith, walking just behind Hort, said to him, "Are you positive these natives aren't dangerous?"

Hort halted and faced him. "I've been living near them or with them for almost three years. I've spent most of my time with them, every day, and I've never seen a fight or even a strenuous argument. I'd say they're extremely dangerous, but not in the way you're thinking."

They moved on. Suddenly they came upon a river, which they crossed on a boat rigged as a crude ferry. They regained the path on the opposite side and moved along it at a brisk pace. The forest unfolded monotonously along the path. The night and the com equipment reduced all colors to gray, and the huge flowers on many of the trees had folded delicate petals into strangely shaped defenses against the darkness.

They ferried their way across another river. The explosions were becoming more distant, but Vorish, watching from the safety of the *Hiln* while his men moved farther and farther into an unknown forest, became increasingly concerned.

Smith asked, "Have they ever set off explosives before?"

"No," Hort said. "I didn't know they had any."

"They sound like potent charges. One of them could make a scrap heap of a rather large spaceship."

Hort had no comment. Vorish was on the verge of halting them when suddenly Hort dropped to his knees on the path.

"Stand back!" he snapped.

Smith knelt nearby, holding a light, and one of the navs pointed a scanner. Vorish scrutinized the projected image of the nondescript mass Hort was studying and made nothing of it.

"What is it?" Smith asked.

"I don't know. Can you move the light—there. Darned if it doesn't look like—"

Suddenly Hort began to laugh. The navy men crowded around him and bewilderedly studied the clutter of debris on the path while Hort slumped to the ground convulsed with laughter. He thumped helplessly on the packed dirt with his fist. At irregular intervals the explosions boomed a bizarre accompaniment.

Finally Hort controlled himself sufficiently to be able to speak. "It's the gourds," he gasped.

"It's the gourds," Smith repeated. He was becoming angry. "Is that supposed to tell me something?"

Still laughing, Hort struggled to his feet. "Langri has these enormous gourds. They're bigger than houses —in fact, the natives actually use segments of them for the roofs of their dwellings. They come in all shapes and sizes, and they're used for everything from furniture to utensils. I've been wondering ever since I came here how the damned things reproduce, and now I know— they explode and scatter their spores."

Smith said bitterly, "Do you mean every alien on the planet has been woke up, and we've had this lovely midnight stroll through the forest, just because some vegetables are enjoying their mating season?"

An officer entered the control room and snapped attention. "Excuse me, sir, but—"

Vorish raised his hand. "Just a moment."

Smith was nurturing his anger. "How come these gourds decided all of a sudden to have babies the night the navy landed?"

"Obviously the natives know how to set them off," Hort said.

"Sir," the officer said to Vorish, "there's a native—"

Vorish raised his hand again.

"The natives know how to set them off," Smith said coldly. "Just their idea of a friendly welcome, I suppose."

"Or a way to distract your sentries."

"There's a native asking to see you, sir," the officer persisted.

Vorish turned. "A *native?*"

Hort said, "It wouldn't surprise me in the least if your commanding officer were having an extremely interesting conversation with a young native named Fornri."

"Is his name Fornri?" Vorish asked in a low voice.

"Yes, sir."

"I told him he'd get killed if he tried to go through the perimeter," Hort said. "I told him with all those new lights and sentry posts it'd be impossible, and I could make an appointment for him tomorrow, and he said it was too important to wait and the Plan would get him past the sentries."

"What Plan?" Smith asked.

"The Plan behind everything the natives do. You've been listening to part of it."

Vorish leaned forward and turned off the projection. "I suppose all the sentries and patrols have been watching the forest so they can hear the explosions better, and this Fornri walked right up to Sentry Post Number One without being challenged."

"That he did," the officer said grimly. "He had to pass through the perimeter, avoid three patrols, and follow a route that should have been visible to half the rear-line sentry posts, and no one saw him. I'm going to throw twenty men in the brig."

"I'll look into that later," Vorish said. "Well— I've heard Wembling's side of this, so it's only fair that I hear what the natives have to say. Do you suppose Wembling would let us have an interpreter?"

"I wouldn't know about that, sir, but this native doesn't need one. He speaks Galactic."

Vorish nodded his head. "Of course. He would. This is quite an assignment we've drawn here. Everything is perfectly logical and utterly inexplicable. Gourds explode, but only when they're properly asked. A construction site is under tremendous guard with the navy called in to help, and for no obvious reason. Natives speak Galactic, which as far as I know isn't a native language anywhere in the galaxy. Bring this Galactic-speaking native in."

16

He was clad only in a loincloth, and he entered the *Hiln*'s control room with the superb confidence of one about to take possession of it. He said, "Commander Vorish? I am Fornri."

Vorish did not offer to touch hands. He would give this native a fair hearing, but he wasn't pleased about the commotion that had made the interview possible. He especially wasn't pleased because, if his men had been as alert as he expected them to be, this youngster should have been a corpse right now instead of an emissary, and Vorish could think of nothing that Fornri or any other native might have to say to him that couldn't wait until the morrow or even the next week. He indicated a stool, and as Fornri accepted it he moved up one for himself.

Fornri spoke firmly. "My understanding is that you are members of the Space Navy of the Galactic Federation of Independent Worlds. Is that correct?"

Caught in the act of seating himself, Vorish straightened up and stared. He said blankly, "Yes—"

"On behalf of my government, I ask your assistance in repelling invaders of our world."

The communications duty officer so far forgot himself as to exclaim, "The devil!" Vorish managed to sit down on his second try, and he said calmly, "By 'invaders' I suppose you refer to the construction project."

"I do."

"Your planet has been classified Three-C by the Federation, which places it under the jurisdiction of the

144

Colonial Bureau. Wembling and Company have a charter from the Bureau. They are hardly to be considered invaders."

Fornri spoke with exaggerated deliberation. "My government has a treaty with the Galactic Federation of Independent Worlds. The treaty guarantees the independence of Langri and also guarantees the assistance of the Federation in the event that Langri is invaded. I am calling upon the Federation to fulfill its treaty obligations."

Vorish turned to the duty officer. "Let's have the index."

"Shall I put it on that screen, sir?"

"Yes. Dial Langri for me, please."

The screen at Vorish's side flickered to life, and he spoke aloud as he read. "Initial contact in '44. Classified Three-C in '46. There's no mention of any treaty."

Fornri took a tube of polished wood from his belt and slipped out a rolled parchment. He passed it to Vorish, who unrolled it and smoothed it flat. He stared at it so long, and so incredulously, that the duty officer came to look over his shoulder.

"That's the seal of the battle cruiser *Rirga!*" the duty officer exclaimed. "It's a certified copy of the original."

Vorish tapped the parchment with one finger. "Where is the original?"

"It is preserved in a safe place," Fornri said. "We requested copies at the time the treaty was signed, and the naval officers supplied them."

Vorish looked again at the screen. "There's something exceedingly peculiar about this. The treaty is dated two months after the initial contact, and it classifies the world Five-X. That would mean that the '46 action was a reclassification. The index should say so, but it doesn't."

"There'd be no possible explanation for almost a two-year delay in classifying a world," the duty officer said. "But is the treaty genuine?"

"Where would these natives get the knowledge and equipment to produce a forgery on this order?" Vorish turned to Fornri. "If this is genuine, and I see no reason to doubt it, there's skulduggery here on an order I wouldn't have thought possible. Tell me what happened."

The next morning Aric Hort called to keep an appointment made by way of Smith's com equipment the night before. He took Vorish for a walk along the beach, and at a point beyond the construction site perimeter, where the coast curved northward for a short distance, they found eight native boys waiting for them with a boat. They had a swift ride along the coast, past several native villages, and eventually the shore curved west again and Vorish saw the spectacular silhouette of a modern building perched on a bluff by the sea.

"So that's the medical center," he said. "Would you mind explaining—"

"Not until you've seen it. I promised Talitha she could have first crack at you before I stuff you with misleading information."

"Talitha?"

"Miss Warr. Wembling's niece. The medical center is her pet project."

"I gather that you don't think much of it."

"I think it's tremendous," Hort said. "I just wish the natives hadn't had to pay such a stiff price for it. When a man has an infected toenail, we ought to be able to heal him without cutting off his head."

They turned shoreward and beached their boat beside two other native boats that were drawn up on the beach. Someone had gone to considerable trouble to construct a paved walk that curved to the top of the bluff on a gentle slope, but another path, crude but well worn, went directly and steeply to the top, and Hort led him that way without apology.

Talitha Warr received him graciously and introduced him to Dr. Fenell, the Wembling and Company staff doctor who spent two half days a week at the medical center and also was on call for emergencies. Miss Warr was capable of ornamenting any surroundings and also seemed dazzlingly efficient. Dr. Fenell was a gawky young man, obviously inexperienced, and certainly not the sort Vorish would have expected to find in such an adventurous project. He wondered if the man was a failure attempting to rehabilitate himself.

The doctor followed Miss Warr about as though she were the doctor and he the nursing assistant, and he fawned over her at every opportunity. Vorish observed Aric Hort glaring at the two of them. Obviously there was a rivalry here that perhaps accounted for Hort's attitude toward the medical center and made his judgments suspect, but that was no concern to Vorish. He would form his own judgments.

So he politely observed the various tiny clinics, most of them without signs of recent use, from magno and hydrotherapy to nutrionics. He professed to admire the pediatrics ward, with its adjoining children's playground, though he wondered how the native children managed to cope with such radically civilized toys.

What impressed him most was not the clinic but the fact that it seemed to have so little use. The only patients he saw were a few adults seated in the magnificent park that overlooked the sea, and every one of them was a bone-fracture case. Watching them as they came and went in self-powered invalid chairs from the native-type buildings at the rear, he decided to ask his own medical staff to examine this puzzle. Either the Langrian natives were an unusually healthy people, or they were using the medical center only for a few medical problems they couldn't handle themselves.

Otherwise, if Miss Warr expected to overwhelm him with her uncle's generosity to the natives, it was just as well that she would not be seeing the report he intended to file. Vorish had seen medical centers on many worlds. Any time a man in his command became seriously ill far from regular navy facilities, Vorish had to obtain for him the best medical care conveniently available, and he always made it a point to inspect the facilities himself. He would not willingly place one of his men in the care of Langri's medical center. The building and its setting were attractive, but its medical facilities were at best mediocre, and there was no trained staff at all. Miss Warr, for all of her enthusiasm, was a novice, and the doctor could not possibly have the broad spectrum of experience so essential to a medical director. Wembling and Company had in fact made no more than a gesture at providing medical care for the natives.

But Vorish did not denigrate the gesture. He well understood that even a badly run center could produce spectacular results on a primitive world that had been completely without medical care.

"That's the story," Miss Warr said finally. "I insisted that the center be built *first*, and here it is. We've already inoculated the entire population against the worst diseases, and there's a regular inoculation program for children. Diseases that formerly caused certain death now no longer require hospitalization, and we haven't had a death from sickness since the center opened. We're making spectacular improvements in infant mortality, and broken bones, which in the past frequently caused death or lifetime disability, now are routinely handled. I still have nightmares about that child I saw die, and it's the greatest satisfaction I've ever experienced to know that it won't happen again."

"To be sure," Vorish murmured. "I see that you're training native nurses."

"We call them medical assistants. We have youngsters of both sexes studying here, and we let them perform all kinds of routine chores under supervision. As much as possible we convert our cases into medical lessons for them. Of course the natives won't be able to achieve the competence to run the center themselves until they're able to send their bright young people to medical schools on other worlds and make fully qualified doctors of them. That's many years away, but the problem isn't urgent. The resort will have its own medical center, so there'll be doctors available until the natives can provide their own."

"Thank you very much, Miss Warr," Vorish said. "I'll send my own medical officer to visit you. I'm sure he'll be interested."

Vorish and Hort emerged at the rear of the center,

near the native buildings, and they took the paved walk back to the beach. As soon as it had curved out of sight of the center, Vorish said to Hort, *"Now* will you answer my questions?"

"You saw it yourself," Hort said. "She thinks the medical center justifies everything."

"I want to know what you think. I've heard Fornri's story, and I believe him. He couldn't possibly have forged that treaty, and anyway my records officer has come up with an old index tape that he fortunately neglected to discard, and on it Langri is classified Five-X. How did Wembling get the classification switched to Three-C?"

"How does a big-time operator manage anything?" Hort asked bitterly. "Political pressure, bribery, trading favors—if there's a way, he knows how to find it. Probably we'll never know how he did it. The question should be—what can be done about it while there's still time to save the natives?"

"Save the natives? Surely Wembling isn't plotting anything more sinister than stopping their harassment. He started his project with the idea of helping them."

"He did not," Hort said hotly. "Wembling never has any idea except to help himself. He was trying to make a record so he'd get a diplomatic appointment to a world with more potential loot. The moment he got the notion he could make more money from Langri resorts than he could from mining concessions somewhere else, he sent Ayns off to Colomus to get Langri reclassified."

"I see. Even so, if the resort is as successful as Wembling predicts, ten per cent of the profits will produce a whopping income for the natives. Why are they fighting him?"

"Haven't they the right to reject the ten per cent *and* the resort if they don't want either?"

"Of course. That is, they should have had that right under the violated treaty. But it does seem to me that they could have compromised—received the benefits from the resort and at the same time controlled it. Wembling did try to get their permission first, Fornri said. And when he couldn't, *then* he worked the reclassification."

They had reached the beach. The natives pushed the boat into the water and stood waiting for them, but Hort and Vorish turned aside and sought the forest's edge and a fallen tree to sit on. The boys grinned and pulled the boat back onto the beach.

"It's a matter of life and death," Hort said.

Vorish regarded him skeptically. "You'll have to explain that."

"These natives have a precarious existence. Perhaps a small resort, properly controlled, wouldn't affect the world's ecology, but Wembling doesn't do anything in a small way. He's building a huge resort, and he's planning others, and already his construction and the water recreation of his workers is seriously affecting the natives' food supply. If Wembling isn't stopped, there won't be any native population left to enjoy that ten per cent when and if Wembling and Company gets around to paying it."

"Are you serious?"

"Deadly serious. It's a scientific fact that a people can become accustomed to certain kinds of foods and unable to eat others. There are dozens of worlds where local populations are fond of native herbs that make visitors ill."

"The Space Navy can tell you a few things about that," Vorish said. "Our men come from all the member worlds of the Federation. Space Navy ships have to have dietary classifications, so that men accustomed to the same kinds of food can serve together."

"Langri's problem is much more serious than that. For an unknown number of generations, these natives have been existing on a diet composed almost entirely of koluf, a Langrian sea creature. It's an extremely rich and nutritious food, but its components of vitamins and minerals and the rest are peculiar to the world of Langri and unlike any food ever eaten by humans anywhere else. By evolution or adaptation the natives' bodies are accustomed to this, and I'm afraid they won't be able to assimilate normal human foods. And the construction activity is ruining their hunting grounds."

"In other words," Vorish mused, "the natives can't eat anything but this koluf, and Wembling and Company are destroying it."

"Not 'destroying.' Driving it away. As far back as the natives can remember, koluf always have followed regular feeding routes along the coast. Now they're changing them."

"I see."

"Would it be possible to have your medical staff investigate this for me?" Hort asked.

"The ability of the natives to eat normal food? Certainly. Now what's this about a Plan? And what are 'conjunctions'?"

Hort chuckled. "Fornri means 'injunctions,' and there've been a lot of them. The court held up Wembling's work for months."

"I heard about that. It cost the natives a fortune and they lost every case."

"It bought them some time, though, and that's what they say they need. Time for the Plan."

"And what's the Plan?"

"I don't know. Whatever it is, they believe in it absolutely. The Plan said Fornri should see you the moment you landed, so he insisted on seeing you last night. I tried to convince him he'd get himself killed, and he said he'd follow the Plan and be perfectly safe and every hour was important. Now you know as much about it as I do."

"He easily could have got himself killed," Vorish said. "On the other hand, he didn't, so maybe he *was* perfectly safe. All things considered, this seems like an extremely complicated problem." He got to his feet. "I have an appointment with Wembling, and it wouldn't do to keep a busy and important man waiting."

They walked toward the boat, and the grinning boys launched it again and stood waiting for them.

"I don't think the natives can beat Wembling in court," Vorish said. "He'll have too much money, and too much influence, and the trickiest lawyers money can buy.

"Where do you stand in this?"

"Squarely in the middle," Vorish said. "I'm abso-

lutely impartial, and Wembling isn't going to like that.
I'll protect him from the natives, but I'm also going to
protect the natives from Wembling, in every way I can.
And while I'm doing that, I'm going to report this
situation at once, in more detail than Fleet Headquarters will like, and request action to get the treaty
restored. The problem on this world isn't what the
natives can or can't eat. The problem is a treaty that
was negotiated in good faith on both sides and now has
been brazenly violated. The honor of the Space Navy is
involved."

"You don't realize how potent Wembling's influence
is. Your headquarters will file that report and forget it."

"Then I'll take action to get it unfiled," Vorish
said with a grin.

The natives weren't talking about their Plan, but
Wembling talked rather too much about his. He took
Vorish and Smith to his planning office, where an impressive scale model of the resort was on display. There
he bit a capsule, breathed pungent colored smoke into
their faces, and orated statistics.

"A thousand accommodations," he said proudly,
"and most of them suites."

Smith stooped for a closer look. "Are those things
on the beach terrace *swimming pools?*"

"Right. There'll also be an indoor pool. Some
people can't stand even mildly salty water, you know,
and some will be afraid of the ocean creatures, even
though there's no danger. Well—what d'ya think of it?"

"It's very—impressive," Vorish murmured.

"There'll be two main dining room and half a
dozen small ones that'll specialize in food from famous
places. I'll have a whole fleet of over- and underwater
boats for recreation and sightseeing. You may not believe it, but there are millions of people in the galaxy
who've never seen an ocean. Why, there are worlds
where people don't even have enough water to bathe
in. Some worlds even have to import their air. If their
populations can come to Langri now and then and live
a little, they'll need a lot fewer doctors and psychiatrists.

This project of mine is nothing less than a service to humanity."

Vorish and Smith exchanged glances. "From the looks of this, the only humanity you'll benefit will be the poor, broken-down millionaires," Vorish observed.

Wembling waved a hand disarmingly. "This is only the beginning. Have to put the thing on a sound financial basis right from the start, you know. Later there'll be plenty of room for the little fellows—not in water-front hotels, of course, but there'll be community beaches and hotels with rights of access and that sort of thing. My staff has it worked out. Once this resort opens for business—"

The construction sounds outside the window had halted. Wembling dashed for the door, with Vorish and Smith close on his heels. Once outside, they stopped and watched him sprint to the nearest work point, where three of his hammerheads were struggling with a native.

The young man had attached himself to a girder that was about to be swung aloft. The workers were trying to remove him, but he clung stubbornly. Wembling dashed up waving his arms angrily and shouting orders. None seemed to be needed. The workers had to remove the native without harming him, and they were doing their best. Eventually they managed to pry him loose and carry him away.

"What can they possibly gain from that?" Smith asked.

"Time," Vorish said. "Time for their Plan."

"Has it occurred to you that this Plan might consist of a genuine uprising with real explosives?"

"No, and from what I've seen of the natives, that's the last thing I'd expect. What do you think of Wembling?"

"He's a self-activated power unit."

"Much as I loathe the man, I have to admire the way he gets things done," Vorish said. "I'd hate to be a native and have to fight for my life against him. They're intelligent enough to know they can't evict him with force. I'm afraid, though, that they're trying to match wits with him. They don't stand a chance that way, either."

Wembling got the work started again, and then he trotted back to join them. "If you'd put in the kind of defensive line I want, I wouldn't have that trouble," he complained.

"We both know I'm not going to do it," Vorish told him. "An electronic barrier would cost a fortune, and the dead natives it produced would be my responsibility. I wouldn't even suggest it. At the very worst, the natives are only a minor nuisance to you."

"They make the men nervous. Everyone has to keep alert every minute so he won't accidentally kill one of the puggards."

"That should make them highly efficient workers," Vorish observed dryly.

"Maybe, but the natives mucking about the project slow me down. I want 'em kept out."

"Frankly, I think you're exaggerating the problem. One or two interruptions a day doesn't slow you down much—certainly not enough to justify keeping a naval battle cruiser here. However, I have my orders. I'll use everything I have short of violence to keep them out."

Wembling grinned good-naturedly. "I guess I can't ask more than that."

He looped his arm through Vorish's and led him back to the planning office.

17

The *Hiln*'s medical officer refused to pose as an expert nutritionist, but he saw nothing absurd in Aric Hort's notion that the natives might be unable to assimilate other foods after living on koluf for generations. "It's easily tested," he said. "Let's put some natives on navy rations and see what happens."

Hort arranged the experiment, and nothing at all happened. Vorish gratefully marked it off as one less thing to worry about.

As the days spun out into weeks, he dutifully tightened his protective screen around the construction site, his men became better versed in the natives' infiltration tactics, and work stoppages decreased almost to zero. Wembling was pleased, and the construction project began to take on a skeletal resemblance to the lavish model in Wembling's planning office.

Vorish saw Aric Hort only on the infrequent occasions when he wanted information. The only natives he saw were those captured on the construction site. He politely declined invitations to native festivals, just as he declined Wembling's social invitations. The air of impending tragedy at the native villages, and the natives' blind faith in a futile Plan, disconcerted him. He easily could have become too sympathetic to them. On the other hand, Wembling was able to exude charm and infectious enthusiasm when he chose, and too much exposure easily could have biased Vorish in the opposite direction.

He saw himself as the impartial referee in a dispute, and if he got too familiar with either party, that impartiality might suffer. It disturbed him deeply that he was increasingly convinced that Wembling was right: the resort *would* be a splendid asset for Langri and its people. Hort's and the natives' fears undoubtedly were silly bugaboos that would be forgotten without regret once the benefits of the resort became a reality.

Concerning the shamefully violated treaty, though, he had no choice but to fight fiercely for justice and a full restoration of the natives' control of their own destiny.

The dilemma seemed irreconcilable.

Because the natives were declining something that obviously would benefit them greatly, perhaps the resort should be forced upon them, as one forced a child to take the medicine he needed. On the other hand, Aric

Hort, an anthropologist, stoutly maintained that whole populations had been destroyed by such stupid benevolence, and he could cite which ones they were.

If Wembling's activities were interfering with the natives in any way, Vorish couldn't detect it. The hunting fleets went out daily, and the invitations to attend the natives' feasts and festivals arrived with monotonous regularity. He could not share Hort's belief that the resort posed a threat to the natives' existence.

And yet there had been a treaty, and there was such a thing as honor—the Federation's and the Space Navy's. And if the resort offered benefits for the natives, Vorish wasn't overlooking the fact that it would benefit Wembling much more. The treaty had to be reinstated, following which Wembling could do what he should have done in the first place: convince the natives about those lavish benefits, and build the resort with their consent. Perhaps they would let him have ten per cent, in which case it would be interesting to see if he still considered that share as munificent as he had when he was offering it to the natives.

As Hort predicted, headquarters had ignored Vorish's report on the treaty. When he politely asked what action was being taken, headquarters gave him a polite Z in response: "We assume authority and responsibility."

Then Hort came to see him and spoke tersely, and when he left one of Vorish's worries had been restored: the natives they thought were participating in the food test had been cheating. They ate little if any of the navy food and continued to eat native food, and the test was a farce.

"They claim they were so hungry they had to," Hort said glumly. "That ought to tell us something. I hope so, because it's as much as we're likely to learn."

If Hort could find volunteers who seemed to understand the experiment, they would try again. He was not optimistic about his success. A native accustomed to koluf meat would have to be a genuine martyr to agree to subsist on Space Navy rations, even in a short experiment.

While Vorish was still meditating this restored worry, Wembling came with a request for expanding the protective perimeter around the construction site. He wanted to enlarge it. He also wanted to begin work at a new construction site far down the coast.

Vorish brusquely refused. He had insufficient men for the area they were screening now. Further, he was becoming concerned about them. They had been vegetating on this paradise planet long enough. Specialists who didn't use their skills soon stopped being specialists. It was time he took the *Hiln* back into space where it belonged.

Talitha Warr invited him to dinner at the medical center. Vorish persuaded himself that this was neutral ground and went, and the food she served was delectable beyond description.

"It's koluf," she explained. "It's the staple of the natives' diet—imagine a diet with a staple like that! But never ask to see a live one, or your koluf palate will be ruined for months."

The next day Vorish sent for Aric Hort and inquired as to the possibility of obtaining enough koluf for an occasional navy meal.

Hort regarded him with horror. "I keep telling you that the natives don't have enough for themselves. Don't you believe me?"

"I somehow never made the connection," Vorish confessed. "I know it's their principal food—we talked about that—but Miss Warr was serving it, and—"

"The hospital has a priority, but the food supplied to it is supposed to be for the sick. And because Talitha always gets anything she asks for, she won't believe there's a shortage."

"I see."

"No, you don't. I *know* the natives aren't getting enough to eat. The koluf catch is down at least a fourth. They're starving, but so slowly that it's hardly noticeable. As the catch continues to drop, which it will, they'll starve more quickly. We *must* find a dietary supplement. I'd like to try another experiment."

"What sort of experiment?"

"Since some of your men are living in Wembling's dormitories, could we bring a few native children to the *Hiln* for a short stay? They could be fed nothing but navy food—they couldn't cheat if we kept them on the ship—and perhaps we could learn something."

"Perhaps," Vorish agreed. "Find out if the natives are willing, and I'll find out whether my medical staff would object to running a nursery for a few days."

The medical staff didn't object; the natives did. They saw no need for such an experiment. They had their Plan. Hort promised to continue his efforts to persuade them.

First there was the violated treaty, and then there was Vorish's report that headquarters had tried to Z out of existence, and now the independent world of Langri had sunk so low that the natives were unable to confer privately with their attorneys. Wembling monitored their communications center and read all of their messages. They were afraid to send letter mail on his supply ships, because they knew that he would read that, too.

Lieutenant Commander Smith discussed the problem with Fornri, and then he brought it to Vorish.

"The natives certainly have a legal right to private communication with their attorneys," Vorish said, "but since headquarters maintains that no Langri problem exists, it wouldn't be wise to involve ourselves in an official solution to a non-existent problem."

"How about a private solution?" Smith suggested. "I'll send the communications as coming from myself, and I'll ask the attorneys to suggest some way in which they could be representing me—just in case anyone inquires. As for their letters to the natives, they can double-wrap them and address the outer to me. I'll pledge to deliver the inner one unopened."

"Good idea," Vorish said. "There's no naval regulation that forbids your forwarding a friend's mail."

"Too bad headquarters Z'd your report. I thought they'd have to react one way or the other—either with a public fuss or with a private order to keep your mouth shut."

"They will," Vorish promised grimly. "Wembling was in this morning, and he took me for a tour of the territory he wants to add to the construction site. Know what he intends to put there? A golf course! This afternoon I'll see Fornri about it. And yes—I'm certain I can get a reaction to my report."

As Vorish walked along the central avenue of the native village, cordially exchanging greetings with the natives he passed, he noticed Talitha Warr seated a short distance up one of the curving side streets. Beside her was a child swathed in blankets, and her attitude was grave and intense.

He turned aside and sat down beside her. "What do we have here?" he asked, scrutinizing the child's small, serious face.

"It's something new," she said. "A number of the children have come down with it, and we haven't been able to figure out what it is."

"Nothing serious, I hope."

"We don't know. They get sick and they stay sick, and we haven't the facilities to handle an epidemic. All of our beds at the center are filled."

"Are only the children affected?"

She nodded. "The young children. They're a stubbornly healthy people, but this world has some very peculiar diseases."

Vorish took leave of her and walked on up the central avenue.

At the isolated hut beyond the village, Fornri stepped out to meet him. They touched hands, and Vorish unfolded a large map onto a gourd table.

"Did Aric tell you what I wanted to talk about?" he asked.

"Yes."

"This is a map of Wembling's construction site and the land beyond it. He wants to push the perimeter back into the forest so he can clear land for a golf course. Do you know what golf is?"

"Airk explained it to me," Fornri said.

"If you don't see the point, don't let that bother

you. Some people who play the game don't see the point. This new territory would lengthen the perimeter enormously, and I've already told Wembling I haven't sufficient men. I think he'll go ahead and use his own men for guards."

"Perhaps we could ask our attorneys to make a suit about this golf course," Fornri said. "The charter says Mr. Wembling can develop our world's natural resources. Is golf a natural resource?"

"I don't know," Vorish said. "It sounds like the sort of question attorneys would enjoy immensely. By all means suggest it to them. This is what I wanted to see you about. There's an abandoned village in the forest." He pointed to the map. "Here. Did Wembling move your people out of there?"

"No."

"I'm sorry to hear that," Vorish said, grinning rue-fully. "If he'd forced your people from their homes, I could have done something about it. Why is this village off by itself in the forest when all the others are located on the coast?"

"It is the village of our teacher, and it is no longer in use."

"Teacher?" Vorish echoed blankly. "What sort of teacher?"

"Every sort," Fornri said with a smile.

"You interest me." Vorish helped himself to a gourd chair. "Tell me honestly. Does this village have some special meaning for you?"

"It has a very special meaning."

"Teacher? Guru? Philosopher? Prophet? A very special meaning, you say."

"Yes. Very special."

"And a village with a very special meaning—especially if the teacher is a religious leader—can become a shrine," Vorish suggested. "Could we say that you left it exactly as it was in memory of your teacher?"

"Yes. That is true."

"And you have permitted no feet to profane it since his parting. I like that. It just might be the angle I've been looking for." He grinned at Fornri. "I think

I'm going to get you some time for your Plan. I also think I'm going to get my report unfiled."

On his way out of the village Vorish encountered Aric Hort, and the two of them walked together toward Vorish's boat.

"Did you see the sick children?" Hort asked.

"Miss Warr was telling me about them. I gather that this world has some rather peculiar diseases."

Hort turned on him furiously. "There wouldn't be any disease if the children weren't weak from hunger. The whole population is weak from hunger, but the children are the most susceptible to the disease. Neither she nor her precious doctor will face up to that."

Vorish said, "As long as there's no proof—"

"When the koluf catch is down more than a fourth, what more proof do you want?"

"Have the natives consented to your experiment?"

"We'll start tomorrow."

"Strange anyone should have to be hungry on such a fertile world," Vorish mused, looking at the magnificent growth of forest.

"Don't you know that human food won't grow here?"

"No. I hadn't heard that."

"When we first came here I got Wembling to import all kinds of seeds," Hort said. "The few things that grew were mutated and nutritionally suspect."

"So the natives are forced to eat koluf, which would be a wonderful fate if they had enough of it."

"Right. The water activity by construction and naval personnel, the machinery and construction noises transmitted through the water, the pollutants that are dumped offshore—all this and maybe other things are driving the koluf into deep water where the natives can't catch them. The situation is going to get a lot worse, and it may never get better because once the resort opens the tourists will ruin the hunting grounds much more thoroughly. Yes, the natives are hungry, and the children are showing the effects of it first."

"Strange," Vorish said. "One would think the

medical center would detect a thing like that immediately and do something about it."

Hort said bitterly, "The most the medical center can do is make it possible for the natives to starve to death in perfect health."

On his return, Vorish went to see Wembling. "About that golf course," he said. "What do you plan to do with the native village?"

"Knock it down," Wembling told him. "It's abandoned. Probably it's been years since the natives have used it."

"Let's go have a look at it," Vorish suggested.

Wembling went willingly. Probably he hoped to persuade Vorish to extend the perimeter. His machines, well guarded, already were biting deeply into the forest. Wembling led the way around them and along a path that led to the village. It consisted of an oval-shaped clearing with a cluster of native dwellings at one end.

"See? It's just an abandoned village," Wembling said.

He began poking into the huts. Vorish, looking about him, saw an utterly strange object: native cloth stretched between two trees and plastered with a smooth layer of clay, and the dried clay bristled with mathematical symbols. "What the devil's this?" he exclaimed.

Wembling emerged from a hut. "It's been abandoned for years," he called to Vorish. "Anyway, I couldn't possibly leave it here. It's right on the eighth green."

Vorish was staring at the math symbols. "Why—it's a problem in celestial navigation! Then this *is* a teacher's village! But what would the natives want with mathematics on this order?" He turned away shaking his head.

Vorish joined Wembling as he emerged from investigating another hut. "Sorry," Vorish said. "I can't let you touch this place without the natives' permission."

Wembling playfully prodded him in the ribs. "Don't be silly. You wouldn't tie up my whole project for a few grass huts. Let the natives sue me. The court won't stop me—it'll just award them the value of the huts, which can't amount to more than a credit and a half, and the suit will cost them fifty thousand. The faster they use up their money, the sooner they'll stop harassing me."

Vorish said sternly, "The navy is not here for your exclusive use. My orders specifically call for the protection of the natives and their property, just as I protect you and your property. Maybe the court won't stop you, but I will."

He strode away, leaving Wembling to glare after him. "But he thinks I'm bluffing," Vorish told Smith afterward. "I notice he has the machines pointed at the village. Some people can't resist calling a bluff, even if they know it'll explode when touched."

"I hope you realize that you're sticking your neck out," Smith said.

"A naval commander who's afraid to stick his neck out isn't worth a damn."

When the machines broke through into the village clearing, Vorish had his men waiting. He stood with Smith on the high ground near the landing field and watched Wembling waddle up to a work crew, gesture, and step back. A machine edged forward and smashed the nearest hut. Vorish signaled his own men into action. An armed navy squad moved down the slope, weapons at the ready, and took possession of the village. The machines clanked to a stop, and as Vorish and Smith approached, Wembling stormed to meet them.

"Did you get the natives' permission for this?" Vorish demanded.

It cost Wembling an effort to master his rage. "I have a charter. How I use it is none of your business."

"I think it is," Vorish said. "Shall we have a legal test? Maybe the court will award you the value of the huts." He turned to Smith. "Place these men under protective arrest and stop all work on the construction site. A sacred place has been desecrated, and we'll have to use the utmost care to prevent a native revolt."

He went back to his quarters on the *Hiln* and worked on his report. Smith came in later, grinning broadly.

"Well, it's done," he said. "Wembling is confined to quarters. His project is closed down and his entire force has an indefinite vacation. The workers are delighted and Wembling is apoplectic. Are you sure that's what you wanted?"

"That's what I wanted. There's a massive conspiracy to cover up Wembling's shenanigans here, and I know of only one person who has enough influence, and is capable of making enough noise, to force headquarters to take action."

"Who's that?"

"Wembling. You and I have to use the chain of command. He can broadcast complaints in all directions, at the top of his voice. If he gets mad enough, he will."

"He's mad enough. He's sending messages furiously. I was going to suggest closing his com center."

Vorish shook his head. "I want every message he sends to go through promptly. About the time headquarters grasps the significance of my report, his complaints will hit it from a dozen different directions. I'd like to see it Z Langri this time!"

Wembling's work had been at a dead halt for three weeks when Vorish next called at the native village. Talitha Warr had taken over a large dwelling to use as a children's hospital, and he saw her at work there, though she was much too preoccupied with her young charges to notice him.

He wondered if Hort had told her of the sober preliminary report from the *Hiln*'s medical staff: the children in Hort's experiment were indeed undernourished, all of them, and as far as the staff could determine, navy rations did nothing to correct that. The experiment was continuing, but the staff was disposed to give Hort's theory a qualified endorsement: the natives were so thoroughly adapted to their diet of koluf that only a very similar food could successfully supplement their diets. The staff now was attempting to figure out what might constitute a similar food.

In the grove of trees at the top of the avenue,

Fornri and Aric Hort were seated in gourd chairs talking quietly. They made Vorish welcome and called for another chair and drinking gourds. Nearby, several elderly natives lay talking in hammocks that swung gently in the sea breeze. Vorish noted their leisurely conversation and long, meditative silences and reflected on the wisdom of the natives in placing the burden of leadership on Fornri and not on the Elder. The menace of a Wembling could not be coped with by the hammock talk of the elderly.

Fornri said anxiously, "Is it true that you will suffer harm from helping us?"

"I'll be threatened with all kinds of dire consequences," Vorish said. "I already have been, by Wembling, as recently as this morning. The worst that's likely to happen is that I'll be recalled and spoken to sternly. Anything more serious would require a public airing of this mess, which is the last thing Wembling's friends want."

"The commander is an optimist," Aric Hort said. "He's bought time for your precious Plan, and he may pay for it with his naval career. There's an admiral on the way here, and his first action will be to turn Wembling and his men loose and arrest Commander Vorish."

"This particular admiral is an old friend of mine," Vorish said with a smile. "If he arrests me, he'll do it affectionately."

Hort gestured disgustedly. "If Wembling has anything to say about it—and he will—he'll have the commander's ears on a platter, barbecued. I'd feel much better about this if you'd made some use of the time that he bought. If your Plan is to hold out and harass Wembling until he goes away, I promise you that he won't."

Leaving the village, Hort and Vorish found Talitha Warr sitting at the edge of the beach. She had been gazing morosely out to sea. "I can't understand it," she said. "The sick list grows longer every day."

Hort had been in a savage mood throughout the interview with Fornri, and now he turned on her furiously. "You can't understand it? You mean you *still* can't see what is happening? Are you blind?"

"What—what do you mean?"

"An entire population is in the preliminary stages of starvation, and you can't understand why the sick list grows. Do you know how many koluf this village caught yesterday? Just two, and they were small. Normally it takes sixteen to twenty to feed a village this size. Try eating one eighth of your usual diet and see how your strength lasts."

She tried to meet his eyes and failed. For a suspenseful moment she stared at the lines her foot was drawing in the moist sand. Then she got to her feet and walked toward the village.

Hort called after here, "Where are you going?"

She did not answer. Vorish and Hort exchanged glances and followed after her. She went to the large dwelling she was using for a hospital, and they waited outside while she moved slowly from one child to another. When she emerged her face was white.

"I *was* blind," she whispered.

"Have you looked at the old people lately?" Hort demanded. "The koluf hunters have to keep up their strength—hunting koluf is a tremendous physical struggle, and there'd be instantaneous starvation the moment the hunters became weak. The hunters eat first, and the old people who contribute the least and have the least to lose eat last. They lie in their hammocks and wait for death. Haven't you noticed that a fire of death is almost a nightly occurrence at every village?"

"I was blind," she whispered again. "But why didn't Dr. Fenell recognize it?"

"Malnutrition isn't a civilized disease. He probably never saw a case before."

"Uncle will have to import food for the natives."

"It's too late," Hort said. "That should have been thought of before the construction started. Commander Vorish's doctor has been trying to feed navy rations to the native children. He hasn't been able to find a food that gives them a significant amount of nourishment. Humans accustomed to eating nothing but koluf can't assimilate other foods."

Talitha buried her face in her hands. "It's my fault.

I suggested the resort to Uncle. I talked him into it."

"Maybe you did or maybe you didn't," Hort said grimly, "but I don't think anyone is going to talk him out of it."

Vorish turned out an honor guard when Admiral Milford Corning arrived on the command cruiser *Maldaro*. The admiral, a crusty, fussy little officer whose men affectionately called him—out of his hearing— "the Old Woman," paused at the top of the ramp to receive Vorish's salute, and then he marched down and touched hands with him.

He said, "Good to see you, Jim," and Vorish responded, "You're looking well, sir," and they moved off to inspect the guard.

When they reached the end of the last line, Corning said, "That's as much ego lub as I can stand for one day. Now let's go where we can talk."

"Your quarters or mine?" Vorish asked.

The admiral sniffed the sea air. "Jim. I've been in space for six months. Let's have a look at that beach."

They strolled out beyond the perimeter and seated themselves on boulders where the surf washed gently beneath their feet. The devastation of the construction site was hidden from them; the nearest sentry was fifty meters away. Corning sniffed the sea breeze again, and observed, "Nice place here. Your men look as though they'd enjoyed it. You're looking pretty good yourself." He paused. "Jim, just what *is* going on here?"

"I don't suppose headquarters showed you my reports," Vorish said, "so I had copies made for you."

He handed them to Corning, and then he walked a few paces along the beach and stood watching the lapping waves while the admiral quickly perused the reports.

Finally Corning said, "All right—I've read enough to get the idea. I'll go through them carefully tonight. What official action did they take?"

"None," Vorish said.

"You mean—you formally submitted these reports, and headquarters took no action at all?"

"Neither report was acknowledged. When I asked to be informed as to action taken, headquarters Z'd them."

Corning's lips shaped a soundless whistle. "I agree with you absolutely. It's a damnable mess, and eventually heads will roll, but that's no concern of yours. Your duty was to report the situation, which you did. Sit down here."

Vorish perched himself on an adjacent boulder.

"Now then. What's this nonsense about a few native huts?"

"According to my orders, I'm an impartial referee here," Vorish said. "I'm to maintain the peace, which means that I protect Wembling against any excesses perpetrated by the natives, but I also protect the natives against infringement upon their customs, property, sacred places, and so on. Paragraph seven."

"I've read it."

"The idea being—I assume—that if the natives are treated properly Federation citizens and property are less likely to need protection. Those few huts are called, by the natives, 'The Teacher's Village,' and the place seems to have a religious significance to them."

"Ah! That would make it a sacred place in terms of your orders. I take it that Wembling busted right in and started tearing the place apart."

"That he did."

"And you'd warned him ahead of time that he had to have the natives' permission, and he laughed it off. Up to that point your conduct was not only proper but commendable, and no one will fault you. But why did you have to close Wembling down and stop his work completely? Why didn't you just make him put his golf course somewhere else? If he'd complained about that, he'd have been laughed at. By stopping his operation you've cost him time and money, and now he has a valid grievance—and he has plenty of political influence."

"I closed him down for his own protection," Vorish said.

"His own—*protection?*" Corning echoed blankly.

"He'd defiled a sacred place. If the natives had

retaliated, I would have been responsible. So I placed him under guard and restricted his workers."

Corning burst into laughter. "That's very good! For his own protection! All right—I'll support that. I think I can keep you from being shot."

"Is that what they were planning?" Vorish asked with a grin.

"They were—are—planning to do their worst," the admiral said soberly. "I don't like it, but I have my orders. You'll return to Galaxia on the *Hiln*, under arrest, to stand court-martial."

"I'm glad to hear that. I'm looking forward to describing Wembling's iniquities for the public record."

"That's the last thing headquarters will want, and if you insist on a public court-martial they'll probably tell you to forget it and give you a commendation. So insist."

"I'll insist," Vorish promised. "A private hearing wouldn't accomplish a thing—except maybe get me shot. I'm glad I'm leaving Langri in capable hands."

"Not in my hands, you're not," Corning said. "Not for long. The 984th Squadron is on its way to take over. Eleven ships. Headquarters is taking no chances on the Langri situation getting out of hand. The commander is Vice Admiral Ernst Dallman. A good man. Know him?"

18

Submaster Jarvis Jarnes presented himself to the court in the only manner possible—with temerity. Although the Justice His Eminence Blorr Figawn had not precisely said so, his manner on the occasion of Jarnes's previous appearance clearly indicated that His Eminence was sick of the sight of him, and His Eminence had a long memory. And Jarnes himself had lost track of the number of unsuccessful actions he had undertaken for the people of Langri.

His Eminence greeted Jarnes with resignation and a prolonged scowl. "Must we go through this again, Submaster Jarnes?"

"It is of crucial import, Your Eminence. The natives of Langri—"

"Ah, yes. Those poor natives. If there were any possible succor, I assure you—" He paused and then said sternly, "What is it this time?"

"A petition for an injunction, Your Eminence."

"I suspected as much."

"It concerns Wembling and Company's use of its Langrian charter, Your Eminence."

"Submaster Jarnes, are you—the words are those of your honorable opponent and the counsel to Wembling and Company, Master Khorwiss—are you inflating trivialities again?"

"I hope not, Your Eminence."

"So do I. You may proceed."

His expression of polite boredom matched that of Clerk Wyland, who was seated beneath the justice's projection. There were no spectators. "I'll be brief, Your Eminence," Jarnes promised. "I am petitioning for a court-directed work stoppage and a thorough review of the 'natural resources' clause in Wembling and Company's charter."

"Again?" the justice asked politely.

"The survival of the world's population is at stake, Your Eminence. The plight of the natives is desperate. I have proof—"

"I am well aware of that plight, Submaster Jarnes. You have brought it to my attention repeatedly, and while I no doubt have my weaknesses and foibles, I do not number a poor memory among them. Nor do I stand second to anyone in my sympathy for those poor natives. Unfortunately, I must apply the law and observe the rulings of Higher Court. What is the basis for your challenge this time?"

"Golf courses, Your Eminence."

"*Golf* courses?" the justice repeated incredulously.

"Yes, Your Eminence. Wembling and Company plan the construction of a number of golf courses of unusually large size—one could even say absurdly large size. The number is far in excess of the possible needs of the resort under construction, and most of them will be in locations impossibly remote from the resort. Obviously they're a subterfuge, Your Eminence. They are camouflage for a land grab that will further endanger the native population's chances for survival, and Wembling and Company intend—"

The justice waved a precautionary finger. "Opinion of the plaintiff's counsel is not evidential. Can you prove they're a subterfuge?"

"By the time the real intention of Wembling and Company becomes apparent, it'll be too late for legal action."

"We must test the situation on the basis of the known facts, Submaster Jarnes. Wembling and Company's project *is* a vacation resort. I suppose it *is* perfectly in order for people on vacation to play golf, and Higher Court has affirmed that the charter provision allowing Wembling and Company to develop the world's natural resources can legally cover the construction and operation of a resort. Precisely what new question are you raising, if any?"

"Two questions, Your Eminence. First, whether the charter permits golf courses; and second, if it does, whether it permits golf courses in this irrational number and on this unreasonable scale. The golf courses require the clearing of vast stretches of forest, Your Eminence. In other words, these golf courses, which Wembling and Company presumes to build under a charter permitting the development of natural resources are resulting in the irrational destruction of natural resources.

"Have you searched it?"

"Yes, Your Eminence. I find no ruling that would apply."

"Then I would have to view the golf courses as adjunct to the vacation resort and thus properly covered by the charter. Believe me, my sympathy is with the natives, but I cannot make law to succor them. You'd have to apply directly to Higher Court for your injunction, and I doubt that it would hear you."

"Yes, Your Eminence. I will weigh that. Would you then consider enjoining Wembling and Company from further disruption of the ecology of the world of Langri?"

The justice stared for a moment. Then he smiled. "Very ingenious, Submaster Jarnes. Tell me frankly. At this stage is there any aspect of Wembling and Company's activities that could be continued without further disruption of the ecology of the world of Langri?"

"We would request the injunction only as concerns *new* activities, Your Eminence."

"Such as golf courses?"

Jarnes said feebly, "Well—"

"Ecology is such a large word, Submaster Jarnes. It covers so many things—among them things already granted to Wembling and Company by Higher Court. Should I enjoin Wembling and Company from further disruption of the world's ecology, would I not be infringing upon rights already granted? If a tourist takes a deep breath, doesn't that alter the ecology? The breathed portion of the atmosphere has been converted from oxygen prime to carbon dioxide prime. No, Submaster Jarnes. Higher Court has affirmed the right of Wembling and Company to build and use resorts on the world of Langri, and that right is now beyond my power of enjoinment. Those poor natives—but of course I must observe the law and the decisions of Higher Court. Are there any promising possibilities on the political front?"

"It is very uncertain, Your Eminence. Too many politicians are interested in injustice only when they can make political capital of it."

"To be sure," the justice said sympathetically.

"There's one comforting thing about the law. When asked it will answer. It may say it doesn't know, but at least it speaks."

"Nevertheless, the law permits the destruction of an entire world population so that Wembling and Compang can have a prosperous resort."

The justice frowned and then regarded him perplexedly. "Mmm—a charter to develop natural resources should not permit the extermination of human life. If you can put *that* in the form of a legal petition I will grant you relief immediately."

"I've been trying for months, Your Eminence. It can't be done."

"And unfortunately, there's no way I or any other justice can rule on a petition you cannot present. Most unfortunate, but true. Those poor natives—"

19

Admiral Ernst Dallman stood at the window, as he had so often since Wembling gave him office space in this complete wing of the resort, and stared at the specks of color on the horizon. They were native hunting boats, and he kept a pair of binoculars at hand to use when he wanted to study them.

His intercom rasped, "The *Spolon* has landed, sir. Captain Protz is on his way down."

Dallman thanked the intercom over his shoulder and reflected again that he would have to fire the young man who served as desk ensign. He had tested well, but with each passing day he sounded more raspy. Such an unpleasant voice, abruptly intruding upon a commanding officer's most intimate thoughts, could reduce his efficiency by fifty per cent.

He raised his binoculars and watched the hunting boats until he heard voices in the corridor. The desk ensign asked, "Have a nice leave, sir?" Captain Protz responded, "The usual." Then Protz entered through the open door and dropped it shut behind him. Dallman stepped to meet him; Protz saluted, and then they touched hands.

"What's 'the usual'?" Dallman asked.

"The usual? Oh, you mean—yes. The usual leave. Crowded, with dreary treks to visit relatives."

Dallman seated himself at his desk and indicated a chair for Protz, and the captain dropped into it wearily. "Well, I did it," he said. "I planted copies of the treaty and of Vorish's reports and yours with every opposition politician and with all the major news and political commentary services. I'm not hopeful, though. When I talked with the natives' attorneys, I found they'd already done something like that. Still—if it's said often enough, someone might start believing it."

"Our hitting them with it a second time might possibly convince someone," Dallman agreed. "Unfortunately, when the explosion comes, if it does come, it'll be much too late. Have the attorneys run out of ideas? Wembling wasn't hit with an injunction all the time you were away."

"They didn't confide in me. Maybe the natives have run out of money. So that's why Wembling got so much done. That and his flimsy building techniques. I stopped to watch on the way over. They roll the film on, spray it, and suddenly it's as solid as metal—the foreman claimed. It still looked like film to me. At this rate, Wembling will be open for business in a few weeks. Still, if some politician has the guts—"

Dallman shook his head soberly. "It's got to happen now, or he'll be too late. Look here."

He went to the window, and Protz joined him there. "See those hunting boats off the point?" Dallman asked.

"What about them?"

"They don't catch anything. I've watched them for hours. Every day they're there, patiently searching back and forth, but they never catch anything. The natives are starving."

"Can't we make Wembling feed them?" Protz asked.

"We still haven't found a food they can or will eat. They're a proud people, Protz, and they don't want handouts. Especially they don't want handouts from Wembling. The perplexing thing is that they're so cheerful. They're confident they have a Plan to blast Wembling and his resort right off the planet."

"Have you found out what it is?"

Dallman shook his head. "I only hope that when it fails, as it must, they don't lose their heads and attack us. It'll be a sad day for the navy if we have to slaughter starving natives to protect the corrupt interests of a Wembling."

The desk ensign's voice rasped, "Mr. Wembling is on his way up, sir."

Protz turned away. "Excuse me. I haven't unpacked yet."

"Go ahead," Dallman said. "I wish I could go somewhere and unpack something."

Protz dropped the door open and went out. Dallman heard Wembling's voice outside. "Oh, hello, Captain. Have a nice leave?" And Protz's answer, "Very nice, thank you."

Then Wembling entered. "Morning, Ernie."

"Good morning, Harlow."

Wembling sauntered up to Dallman's desk and dropped a folio with a thud. "Here's more paperwork for you. Come down to the lounge for a drink?"

Dallman absently lifted the folio and set it down again. "Why not?"

The upper levels of the finished wing were used for office space. The lower level served as a lounge for Wembling's supervisory personnel and the naval officers. Wembling used it as a training school for waitresses, cooks, and bartenders who later would work in the resort. Normally Dallman avoided the place—its dim interior was always crowded with off-duty personnel, and the strumming, whining music sometimes was so loud that he could feel the beat in his office two levels above.

But when Wembling entered, the volume of sound was turned down instantly, and the lights were turned up. The hostess dashed out to greet them and signaled a waitress, and when they reached their favorite table —hurriedly evacuated for their use—the waitress was waiting with their favorite drinks. Dallman seated himself; Wembling captured the waitress' arm and remained standing.

"Ernie!" he exclaimed. "You didn't notice! The uniforms came! How do you like this one?"

He turned the waitress around, posing her. To Dallman the uniform looked like a few spangles and frills without a costume, but he made no comment.

Wembling released the waitress and pounced on another who was passing by. "Just a moment, Farica. How do you like this one, Ernie? I can't make up my mind."

To Dallman it looked like the same costume with a different arrangement of frills. Wembling posed the second waitress, he extremely serious, she giggling. Finally he seated himself and looked after her as she walked away.

"You're going to have several lounges and dining rooms," Dallman said. "Why don't you put a different costume in each one?"

"Hey—why didn't I think of that?"

They sipped their drinks in silence, and Dallman, looking through a gap in the heavy draperies, watched the specks of color on the horizon: starving natives, searching the waters with heroic patience for food that long since had been driven elsewhere.

Wembling set his tumbler down and raised two fingers. The waitress was waiting for the signal, and she rushed over with fresh drinks.

"Trouble this morning on Site Four, Ernie,"

Wembling said. "The usual—native sneaked in and stopped the work. Can't you put more sentries there?"

Dallman shook his head. "I just don't have enough men."

"The puggards are changing their tactics—now they don't lie down and wait to be carried away. They run about and make the work force catch them. This one held up work for half an hour. Can't you give me more sentry posts there?"

Dallman shook his head again. "No. Can't be done."

"You're doing a fine job, Ernie. I'm putting in a good word for you at Naval Headquarters. But go down to Site Four this afternoon, like a good fellow, and see why the natives keep breaking in there."

"Why are you scattering those stupid golf courses all over Langri?" Dallman asked. "If you'd keep your operations in one place, I could look after you properly."

"Politics and the law," Wembling said, grinning at him slyly. "Stay away from them, Ernie. You have superior brains and talent, but it isn't that kind of brains and talent."

Dallman shrugged good-naturedly and said nothing, though he was reflecting that the galaxy would be a far better place if even fewer people had that kind of brains and talent. The hunting boats were tacking toward shore, and he could make out the black lines of the boats beneath the sails.

Wembling said suddenly, "By the way—whatever happened to Commander Vorish?"

"The last I heard, he'd been promoted to captain, and he was taking the *Hiln* on training maneuvers."

"You mean—they didn't fire him?"

It was Dallman's turn to grin slyly. "They investigated him, and then they handed him a commendation for handling himself well in a difficult situation. My assumption is that the trumped-up charge would have resulted in more publicity than certain persons thought desirable, so Vorish was patted on the head and told to forget it. I could be wrong about that—I don't know anything about politics and law. Did you want him fired?"

Wembling looked startled. "I? Certainly not. I had no grudge against him. There's no profit in grudges. We both had jobs to do, but he went at his in the wrong way. If they kicked him out, I'd have offered him a job. He was a good man, and he understood these natives, and I can use someone like that. I'm going to have a huge enterprise here, and I'll need all the good men I can get. If you ever leave the navy, Ernie, come back to Langri. I'll have a place for you."

"Thanks. I'll remember that."

Wembling finished his drink, slapped the table with both hands, and pushed himself to his feet. "Come down to Site Four with me this afternoon?"

"I have a full schedule, but I'll send someone."

Wembling nodded and waddled away. Dallman nursed his drink for a time and watched the tacking hunting boats. The music became louder the moment Wembling left, and the dancing that accompanied it became disconcertingly frenzied, and finally he fled back to his office.

Again he stood at the window watching the hunting boats. For half a day he had been trying to decide what to do about a joint report submitted to him by Aric Hort and Talitha Warr. It detailed the mortality rate at each native village during the past month, with an attested statement from Wembling's own doctor concerning the natives' physical condition. It also contained a bleak forecast concerning future mortality. The report was a model of its kind—detached, concise, and bristling with verifiable facts, and if, as he had done with their previous reports, he forwarded it to headquarters with a covering letter pointing out that Wembling's resort project was exterminating the natives, headquarters would file it without comment.

Headquarters undoubtedly wished that he would cease and desist, but it dared not complain. His orders made him responsible for the welfare of the natives *and* the protection of Wembling's rights under his charter, and there was no provision for the possibility that these two responsibilities would be irreconcilable.

Somewhere in the upper strata of political power, there were persons who had conspired with Wembling to violate a treaty solemnly entered into by their government, and if they knew about Dallman's dilemma they would be badly frightened. They would exert all of their influence to consign such reports to the file and keep them there, and they would willingly allow an entire people to die because they could not save them without revealing their complicity in a vile conspiracy. In the end the fermenting scandal would explode anyway, and everyone concerned would be destroyed except Wembling.

That would come much too late to help the natives.

Dallman's problem was to send the report where it would be studied and acted upon, and if such a place existed, no one he had consulted knew where it was.

Finally he gave it up and attacked the pile of work on his desk.

It was midafternoon when he became aware of the vibrating roar and whistle of a spaceship in landing approach. At first he scowled irritably, and then he sprang for the window. The shrieking roar shook the building as the ship passed close overhead. Dallman caught only a glimpse of it, and he turned and raced for the door.

The white-faced duty ensign was looking out from under his desk. He scrambled to his feet in embarrassment and asked, "What was it, sir?"

Dallman ran past him without speaking. Outside the building, several construction workers were climbing out from under a machine. A driver was still hiding under Wembling's conveyance. Dallman hauled him out and had himself driven at top speed to the landing field.

Captain Protz was standing at the top of his ship's ramp, angrily staring into the distance. Dallman called to him, "Where did it land?"

"Off in the forest somewhere," Protz said. His face was flushed with anger. "What idiot was it?"

"I don't know. Suppose we try finding out."

"When we do, I want the captain's license. He came in without clearance, he violated every landing procedure on the list, and then he missed the field by at least twenty kilometers."

Their investigation lasted all of five minutes and produced two negatives: the ship was not a naval craft, and Wembling's supply chief disclaimed any knowledge of it—he had no ships due. In the meantime, a reconocopter was taking the tops out of trees back in the area where the ship was presumed to have come down. The pilot saw no trace of it.

"This can only mean one thing," Dallman said. "The natives have visitors."

"Why do you say that?"

"I think that landing approach was neither inept nor accidental. It was done deliberately, to avoid any chance of an interception. The natives probably have the ship thoroughly hidden by now, which means that neither a reconocopter nor a ground search would have a chance in a million of finding it."

"A ground search is out anyway," Protz said. "I wouldn't order men into that forest. Anyway, I don't suppose there's a portable detector on Langri."

"I certainly don't know of any."

"What possible business would an outsider have with the natives?"

"How about smuggling arms?" Dallman suggested.

Protz groaned. "In that case, we'll *have* to make a ground search. But even if we found the ship, the arms would be unloaded and hidden."

"If they attack us, we'll have to smash them," Dallman said despondently. "I'd hoped I could get through this assignment without a shot fired at the natives. I'd much rather shoot Wembling."

20

A broad band of light marked the construction site perimeter, and on the landing field each ship stood in its own bright oval. The humped silhouette of a reconocopter, small cabin perched over enormous, circular turbine housing, stood at the edge of the landing field. As Dallman and Protz approached it, the pilot jumped down and snapped a salute.

"Ready any time you are, sir," he said.

"Pity Langri doesn't have a moon," Protz observed, looking about him. "It'd be charming by moonlight."

"Mention that to Wembling," Dallman said. "He'll have one built."

They climbed aboard, and the reconocopter shot upward steeply and moved off along the coast, still climbing. Staring down into utter blackness, Dallman suddenly saw a patch of light on the horizon. As they gained altitude, more patches came into view.

He touched the pilot's shoulder. "Can we have a closer look?"

They dropped precipitously and drifted over a village at low altitude, and the patch of light resolved into rows of fires that turned the village oval into a blaze of light. There seemed to be a great bustle of activity, but what it signified Dallman had no idea.

"You say this isn't normal?" he asked the pilot.

"Definitely not normal, sir. They fix their evening meal about dark, when the hunting boats get in. When they have something to fix, that is. Sometimes they don't.

Once they've finished their meal you can fly the whole coast without catching a glimpse of light except at the construction sites."

"It's a shame that we know so little about these natives," Dallman said. "I never have an inkling of what Fornri's thinking about, and I doubt that Aric Hort understands him any better than I do. The Colonial Bureau should have sent in a team to study them." He turned to Protz. "What do you make of it?"

"It's suggestive, but darned if I know what it suggests."

"I know what it suggests," Dallman said grimly. "A strange ship lands this afternoon, and tonight every native on the planet is staying up all night. They're getting ready for something. We'd better go back and make a few preparations of our own."

The pilot turned back. When they reached the landing field, Dallman strolled over to the perimeter and walked the sentry path for a thousand meters, meditating the uncanny quiet of the night. Protz followed behind him without speaking.

"Going to double the sentries?" he asked finally.

"Could you work out a staggered relief system to place all the sentries on duty from four hundred on?"

"Of course."

"Let's do it that way. Since most of the natives are still at their villages, it should be several hours before anything happens here. I'm going to get Wembling out of bed. I'll tell him to issue orders immediately—his men are to have the day off tomorrow, and they're restricted to quarters until further notice. That'll apply to him, too. He can put his commissary to work right now packing meals for the men to eat in quarters."

"He'll howl," Protz said.

"He'd better not howl to me. I want all the site commanders alerted. For the time being we're going to forget Wembling's golf courses and shorten sentry lines to effectively protect workers and equipment. I'll also tell ordnance to place a reserve of arms at each site so the workers can be armed if that proves necessary."

They returned to the landing field, and Dallman

walked over to a waiting conveyance and climbed into it. "I want to see Hort the first thing in the morning," he said. "Wembling's niece, too, if she'll come. Tell me—if you were a native and you wanted to stop Wembling's work, what would you do?"

"That's easy. I'd kill Wembling."

"All right," Dallman said disgustedly. "I'll give him an armed guard."

Dallman slept at his desk. He woke up occasionally to monitor reports, but nothing was being reported but negatives. All of the larger native villages were alight with numerous small fires, but if the natives were stirring anywhere else, no one saw them. Finally Dallman chose to ignore the reports and sleep.

The intercom rasped him to wakefulness and reminded him that he'd decided the day before to replace his desk ensign. "Captain Protz is here, sir. With Miss Warr and Mr. Hort."

Dallman stirred sleepily, yawned, and lowered his feet. "Send them in."

He stood up to greet them, and with Protz's help he pulled chairs into position and got the three of them seated. "Nice of you to come," he said, wearily dropping into his own chair. "I urgently need the answer to a question. What's going on?"

Hort and Miss Warr exchanged startled glances and then looked at him blankly. Protz said, "They won't be able to help us much. They don't know anything about the fires. They didn't even know a ship landed yesterday."

"There wasn't any mention among the natives of a ship landing?" Dallman asked them.

They shook their heads.

"Did you notice *anything* about the natives yesterday that seemed unusual?"

"They were a little hungrier than they were the day before, but there's nothing unusual about that," Hort said. "What's this about a ship?"

"I don't know, except that there was one," Dallman said. "It landed in the forest some twenty kilometers from the coast." Absently he got to his feet and went to the window. "How does it happen you don't know about the fires? Aren't you two usually at one of the villages until after nightfall?"

"Usually," Hort agreed. "Yesterday—well, it seemed natural enough at the time, but now that I think about it—anyway, we were sort of escorted away yesterday afternoon."

"Asked to leave?"

"Nothing like that. Fornri said he was going to the next village, and he offered to walk with us as far as the center. If eviction was what he had in mind, I'd have to admit he managed it very neatly. What kind of fires were there?"

Dallman turned again to the window. He gazed at the horizon for a moment, and then he leaned forward, staring. "Look!"

The other three bounded to the window. "What is it?" Protz demanded.

"Look—off the point."

All of them stared. "There's nothing there," Protz announced.

"Right." After so many hours of uncertainty, Dallman's grimness had become fatalistic. "Every day since I arrived here, there's been a hunting fleet working off the point—until today."

"I was about to tell you that," Protz said reproachfully. "The reconocopter pilot just reported—none of the hunting boats are working today."

"I see. Yesterday a strange ship arrives. Today all the natives on Langri take the day off. What *are* they doing?"

"All the pilot could tell me is that they're congregating in the larger villages," Protz said.

"At this point there's only one thing to do. We'll have a frank talk with Fornri."

"How many men do you want to take?"

"None. Miss Warr and Hort if they want to come. We aren't trying to coerce the natives. We're just asking the favor of some information."

They circled widely to approach from the sea and make an unobtrusive landing on the beach below the village. The pilot remained with the reconocopter; Dallman, with Protz, Hort, and Miss Warr trailing after him, walked slowly up the slope to the village. As they reached the point where the first curving side street intercepted the main avenue, he paused and looked about him incredulously.

The natives were in festival costume, and the atmosphere was one of celebration. They greeted their visitors with smiles and made way for them respectfully as they moved slowly up the central avenue. And despite their emaciated appearances, they seemed not merely cheerful but happy.

Cooking fires blazed in the central oval. When they reached it, Dallman paused again and sniffed appreciatively. "They're certainly starving in style. That smells delicious."

"It *is* delicious," Hort said bitterly. "What there is of it. The natives will get about as much as you did—a smell."

"It was enough to remind me that I missed breakfast," Dallman said good-naturedly. They moved on, and at the other side of the oval he halted abruptly. "What the devil!"

They stood gazing perplexedly up the central avenue. At the top of the village, before one of the larger dwellings, a long line of natives stood waiting quietly.

Then Fornri saw them. He came hurrying toward them, but whether his action suggested either alarm or resentment at their presence, Dallman could not say. The native's face remained expressionless.

"Why are you here?" he asked.

"To observe," Dallman said.

"In the past you have not interfered in the lives of my people. Is that to change?"

"Certainly not," Dallman said. "I have no intention of interfering."

"Then your presence is not required. What is happening here concerns only ourselves."

"Everything that happens on this world concerns me," Dallman said firmly. "I intend to know what is going on here."

They faced each other, Space Navy admiral and Langrian native, and Dallman had no doubt that he was the more nervous of the two. The silence seemed interminable. Finally Fornri spoke. "I know that you have been a good friend to my people. All of you have, but you also have duties and obligations that concern others. Our fear on this day is that Mr. Wembling may attempt to interfere with us."

"He won't," Dallman promised. "I've confined Wembling and all of hs workers to their quarters. If what you are doing concerns only yourselves no one will interfere."

"Very well." Fornri paused, and then he said proudly, "We are holding an election."

"An—election?" Dallman felt Protz's grip tighten on his arm. He turned and looked blankly at him. Hort and Miss Warr were looking just as blankly at each other.

"We are electing delegates to a constitutional convention," Fornri said.

Dallman gazed past Fornri at the line of waiting natives. He thought, "What an idyllic setting for an election!" Holiday atmosphere, a magnificent view of the sea, a feast in preparation, citizens waiting their turns at the polling booths in a woven grass hut—the principles of democracy had never been more strikingly portrayed.

None of them spoke. Probably none of them could speak—Dallman could not.

"When the constitution has been approved," Fornri went on, "we shall elect a government. And then we shall apply for membership in the Galactic Federation of Independent Worlds."

"Is it legal?" Protz blurted.

"It is legal. Our attorney is advising us."

"Is it the Plan?" Hort asked eagerly.

"It is part of the Plan," Fornri said. "We could have done it sooner, but we did not know that we needed only sixty per cent literacy. We have more than ninety per cent."

Dallman, sensing the solemnity as well as the importance of the occasion, snapped to attention. "I am honored to present my congratulations, and I'm confident that I can include those of the Federation Government. And I give you this pledge: no one will interfere with any of your steps toward self-government, at any time. If anyone tries, notify me at once."

Fornri gave the jerky bow that he sometimes affected when speaking with outsiders. "In behalf of the people of Langri, I thank you."

"I suppose your government's first official action will be to evict Wembling," Protz said lightly.

Fornri's politely blank expression did not change. "We shall of course be guided by the law."

With a final glance at the polling hut, they turned and walked slowly back to the reconocopter. The pilot was waiting to assist them aboard, but instead they turned again and looked at the village.

"And that," Protz murmured, "will finish Wembling."

"At least we've solved the mystery of the unknown ship," Dallman said. "It was their attorney, coming to advise them and help them draw up a constitution. As for finishing Wembling, you're wrong. The Wemblings in this universe don't finish that easily. He's ready for this. You might even say he's been expecting it."

"What can he do?" Protz demanded.

"No court of law would make him give up what he already has. The bribery and political connivance that got him his illegal charter won't be part of the official record, and the court can't take note of them. It will have to assume that Wembling acted under his charter in good faith. *Now* we know why he's been laying out all those enormous golf courses. That land was legally developed by him, under an official Federation charter, and the court will let him keep it."

Hort and Miss Warr turned on him aghast. "That can't be true!" Hort exclaimed.

"Ah, but it is. Wait and see. And once the court

confirms his ownership of all that land, he'll be free to use it any way he likes. He can put up dozens of resorts and flood the coast with tourists. If the natives try to stop him, the Federation courts will support Wembling —with force, if necessary."

Dallman gestured at the distant election lines. "Do you realize what a tremendous accomplishment that is? Ninety per cent literacy from nothing. How they must have worked! You two—" He spoke to Hort and Miss Warr. "Did you know the entire population was learning to read and write?"

"I've been teaching the children," Hort said. "But only children from the villages close by."

"Then the children taught the adults, and the villages close by taught others. They did this thing themselves, and they did it secretly, and in all of human history few people can have worked harder or achieved more. Ninety per cent literacy. And they were beaten before they started. The poor devils!"

21

In the course of his legal career, Submaster Jarvis Jarnes often had experienced despondency—any attorney who lost a close judgment experienced despondency—but what he felt now was bleak despair. The sugary visage of Master Khan Khorwiss, eminent counsel of Wembling and Company, who faced him across the chamber's computer consoles, added another measure of bitterness for the quaffing.

Khorwiss was waiting patiently, hands clasped behind his head, robe thrown back carelessly, the merest flicker of a smile playing on his lips, and occasionally he shot a scornful glance at Jarnes, who was rechecking his reference disks and arranging his notes. Like most masters of the old school, Khorwiss disdained such last-minute priming. *Prepare your case in your office and play it in the chamber.* Obviously his case was prepared to the last reference code, and he was as confident of winning as Jarnes was certain of losing. Jarnes's own case was as thoroughly searched and briefed as human effort could make it, but the most he could hope for was that Khorwiss might be guilty of overconfidence. In that unlikely event Jarnes would have the pleasure of slipping him a nasty jolt or two, but he had no illusions that this could possibly affect the outcome.

He could not imagine any attorney, much less Master Khan Khorwiss, playing a case as strong as that of Wembling and Company so carelessly as to lose it. Jarnes's only chance lay in tricking the computer, a reckless gambit much discussed among young attorneys but as far as he knew never employed successfully. Since his case was lost, he had nothing further to lose by gambling.

His despair was not brought on by the prospect of defeat—what was one more defeat after so many? Every attorney knew that one sometimes had to concede points to win a case and lose first cases to win the last. But following this defeat he would take the one blundering step that would destroy the Langri cause utterly. He had protested and argued frantically, but the natives insisted, and they were his clients, and he had no choice. It was part of the Plan, they said.

They would not tell him their Plan.

The JUSTICE IN SESSION sign glowed to life at the back of the room, and a moment later the scowling, brightly robed image of Justice Figawn appeared. Clerk Wyland jerked to respectful attention, and the two attorneys arose and bowed. Figawn bent low in acknowledgment—without, however, relinquishing his scowl. As soon as they had seated themselves, he faced Jarnes and spoke his mind with more than his usual bluntness.

"Again we have the People of Langri versus Wembling and Company. Submaster Jarnes, my patience—which I never claimed to be limitless—has long since been exhausted by these baseless actions and petitions. Once again I offer my entire sympathy to those poor, starving natives, but—"

The justice turned his irritated gaze on Khorwiss, who had got to his feet and stood waiting. "Well, Master Khorwiss?"

"May I speak, Your Eminence?"

"You have leave, Master Khorwiss."

"Your Eminence, I beg permission to present the petition of Wembling and Company against the People of Langri."

Figawn stared at him for a moment before turning incredulously to Clerk Wyland. "Wembling and Company are suing the natives?"

"They are, Your Eminence," the clerk murmured.

"At least it's a change. You may proceed, Master Khorwiss."

"This morning, Your Eminence, the Federation Congress granted the world of Langri independent status and membership in the Federation. Naturally this alters the status of Wembling and Company."

A flicker of a smile touched the justice's face. "No one will ever accuse you of overstatement, Master Khorwiss. It does indeed 'alter the status.' Wembling and Company's charter is automatically voided."

"Wembling and Company are petitioning for confirmation of ownership of lands properly and legally developed by them under the charter," Khorwiss said. "There is of course substantial legal precedence for such a petition, Your Eminence, as we are prepared to demonstrate."

He seated himself with a smug glance at Jarnes.

Justice Figawn turned. "Have you a challenge, Submaster Jarnes?"

Jarnes got to his feet. "Your Eminence, the people of Langri naturally challenge the claim of Wembling and Company to lands usurped under an illegal and corruptly granted charter."

Khorwiss leaped to his feet. "Exception!"

"Silence!" Figawn snapped. He turned to Jarnes. "Surely I need not inform you again, Submaster Jarnes, that this court has no jurisdiction over the status of that charter. You may play your cases, gentlemen."

The attorneys resumed their seats, and Clerk Wyland spoke. "Do Wembling and Company stand ready to present their petition?"

Khorwiss bowed deeply.

"Do the people of Langri stand ready to answer that petition?"

Jarnes bowed. Clerk Wyland activated the computer; Jarnes leaned forward intently, hands alert on his own console, waiting for Khorwiss' initial reference.

It came with a sharp *ping,* and the symbols appeared at the top of the left, the plaintiff's screen. Jarnes absorbed them with a glance; regretfully he matched the reference from his own slender stack of reference disks. Another *ping* sounded, and his reference appeared in symbols atop the right-hand screen. The third *ping* followed almost at once, and both references vanished; the computer had rated them equal.

Jarnes glanced across at Khorwiss and found Wembling's attorney watching him with a faint smile on his face—perhaps a surface reflection of the old attorney's pleasure in playing a case that could not lose. In his own comparatively brief career Jarnes could not remember having experienced that pleasure.

Khorwiss disdainfully posted three references in rapid succession and then sat back to see what Jarnes would make of them. Tongue firmly in cheek, Jarnes posted one of his feit disks—a reference of dubious value. It appeared and instantly swept Khorwiss' references into oblivion, leaving the left screen blank. But almost immediately a gong sounded, Jarnes's feit reference disappeared, and Khorwiss' references were restored.

Clerk Wyland spoke. "The computer disallows it, Submaster Jarnes. Reversed by decision of Higher Court."

Jarnes nodded with feigned apology. Khorwiss'

momentary consternation offered some slight compensation for the ignominy of having to play a case with such slight support. He touched the keys that directed more of his slender stack of reference disks into the play. It cost him five of them to match Khorwiss' three postings, and two more to match another.

With an eye on his diminished references, he played again from his stack of feit disks. Again the gong sounded, and Clerk Wyland observed laconically, "Voided by legislative act, Submaster Jarnes." Another feit disk, another gong. "The computer says irrelevant, Submaster Jarnes."

Khorwiss, scenting an easier victory than expected, began to pile up unanswered references. Jarnes waited until the lengthening list reached the eighteenth line. Then, with the stage set, with Khorwiss' plump, smug face radiating victory, Jarnes stroked the keys.

The *ping* sounded; his reference symbols appeared on the right screen. Almost instantly came the *ping* of response, and Khorwiss' entire list disappeared.

All of it. For a suspenseful moment the master attorney was too dumfounded to protest. Then he came to his feet screaming. "Exception! Exception! *What reference is that?*"

Jarnes answered calmly, "The reference is as stated: *Rulings of Governmental Commissions, 5/19/E/349/K.*"

"That's no reference!" Khorwiss proclaimed indignantly.

"Shall we permit the court to decide?" Jarnes asked him politely.

Justice Figawn was consulting his own computer. After a moment he turned toward them. "I find no indication that the commission intended its ruling to have legal precedence. The reference is denied because of single-case applicability."

With a *ping* Jarnes's reference was wiped out and Khorwiss' list restored. He shrugged philosophically; a gamble with a feit reference was excusable only when one didn't expect it to work.

He played his remaining references with deliberation, one at a time. When he succeeded in reducing Khorwiss' list to six, Wembling's attorney insolently added another dozen.

Finally, his references exhausted, Jarnes turned to the most promising of his feit disks. The computer greeted each one with a gong, and Clerk Wyland's voice took on an edge of impatience that matched Justice Figawn's deepening scowl as he observed, "The computer says irrelevant, Submaster Jarnes." Khorwiss was grinning broadly.

Finally Jarnes got to his feet and faced the justice. "That's all I have, Your Eminence."

Justice Figawn nodded politely. "The court confirms the ownership by Wembling and Company of land on the world of Langri properly developed by them under charter. Does your petition include the required legal descriptions, Master Khorwiss?"

Khorwiss arose. "It does, Your Eminence."

"It does? Yes—I have it here." Figawn paused to skim through the descriptions. "Master Khorwiss," he asked politely, "how many golf courses does one resort require?"

Khorwiss remained discreetly silent.

Figawn turned to Jarnes. "May I have your counterpetition, Submaster Jarnes?"

"I have none, Your Eminence," Jarnes told him.

Figawn stared at him. "Do you mean to say you're going to accept these claims as stated?"

"That is the wish of my clients, Your Eminence."

"Anyone but a nitwit could tell with one glance that many of these claims are preposterous," Figawn announced.

"Your Eminence!" Khorwiss exclaimed.

"Surely you're not going to let this petition stand without protest," Figawn said to Jarnes.

"I have no choice but to observe the wishes of my clients, Your Eminence. They do request, however, that Wembling and Company be required to file a certified and attested statement of investment for each parcel of land claimed so as to demonstrate the validity of the claim to this court's satisfaction. I shall insist on an accounting of Wembling and Company's expenditures for each parcel."

Figawn regarded him gravely. "You are of course bound by the wishes of your clients." He turned to Khorwiss. "I so rule. Wembling and Company are instructed to prepare the desired certified and attested statements, and I myself will then carry out the wishes of the people of Langri by allowing such claims as the developmental investment justifies—in accordance with legal procedure, of course. Is there further comment? None? *Let justice be done.*"

His image faded. The JUSTICE IN SESSION sign darkened. Khorwiss quickly gathered his disks and records and went out grinning. Jarnes wearily began the methodical packing of his own reference disks.

Clerk Wyland leaned over and spoke to him. "Submaster Jarnes—a word, please. My understanding was that even one resort on Langri would seriously deplete the natives' food supply."

"That is correct, sir."

"Surely the people of Langri can perceive that Wembling and Company will use this lavish gift of land for the construction of innumerable resorts."

"I'm sure that they can," Jarnes said politely. "In fact, I brought that possibility to their attention very forcefully. However, they not only requested the action taken, they demanded it, and I had no choice but to carry out their wishes."

"Surely if you had explained to them . . ."

"I did explain," Jarnes said.

". . . and demonstrated to them . . ."

"I did demonstrate"

". . . and described the inevitable result . . ."

"I did describe the inevitable result, not once but repeatedly."

"Well!" Clerk Wyland drew back and regarded him indignantly. "I'll be interested to see what happens, and I'm certain that I'll find out. The people of Langri will soon be back here screaming for relief. Unfortunately, *that* petition will come much too late."

He stomped away angrily. Jarnes felt like weeping,

and he turned away for a moment before resuming his packing. Saltwater corrosion in an attorney's reference disks was a sure sign of immaturity.

22

The village was deathly quiet. Pausing in the street outside the improvised hospital, Talitha Warr tried to remember the last time she'd heard singing there. Once the natives had accompanied every mood with an appropriate song, from the tender love melodies of the youths to the stirring chants that were used with heavy work and the burying of koluf; but now so many natives were weak from hunger that the heavy work went undone, and the few koluf that were caught were buried in tragic silence.

There were no more songs—only lamentations for the dead, and she heard one beginning now. Shivering, she walked despondently down to the beach, where Aric Hort was to meet her. He was sitting alone on the vast stretch of sand. There were no more native children well enough to play there.

She said, "Did you hear?"

He nodded. "The natives gave your uncle everything he asked for."

They set out along the beach for the medical center, and for a time they walked silently, keeping their eyes on the unmarked, wind-rippled sand. "It was their last chance for help from the courts," Hort said finally. "Fornri doesn't even seem worried. He says it's part of the Plan."

"I have an appointment with Uncle tomorrow,"

she said. I'm going to try again to persuade him to hire an experienced nutritionist. We've *got* to find something they can eat. If only they would trust us—"

"But they won't," Hort said. "If one thing is more responsible than any other for the mess they're in, that's it. They need help desperately, and they won't trust anyone. Turn your head slowly and look at that bush on the ridge."

She did as he told her and saw two native children peering at them from behind the bush. "It's only a couple of children," she said.

"Any time you can see two, there are ten others you can't see. Weak as they are, they follow every alien on Langri who takes a step away from the construction sites. They watch his every move and carry regular reports to a secret native headquarters. They've been doing that from the moment your uncle set up an embassy, and they're still doing it, malnutrition or not. One would think that by this time they'd trust you and me, but they don't. We're followed everywhere we go. Didn't you know?"

She shook her head. "I'm not surprised, though. Certainly they have every right—"

He gripped her arm. The two of them stopped and stood facing each other. "Would you join me in an experiment?" he asked. "There's something I've wanted to investigate for weeks, but I know the natives would stop me if they caught me at it. There's only one way I can think of to shake off those children."

She resisted the temptation to look again at the bush. "What sort of an experiment?"

"Come on. I'll show you."

They turned back, left the beach, and crossed the seaside meadow to a forest path. After some distance the path forked; one branch sloped upward steeply, and when they turned into it they saw, far ahead of them, a young native couple walking along slowly in close embrace.

"Where are we?" Talitha asked.

Hort gestured toward the top of the slope. "This is a Bower Hill."

"*Bower* Hill?" she echoed. "I never heard of such a thing." She glanced about her. "I've never been this way before."

"I should hope not!" Hort said with a grin.

"Now what do you mean by that?"

He shook his head and took a surreptitious backward glance. "We brought the whole flock with us," he said disgustedly.

"Was that the experiment? Did you think they wouldn't come here?"

"I hoped they wouldn't, but they probably want to make certain where we're going."

"So where *are* we going?" she asked.

"To the Bower Hill."

As they approached the crest she saw why the word "bower" was used—along each side of the path were openings into small forest glades. In one of them she saw the young couple they had followed up the path lying in close embrace. She averted her eyes and then turned a puzzled gaze on Hort; he was looking behind them again, and they walked on for some distance. Then, before she quite knew what was happening, he had drawn her into a bower on the opposite side of the path.

She struggled furiously as he tried to embrace her. "So this is your idea of an experiment!" she snapped. She beat futilely against his face with her fist.

"Hush!" he whispered. "It's the only way to get rid of the escort!"

She continued to struggle. "With you, a girl needs an escort!"

"Hush! If it isn't a good act, they won't leave!"

Then his lips found hers, and she stopped struggling.

A moment later, an hour, an eternity, she lay in his arms on the soft, springy blanket of pliable fronds, and she opened her eyes bewilderedly when he suddenly released her and raised himself up.

'I think they're gone," he whispered.

"Good for them," she said, and pulled him back. His beard caressed her face and his lips sealed her

eyes, and she heard his whispered words with a wild
surge of joy. "If we had only ourselves to think of—
they call this world paradise, but it wasn't, not until
you came. But the natives—"

Her joy took flight, and reluctantly she pushed
herself into a sitting position. "The natives are starving.
What was it you wanted to find out?"

He got to his feet and helped her up. "There's a
path they keep concealed. I'd like to find out where it
leads." He went to the bower opening and cautiously
looked down the path. Then he returned to her.
"They're gone. It was a magnificent act."

She went willingly to his arms, and when they
finally drew apart she said, "You're rather convincing
yourself, but was it necessary to climb up here for our
acting?"

He smiled at her. "You really don't know where
you are?"

She shook her head.

"It's a Bower Hill. There's one for every two or
three villages, and they're the places where the young
people do their courting. They're the only locations on
Langri where there's a right to privacy. Come on—
they'll be waiting for us at the bottom of the hill, so
we'll have to sneak out the back way."

A narrow path, only slightly worn, took them
down the hill in another direction. After watching for a
time to make certain they were unobserved, they sprint-
ed across a meadow to the forest and cautiously skirted
it until they came upon one of the main paths. They
followed it in single file with Hort leading the way. So
well camouflaged was the intersecting path that he
missed it completely and had to fumble in the tall undergrowth searching for it, but finally he found the
place. The opening was cunningly laced together with
vines, and they parted it only enough to squeeze
through.

They found themselves on a broad avenue—not
only was this path wider than any other forest path
Talitha could remember, but the undergrowth had been
trimmed back from it. It had the appearance of a tidy

roadway, and to aggravate the mystery, the path ran absolutely straight. Other forest paths meandered—around trees, away from thickets and bogs, along watercourses—but this one ran as straight as a survey. It turned aside for nothing, and no trace remained of the trees that must have been felled to make its course possible.

They had to get back to the Bower Hill before the children suspected their ruse, so they walked quickly. The wide path provided some consolation: they could walk side by side, and his arm encircled her warmly.

"Did you ever see a forest path that ran so straight?" she asked.

He shook his head. "Nor one so wide."

"What could be back here in the forest that attracts so much traffic?"

"That's what we're trying to find out."

The only obstacle they encountered was a small stream. They waded across, and far up ahead of them the path seemed to end in a blaze of sunlight. A large forest clearing opened before them. It was roughly circular and carpeted with thick grass and flowers. They paused for a moment to look about, and then almost simultaneously they saw it: the rusting, overgrown, smashed hulk of an old survey ship. The forest growth of decades so obliterated its outline that had it not been for the open hatch and the rusting ramp they would have overlooked it.

They ran toward it, and Hort stopped at the foot of the ramp and whistled softly. "Someone came down rather hard. It happened a long, long time ago, but it probably explains a lot of things."

Together they climbed the wobbly ramp and entered the ship. They felt their way cautiously along the dim corridor to the control room, where cracks in the hull permitted the jagged entry of light. There, on the chart table, atop the brittle remains of the charts, was an amazing clutter of objects: the ship's log, a few books, a rusted pocket knife, a broken compass, a rosary.

In the center of the table was a heap of fresh flowers.

"It's a shrine!" Talitha exclaimed.

Hort picked up the logbook. "The ship's log. This may answer questions I've been asking myself ever since I arrived here. Let's take it outside and have a look."

They sat side by side at the top of the ramp and held the log between them. "It's an old-fashioned script," Hort said, leafing through the pages. "Can you make it out?"

"Just barely."

"After the ship crashed, it seems to have been used as a diary, and also—" He stared at it. "Also I don't know what. Let's start at the beginning and see what we can make of it."

So they read together, page after page after page.

His name was Cerne Obrien. He was a little free-booter who had somehow managed to buy or steal a junked government survey ship, and he went batting about the galaxy raising hell and generally having himself a grand puff of a good time. He also did a bit of illegal prospecting when he felt like it, which didn't seem to be often. When the miracle occurred, and he did strike it rich, he actually seemed to resent the fact. He crashed on his way back to civilization, but he remained the freebooter, now lording it among unsophisticated natives. He explored, he prospected for metals, and he added an outrigger to the hunting boats to give them stability in the furious struggles with the koluf.

Cerne Obrien, the wanderer, finally remained in one place because he was unable to leave. He acquired a native wife, rose high in native councils, and became a leader. And down through the years, as they leafed the pages, a subtle change became more and more pronounced. Obrien increasingly identified with the natives, became one of them, and began to worry about their future. He penned in the logbook an astute summary of Langri's potential as a resort planet that might have been written by Wembling, followed by a warning as to the probable fate of the natives. He added, "If I live, this won't happen. If I don't live, there must be a Plan for them to follow."

"Tal!" Hort exclaimed. "It isn't possible! One man couldn't have done all that. He taught the natives government and law and economics and history and science and language and political science and colonial procedure and an entire university curriculum. He even taught military subjects. How could one man—obviously an uneducated man—how could he do it?"

"He did more than that," Talitha said. "He taught them their Plan."

The initial landing, probably by survey ship (government or private). Steps to observe in capturing the crew. Subsequent landings by ships searching for the first ship. How to approach the Space Navy ship. Negotiations, lists of violations and penalties. Achievement of independent status. Steps to follow when independent status is violated. Steps to follow in preparing for Federation membership.

Every detail was there. Everything the natives had done since Wembling's ship touched down was laid out in the form of meticulous instructions for them to follow: the exploding gourds that terrified the Space Navy, the sly tricks and dodges used to interrupt Wembling's work, the directions for their attorney. . . .

Everything. They found themselves gazing awesomely at the natives' cryptic Plan in all of its breathtaking completeness, right up to its final master stroke, laboriously written out by an uneducated man who had vision and wisdom and patience. By a great man. It was a brilliant prognostication, with nothing lacking except her uncle's name, and Talitha had the impression that Cerne Obrien had known more than a few H. Harlow Wemblings in his day.

"Not just one man!" Hort exclaimed again. "He couldn't!"

But he had.

Talitha cast an anxious glance at the lengthening shadows in the clearing. "It's getting late. How long a courtship will they believe from a couple of beginners?"

"I never thought to ask the rules. Well—" Hort closed the book reverently and got to his feet. "Cerne Obrien, we salute you. Someday we want to come back here and read this carefully. Eventually Langri will have its own historians, and they'll venerate it."

"That's what I'm afraid of," Talitha said. "They'll send the name of Cerne Obrien across the galaxy in dryly written tomes read only by other historians. The man deserves a better fate."

Hort returned the log book to the chart table, and the two of them scrambled down the ramp. At the bottom they turned, looked at each other, and then solemnly genuflected. "I wrote down his name and the ship's registration number," Hort said. "Someone, somewhere, may want to know what happened to him."

They left the clearing behind them and hurried along the wide path—the memorial path—that led to the shrine of Cerne Obrien.

"Perhaps verbal tradition will keep his memory a living thing far into the future," Hort said thoughtfully. "Perhaps even now, when no aliens are present, the children gather around a fire and listen to old tales of what the mighty Obrien did and said. But I agree. He deserves a far better fate. Maybe someday we can speak to Fornri about it."

At the concealed entrance to the path, Talitha halted Hort and faced him. "Aric—now that we know what the Plan is, maybe we could help."

Hort shook his head. "Absolutely not. Obrien ordered the natives not to tell anyone, not even their attorney, and he was right. In some ways it cost them, like not knowing the literacy requirements, but it also could be the reason the Plan has succeeded. If your uncle so much as suspected a crafty master plan behind the natives' irrational actions, he'd figure out what it is."

"Then the best way we can help is to know nothing at all and do nothing."

"Right," Hort said. "Let's not tamper with a work of genius and give the natives a handicap of unnecessary assistance."

"All right," she said. "I know nothing. I'll see Uncle tomorrow and beg for a nutritionist. More dratted acting."

"I want you to know," Hort said. "*I* wasn't acting."

They embraced hastily, and then they hurried toward the Bower Hill.

Her uncle had forgotten the appointment. She cornered him in a plush conference room in the finished wing of the resort, and they had a brief conversation before his meeting started. Hirus Ayns was there, along with the entire staff of bright young people Wembling had recruited to build his resorts and run them. They sat around the circular table and talked and joked in low tones, with occasional outbursts of boisterous laughter, while Talitha tried to talk with her uncle.

"Tal," he said firmly, "I wouldn't even consider it."

"You *can't* be so calloused as to exterminate the entire population!"

"Tal, business is business. I gave the natives every chance, and they wouldn't co-operate. They can have their ten per cent of the profits, I'll stand by that, but only after my investment is amortized."

Talitha faced him defiantly, hoping that she looked sufficiently pale and earnest. She said, "Surely—"

"Tal, I have a meeting here. If you want to stay, I'll talk with you afterward."

He got to his feet. "All right. All of you have read the verdict. The court allowed every claim we made. Some were so flimsy that I blushed to submit them, but the natives' attorney was too stupid to object. So that's settled."

He pushed the subject aside with a gesture. "Now that we're safe from further harassment, we can give some attention to long-range planning. We're already recruiting and training the personnel we'll need for this resort, and we'll be ready to open the moment construction is completed. Today's meeting was called to discuss our second resort—what sort of a resort we want and where we should put it. Hirus?"

Wembling sat down, and Hirus Ayns got to his feet. "If I may interpose a remark, I think the natives will give in eventually and work for us."

Wembling shrugged, bit a smoke capsule, blew a smoke ring. "Perhaps. Except for the fact that we'd be able to pay them a twentieth of what imported labor will cost, I couldn't care less. Put it this way: we made them a fair offer and got snubbed. If they change their minds they'll have to come to us. Go ahead, Hirus."

"I call your attention to Site Nine," Ayns said. "By a most fortuitous coincidence, when we laid out this golf course we included a mountain smack in the middle of it."

Laughter erupted around the table. Ayns waited, grinning, until it subsided. "A mountain resort would nicely complement this seaside resort, with the added advantage that a brisk walk or a brief ride down the mountain or inside the mountain will take our guests to the seashore. It's a lovely site. Now then."

He took some drawings from the portfolio that lay on the table in front of him. "We have sketches from three architects for a resort building on this site. Number one: a circular building constructed completely around the mountain." He held up the sketch and then passed it to the young man on his right. "The architect has placed a pavilion on the mountaintop for dining and refreshments or just for the view. There'd be VM shafts inside the mountain for those who wanted the view without the climb. And, of course, shafts leading down to the beaches."

He turned with a frown and directed a question at the doorway. "Yes? What is it?"

Wembling's young secretary had dropped the door open, and he was waiting apologetically. He said to Wembling, "Sir—excuse me, sir—Fornri is here."

"I haven't time to talk with him now," Wembling said. "Tell him to come back later."

"Is that wise, Harlow?" Ayns asked. "After all, he *is* the President of Langri."

"That doesn't give him the privilege of interrupting me whenever he feels like it," Wembling said.

"It isn't a matter of privilege," Ayns said. "It's a question of courtesy."

Wembling turned to his secretary. "Did he say what he wanted?"

"No, sir."

"Maybe he's changed his mind about those land parcels," a young woman suggested.

"Tell him he can't have 'em back, and let's get on with this," another called.

Wembling said to Ayns, "I think you're right, Hirus. It's a question of courtesy. I'll see him and make an appointment to talk with him later." He turned to the secretary. "Send him in."

All eyes were on the door when Fornri appeared. They were curious, Talitha thought, to see how he was taking his defeat. He entered smiling and came to a stop just inside the door.

"I'm extremely busy now, Fornri," Wembling said. "Could we make an appointment for this afternoon?"

"That won't be necessary, sir," Fornri told him. "I only came to deliver your tax bill."

Amidst the circle of blank faces, only Wembling managed a smile. "*Tax* bill? It only goes to show you—even in paradise!" His bright young assistants laughed, and Wembling went on, "All right, Fornri, but it isn't necessary to deliver things like this to me personally. You can leave them with my secretary."

"I thought perhaps you might have questions about it," Fornri said.

He circled the table, giving Talitha a friendly nod, and handed the packet to Wembling. Wembling nodded his thanks and dropped it onto the table. Then, as he dismissed Fornri with a gesture, he glanced down at the summation.

He snatched it up, looked at it again, and leaped to his feet in rage. "*Tax* bill? That's fraud! Extortion! Robbery! No court will permit such a thing!"

The assistant sitting next to him took the packet, stared at the summation, and leaped to his feet, and it passed around the table with the staff members in turn registering rage, astonishment, or indignation. While this happened, Wembling remained on his feet, orating.

"Just because you call yourself a government doesn't mean you can come in here—go ahead, take a look at that. Just because you call yourself a government doesn't mean you can come in here and confiscate —that's what it amounts to, confiscatory taxation, why, that's been outlawed for centuries! Here's an entire world with only one taxpayer, Wembling and Company, and if you think for one moment you can come in here —did you ever see the likes of a tax bill like that? We'll sue and demand damages, that's what we'll do!"

Fornri listened politely, and Talitha, occasionally stealing glances at him, thought his splendidly blank expression nothing less than a work of art. She fought to suppress her laughter while her uncle's voice raged on.

"We'll sue and demand damages. Confiscatory taxation, that's the only way to describe it. Confiscatory and *punitive* taxation, and if you think for one moment Wembling and Company is going to play the sucker and let you get away with an illegal tax grab—"

23

Master Khan Khorwiss pompously struck his most dramatic pose. "Confiscatory and *punitive* taxation, Your Eminence," he thundered.

Justice Figawn leaned forward. "Ah! So that's the tactic. The people of Langri made their bargain, Submaster Jarnes. They cannot unmake it through the agency of taxation."

"Ten-to-one taxes, Your Eminence," Khorwiss proclaimed. "Langri presumes to assess Wembling and Company with an annual tax equal to ten times its total investment. If it fails to pay, its holdings will be confiscated. If it pays it will be forced into bankruptcy. Have you ever heard of such a thing?"

"Now I have," the justice said angrily.

Jarnes leaped to his feet.

"I know, I know, Submaster Jarnes. Those poor natives—but they lose sympathy rapidly when they practice such a flagrant illegalism."

"The references, Your Eminence," Jarnes said politely. "Those tax rates were set properly and legally by the duly elected Congress of the World of Langri, and no Federation court can claim jurisdiction over them."

The justice studied Jarnes quizzically for a moment, and then he said, "Very well. Do you both stand ready? You may play your cases, gentlemen."

Clerk Wyland activated the computer. Jarnes sat back comfortably and waited for Khorwiss to build his case, and Wembling's distinguished counsel did not hesitate. He quickly built a column of references on the left-hand screen. Jarnes, comparing them with his notes, watched patiently; and at the console opposite, Khorwiss' expression gradually became a smirk as he posted one unanswered reference after another.

At one point Figawn, intrigued by such unusual tactics, interrupted with a question. "Are you going to let him play his entire case, Submaster Jarnes?"

"What there is of it, Your Eminence," Jarnes said politely.

Finally Khorwiss slowed his pace, and after each entry he began to eye Jarnes uneasily. Then Jarnes stirred himself, stroked his console, and posted a single reference.

A *ping* sounded, followed instantly by another, and all of Khorwiss' references vanished. Staring at the screen, mouth open, Khorwiss half rose to protest, thought better of it, waited for the computer to correct itself, and finally asked for time and searched the reference.

While they waited, the justice asked, "Have you other references, Submaster Jarnes?"

"Yes, Your Eminence, but I doubt that they'll be needed."

The justice did some searching of his own, read the result, and smiled, shaking his head. "I've never seen that case posted before, Submaster Jarnes. How did you happen to find it?"

"I didn't, Your Eminence. The people of Langri brought it to my attention."

The justice looked skeptical, and Jarnes did not blame him. He found it difficult to believe himself. He'd had the devil's own time tracking the cause down even after he'd been told about it, and when he located it he thought at first that he'd been victimized by a joker. The case was almost identical to Langri's, concerning a world's right to impose uniform taxes, and on appeal to Higher Court the legal principles were laid down firmly for all time in the most comprehensive review of a world's powers of taxation that Jarnes had ever seen. Apparently a world's right to impose taxes had never before been challenged in Federation court, and obviously it wasn't challenged again until now, and a case never cited eventually was dropped from current references.

But someone had remembered it—someone not an attorney, because it was not a legal reference that Fornri passed to him on a soiled scrap of paper, but a scrawled eyewitness recollection of an event remote in time and space. And how did Langri find out about it, when the world's discovery took place long after the event had been forgotten?

Fornri volunteered no information, and Jarnes, not being aware that the scrap of paper might be important, did not ask. If he had asked, probably he would not have been answered. From the beginning the natives carefully told him no more than he had to know, and though this sometimes tried him sorely, he now felt that they had been wise.

And though there were many other references he could have used, though he thought he could have won without this one, it pleased him to let the people of Langri win their own case.

Khorwiss resumed play a moment later, posting reference after reference, and each appeared on the screen momentarily and then vanished. Eventually he began to resort to feit references, and the *pings* were replaced by gongs and Clerk Wyland's reproving voice, "Reversed by decision of Higher Court, Master Khorwiss."

Finally Khorwiss slumped back dejectedly.

"Your reference stands, Submaster Jarnes," Figawn observed. "The tax rate is the local government's prerogative, but it cannot be selectively applied. It must apply equally to all."

Jarnes got to his feet. "It *does* apply equally to all, Your Eminence."

Khorwiss leaped up, arms waving. "Exception! Exception! First, the valuation bases for these taxes are wildly inflated."

"Exception!" Jarnes shouted. "Those values were attested to this chamber by Wembling and Company!"

Justice Figawn imposed order with a gesture. The merest flicker of a smile touched his lips as he inclined his head to Jarnes. "My congratulations, Submaster Jarnes. Your exception is allowed. Wembling and Company did indeed certify the valuations that their counsel *now* calls wildly inflated, and I can and do accept them as a proper basis for taxation. Further, I affirm the right of the people of Langri to set their own tax rates. But I must consider Wembling and Company's charge of selective taxation."

"There is none, Your Eminence," Jarnes said. "The ten-for-one tax rate is applied equally to all."

"Exception!" Khorwiss bleated. "No citizen of Langri owns more than a grass hut. What is ten times the value of a grass hut? Whereas Wembling and Company—"

"Silence!" Figawn roared. He sat back to contemplate the situation. "Will the natives in fact be paying taxes, Submaster Jarnes?" he asked finally.

"Certainly, Your Eminence. The same tax rate

applies to all, and I have the tax rolls here for your examination. Further, I object to that term, 'grass hut.' These are well-constructed dwellings, requiring several days' labor by a crew of highly skilled workers to build them, and no grass is used in their construction. I would like to see my eminent colleague produce an example of the woven fiber matting that is so well suited for dwelling walls on the world of Langri. Only the most skilled of the natives are able to weave it. I offer in evidence a report from one Aric Hort, a trained anthropologist and a deputy marshal on Langri, concerning his own efforts to build one of those maligned grass huts. I further point out that these dwellings are also taxed according to their locations, a variable land-value factor that applies only to community dwelling sites and thus is not imposed on the landholdings of Wembling and Company."

"Accepted as stated," the justice said. "I'll now take your cases on the subject of selective taxation."

This time Jarnes posted a single reference and sat back to enjoy Khorwiss' perspiring efforts to dislodge it. The other counsel's postings appeared, one after the other, and the computer consigned them to oblivion with its mocking *ping*. Khorwiss frantically shuffled his reference disks and frequently turned to the reference console to search something new.

Another posting, and a buzzer rasped. "Duplicated reference, Master Khorwiss," Clerk Wyland said.

Khorwiss shrugged and posted another reference. Again the buzzer sounded. "Duplicated reference, Master Khorwiss."

Justice Figawn leaned forward. "Come, Master Khorwiss. Submaster Jarnes is extending every courtesy and I am permitting unlimited challenges. Have you a case?"

Khorwiss tried again; again the buzzer sounded. Clerk Wyland laughed aloud and then clapped a hand over his mouth in consternation; the justice's tight lips suppressed a smile. With difficulty Jarnes contained his own laughter.

Khorwiss leaped to his feet. "We won't tolerate

this. We'll appeal. It's an outrage, and if this court won't take proper action to prevent it, then Higher Court will. And further—"

Listening to him, Jarnes suppressed a yawn. There would be an appeal, and then another, and with them all of the legal gymnastics the firm of Khorwiss, Qwa-anti, Mllo, Bylym, and Alaffro could devise, but he knew that he had won the judgment.

So did Justice Figawn. He had been busily searching references while the case was played, and now, while Khorwiss raved, he studied the results. Then he inclined his head toward Jarnes and closed one eye in a deliberate wink.

24

The paradise world of Langri still looked hideously scarred, but it was healing. The resort buildings were gone. A solitary freighter stood on the landing field, and a machine was carrying the last of the salvage to it, a mammoth scoopload at a time. Freighters loading salvage had become such a familiar sight that Talitha Warr passed it without a glance.

The resort's vast terrace, designed for thousands of tourists to cavort in oceanside pools, was now bare of its expensive imported tiling, and the Langrian flowers were rapidly restoring it to its pristine integrity. Standing on the beach below the terrace, viewing the sparkling Langrian ocean under the late afternoon sun, was a solitary figure: H. Harlow Wembling. Talitha approached him timidly.

He turned his head when he heard the crunch of

her steps on the sand. Then he looked away. His voice was flatly expressionless. "You're going to stay, then?"

"The government of Langri has invited us to stay. Aric and I are being married tomorrow, in a double ceremony with Fornri and Dalla. Would you like to come?"

"No—no, thank you," Wembling said quickly. "I already told Fornri that I'd finish loading the salvage this evening and leave at once." He paused a moment, and then he muttered half to himself, "What a waste! What a place for a resort!"

A group of natives carrying logs approached them along the beach. They placed the logs carefully, laying out fires for a festival. Then they grinned at Talitha and left. Now that the koluf were returning to the feeding grounds, they had shaken off the horrible grip of malnutrition, but food alone could not account for their transformed appearance. They were *happy*.

Wembling had watched them gloomily. "Getting ready for the wedding celebration?" he asked.

"No. That'll take place at the Elder's village. This is for a special feast tonight. The natives are celebrating getting their world back."

More natives came with logs. Wembling ignored them and stood looking out to sea again. "Well, Tal— you're old enough to know what you want to do, and I wish you well."

"I'm sorry we ended up on opposite sides, Uncle Harlow, but I had no choice."

"That's all right, Tal. This won't ruin me. But what a waste this is—what a place for a resort!"

The purring whine of the machine cut off abruptly. Hirus Ayns came hurrying down the slope from the landing field. "We've loaded everything worth loading," he said. "I think the natives are anxious for us to leave."

"I told Fornri we'd go this evening. We don't have to run away."

"If you want a frank opinion," Ayns said, "I think we do."

Wembling and Talitha turned and looked toward

the landing field. A good portion of the population of Langri was gathering for the festival, and evidently the natives considered the departure of Wembling's last ship the ideal beginning for their celebration. Instead of assembling where the festival was to take place, they were crowding the landing field to watch the ship leave. They had completely surrounded it except for a single lane that had opened to make way for the salvage machine, now being loaded.

"There's a festival tonight," Talitha told Ayns. "They've come to take part in it."

"Let's not make them delay it on account of us," Ayns said. "They might decide to have us provide the entertainment."

"Nonsense!" Talitha snapped; but Ayns obviously was frightened. He started back toward the ship.

"He has a point," Wembling said. "I've nothing to gain from hanging around here." He turned. "Good-by, Tal."

Impulsively she kissed him. Then, as he walked quickly toward the ship, she went looking for Aric Hort. The two of them stood apart from the natives, arm in arm, to watch Wembling's departure.

Ayns already had reached the crowd of smiling natives. He glanced uneasily from side to side as he started up the lane toward the ship. Wembling also was becoming uneasy. He had increased his pace and was overtaking Ayns. Somehow the two of them read malice into the smiling faces that surrounded them, and they broke into a panicky run. Panting, they reached the ramp and scrambled up. Ayns disappeared into the ship. Wembling, breathing heavily, turned at the top of the ramp and looked down on the natives.

Fornri and Dalla stood at the foot of the ramp. They, too, were smiling happily, and Fornri gave Wembling the native salute.

"Well, Fornri," Wembling panted. "No hard feelings, I hope. I tried to do my best for your people, you know. The resort would have been a splendid asset for you. Your ten per cent—"

The smiles had broadened. Wembling paused for

breath, and then he said stiffly, "I'm grateful for the opportunity to salvage the building materials, and I thank you."

"And we thank you for the medical center," Fornri called back to him.

"You're welcome. Sorry you couldn't see it my way. It's such a waste. Why not let us find a stretch of coast where a resort won't interfere with your hunting?"

Fornri did not answer.

"I'll give you twenty per cent of the profits," Wembling said.

He paused and craftily surveyed the faces below him. Ayns had reappeared in the ship's open hatch, and he was looking out curiously.

"Thirty per cent," Wembling said. He paused again and looked about him. "Fifty per cent."

Ayns's mouth dropped open in consternation. Leaning toward Fornri, Wembling called down to him, and the note of pleading desperation in his voice was entirely out of character. "I'll make you rich!"

"We already are rich," Fornri replied.

Wembling turned away. A moment later the hatch closed, the ramp raised, and the natives slowly drew back from the ship. It lifted, and the wild dance of celebration began.

The fires had been lighted, the music had begun, and as Hort and Talitha walked toward the beach, Fornri and Dalla overtook them. Talitha and Dalla embraced happily, and Fornri drew Hort aside and talked seriously with him for a moment.

Hort turned to Talitha. "Guess what—Fornri has a job for us. He wants us to have a look at a certain wrecked spaceship. I had to tell him we found it ourselves."

"Yes. We found it," Talitha said. "We decided it would be best if we pretended we didn't know about it."

The dance lines were leaving the beach to snake through the former construction site. Torches waved everywhere, and the natives were pulling apart the scraps of unsalvageable material left by Wembling.

"What are they doing?" Hort asked.

"We are planning our new capital city," Fornri said. "Mr. Wembling kindly cleared the ground, and now we'll build it the way we want it. They are marking the places for streets and buildings. And parks—we will have many parks."

"Yes. Well—we found the wrecked ship, and we looked through it. It was extremely interesting."

"Have you read the logbook?" Talitha asked eagerly.

"They couldn't," Hort said. "Not in that script. They wouldn't even be able to figure out what it was."

They were walking slowly toward the celebration. "I wonder if you and your people are aware of what a great man Cerne Obrien was," Hort said. " 'Genius' is something of an understatement for him, considering what he did. I suppose in time you'll have buildings and villages and streets and parks named Obrien, but he deserves a really important monument. You should give some thought to that."

Fornri and Dalla were regarding them perplexedly.

"They probably didn't know a world could be named after a man," Talitha said. "What a shame."

Hort nodded his agreement. Then he exclaimed, "Look!"

They were close enough, now, to see what the dancers were doing. They had lettered signs on the scraps of building material, and they were marking off their new capital city—a city planned by dancing. The signs floated past on the way to their destinations: LANGRI UNIVERSITY; LANGRI BOULEVARD; CONGRESS OF THE WORLD OF LANGRI; LANGRI BOTANICAL GARDENS; GOVERNMENT OF LANGRI, ADMINISTRATIVE BRANCH; LANGRI WORLD LIBRARY.

Hort turned again to Fornri and Dalla. "It *is* a shame. Too late to change it now, but you should have named your world 'Obrien.' "

Again Fornri and Dalla exchanged bewildered glances.

"Obrien?" Fornri asked blankly. "Who is Obrien?"

ABOUT THE AUTHOR

LLOYD BIGGLE, JR., is well known to readers of science fiction. He has written more than forty short stories, which have appeared in major magazines, and published two collections. *Monument* is his seventh novel. In 1973 Mr. Biggle was the editor of *Nebula Award Stories Seven*. He makes his home in Ypsilanti, Michigan.

OUT OF THIS WORLD!

That's the only way to describe Bantam's great series of science-fiction classics. These space-age thrillers are filled with terror, fancy and adventure and written by America's most renowned writers of science fiction. Welcome to outer space and have a good trip!

☐ 11392	STAR TREK: THE NEW VOYAGES 2 by Culbreath & Marshak	$1.95
☐ 11945	THE MARTIAN CHRONICLES by Ray Bradbury	$1.95
☐ 2719	STAR TREK: THE NEW VOYAGES by Culbreath & Marshak	$1.75
☐ 12180	A CANTICLE FOR LEIBOWITZ by Walter Miller, Jr.	$1.95
☐ 8276	HELLSTROM'S HIVE by Frank Herbert	$1.50
☐ 10930	DEMON SEED by Koontz	$1.75
☐ 10300	DRAGONSONG by McCaffrey	$1.75
☐ 11599	THE FARTHEST SHORE by Ursula LeGuin	$1.95
☐ 11600	THE TOMBS OF ATUAN by Ursula LeGuin	$1.95
☐ 11609	A WIZARD OF EARTHSEA by Ursula LeGuin	$1.95
☐ 12005	20,000 LEAGUES UNDER THE SEA by Jules Verne	$1.50
☐ 11417	STAR TREK XI by James Blish	$1.50
☐ 11502	ALAS, BABYLON by Pat Frank	$1.95
☐ 11527	FANTASTIC VOYAGE by Isaac Asimov	$1.75
☐ 02517	LOGAN'S RUN by Nolan & Johnson	$1.75

Buy them at your local bookstore or use this handy coupon for ordering:

Bantam Book Catalog

Here's your up-to-the-minute listing of every book currently available from Bantam.

This easy-to-use catalog is divided into categories and contains over 1400 titles by your favorite authors.

So don't delay—take advantage of this special opportunity to increase your reading pleasure.

Just send us your name and address and 25¢ (to help defray postage and handling costs).